LT
F
mAR

HOW TO MURDER
A MILLIONAIRE

HOW TO MURDER A MILLIONAIRE

A BLACKBIRD SISTERS MYSTERY

Nancy Martin

Thorndike Press • Chivers Press
Waterville, Maine USA • Bath, England

This Large Print edition is published by Thorndike Press®, USA and by Chivers Press, England.

Published in 2003 in the U.S. by arrangement with NAL Signet, a member of Penguin Group (USA) Inc.

Published in 2003 in the U.K. by arrangement with the author.

U.S. Hardcover 0-7862-5391-6 (Mystery Series)
U.K. Hardcover 0-7540-7244-4 (Chivers Large Print)
U.K. Softcover 0-7540-7245-2 (Camden Large Print)

The text of this Large Print edition is unabridged.
Other aspects of the book may vary from the original edition.

Set in 16 pt. Plantin by Christina S. Huff.

Printed in the United States on permanent paper.

British Library Cataloguing-in-Publication Data available

Library of Congress Cataloging-in-Publication Data

Martin, Nancy, 1953–
How to murder a millionaire : a Blackbird sisters mystery / Nancy Martin.
p. cm.
ISBN 0-7862-5391-6 (lg. print : hc : alk. paper)
1. Millionaires — Crimes against — Fiction.
2. Philadelphia (Pa.) — Fiction. 3. Women journalists — Fiction. 4. Sisters — Fiction. 5. Large type books.
I. Title.
PS3563.A7267H69 2003
813'.6—dc21   2003047351

With thanks

Many journalists tried to steer me in the right direction: Marylynn Uricchio of the *Pittsburgh Post-Gazette*, Robert Long of Delaware's *News Journal*, Becky Aikman of *Newsday* and the anonymous but excellent staff of *The Philadelphia Inquirer*, *The Roanoke Times* and *Philadelphia* magazine.

Thanks also to Dr. Nancy Curry (sometimes known as Aunt Money), Marian Fiscus, Amy Polk, Samir Arora, Kiryn Haslinger, Tamar Myers, Meg Ruley, Ellen Edwards and Victoria Thompson. And to Barbara Aikman, for her formidable mystery expertise, not to mention a few other things. (Thanks, Mom!)

Grateful thanks to Ramona Long, the best friend a writer ever had.

For Jeff, Cassie and Sarah. See, girls? All those battlefield tours paid off!

Chapter 1

To squander the last dollar left in the Blackbird family fortune, my parents threw a lawn party that would have made Jay Gatsby proud. My father wore a moth-eaten dinner jacket and poured champagne while Mama offered marijuana cigarettes to the ne'er-do-wells of Philadelphia high society who'd come to see how far the mighty had fallen.

At the party's climax, my parents shot off fireworks and presented the Blackbird family art collection to my sister Emma. The Blackbird furniture went to my sister Libby.

Perhaps under the impression that I was the most responsible member of the family — which only means I'm the one who never entered a wet T-shirt contest — Mama and Daddy gave me the Bucks County farm. Then they blew the country for a sunny resort that catered to American tax evaders, leaving stardust in their wake and me with a delinquent property tax bill for two million dollars.

That winter I gave up my Rittenhouse

Square condo and moved back to the decaying splendor of our family homestead. I sold my symphony subscription seats, got a partial refund on a weekend trip to Paris and terminated my charge account at Neiman Marcus, which was probably good for my soul anyway.

I tried to get used to poverty. I really did. But by spring I was down to my last Lean Cuisine, and the tax man had my number on his speed dial.

Which is why I, Nora Blackbird, a former socialite who never really held a job in all my thirty-one years unless you count being secretary of the Junior League, found myself in dire need of a paycheck.

"How's the job hunt?" my sister Emma asked me over our monthly lunch at the Rusty Sabre, the white tablecloth inn in New Hope. She lit up a cigarette after she'd been served her spinach salad and sat back to consider her next move on the food. "Find anybody who wants to hire an expert at organizing charity balls?"

"I do have other skills, you know."

"You're really good at seating charts," said our older sister, Libby, buttering a roll and showing none of Emma's reluctance to chow down. Libby wore her excess pounds to sexy perfection. "A successful seating

8

chart is a work of art. In fact, I'm hoping you'll help us with the wedding, Nora."

Her stepson was getting married soon. Half of Philadelphia knew the details, thanks to frequent bulletins in the papers that documented the union of two old families — the Treese clan of Main Line and Libby's new in-laws, the Kintswells of Society Hill.

Bored with the endless wedding discussion, Emma ignored Libby's gambit to hash it over again. To me, she said, "Maybe the White House needs someone new."

Libby stopped buttering and said quite seriously, "That's not a bad idea."

Emma winked at me. "You do beautiful calligraphy."

"And I can polish silver."

"But seating charts are your gift, really," Libby said.

Emma and I exchanged grins.

The three of us began having our sisterly lunches about eighteen months ago, shortly after Emma and I lost our husbands. Libby had been a widow for several years and remarried, but when Emma's husband, Jake, died in a car crash that nearly killed her, too, and a few weeks later my Todd was shot in a South Philly parking lot, Libby assembled the sisterhood. We took turns being the designated basket case, and to our collective surprise, our lunches were therapeutic. For the first time since our teenaged years, we were close again. We shared our frustration with Mama and Daddy, and argued about how best to cope with being poor (Libby, the oldest and most free spirited, advocated complete denial and Emma, the youngest and most tightly wired, never spent a nickel anyway) and we howled over the things that only sisters can find hilarious, like Aunt Rosemary's shoplifting tendencies and our family's inability to cook a decent meal.

We were not without conflict, of course.

Libby had appeared for our May lunch wearing one of her long, artistic dresses with a plunging neckline. Normally, she sported a beflowered straw hat as if she was ready to fly off to Ascot at a moment's notice. But today her hair was loose and Bardot feminine. Hardly any splotches of paint marred her manicure. All her outfits included matching canvas bags, in which she carried an ever-changing collection of books to share with anyone who came along. Libby had grown up ahead of Emma and me, during the time when our parents lived like minor royalty, so she had a different approach to life. Lady Bountiful in Birkenstocks, often lugging a sketchbook to document important moments. She was an Artist of Life, she claimed. Things like financial survival were irrelevant to her.

Libby shook her knife and said, "No, they already have somebody at the White House. Remember Divvy Moncreath? Her son works there now. He gets along beautifully with the First Lady. They have the same taste in china."

"Divvy Moncreath," I said, "is probably the only woman in America who made a campaign contribution so her son could fold napkins."

"He's brilliant with place settings."

"How do you know that?" Emma asked Libby. She was dressed in riding breeches and boots, as always, and she didn't give a damn that the other ladies lunching nearby cast cool glances at the mud she'd tracked in.

Of the three of us, Emma was the stone fox. A chic, very short and asymmetrical haircut flattered the narrow shape of her head, her sharp-cut cheekbones and wide-set bedroom eyes. The Blackbird auburn hair and magnolia white skin that made me look like a Victorian bride with the vapors was sexy as hell on Emma. Her riding breeches fit her like a pair of gloves, and her boots gave my younger sister a piratical air that suited the look in her eye. Two inches

11

taller than I and with ten pounds strategically rearranged, she could have gotten work as an exotic dancer anywhere.

Em always looked as if she'd just rolled out of somebody's bed . . . with a whip. Libby looked ready to slide *into* the next convenient four-poster. And I — well, I wasn't going to venture under anyone's down comforter but my own for a long time. My husband's death had blindsided me, but it didn't compare to the hell of our last two years together when Todd binged on cocaine, lost his medical research job and showed me what havoc one man's weakness could inflict on the union of two people who loved each other passionately. No, men were too much trouble.

"I already got a job," I announced, intervening before the sisterly sniping developed into a full-blown squabble. "I started last week, so the White House will have to muddle through without me."

"What job?" Libby brightened. "Where?"

"I went to see Rory Pendergast." I smiled at the memory of dear old "Uncle" Rory, years ago our grandfather Blackbird's tennis partner, coming to my rescue. "I asked him for a job and he invited me to write for his newspaper."

"Nora, that's fabulous!"

"He still owns that rag?" Emma blew smoke. "I guess every billionaire industrialist needs a hobby in his declining years."

"How is sweet Rory?" Libby asked. "I haven't seen him in weeks. I should call him, in fact. We have things to discuss."

"This is about Nora," Emma said. "So shut up and listen."

"Rory looked great," I went on steadily. "A little frail, maybe, but still naughty. He's eighty-five if he's a day."

Libby lifted her wineglass in a toast. "And he recognizes talent when he sees it. Writing all those medical articles for your husband has come in handy, Nora. Kudos! Tell us what you'll be doing for the *Intelligencer*. A column for the health section?"

"No —"

"Medical tips?"

"No," I said, taking a deep breath. "I'm writing for the society page."

A short, stunned silence. Libby put down her glass.

Then Emma laughed outright. "Good God," she said. "You're going to write meaningful prose about debutante balls?"

"It's a steady job."

But a job that came with at least one drawback, and Emma immediately hit the bull's-eye.

She said, "Tell me you're not working with Kitty Keough."

I gathered my courage and admitted, "I'm her assistant."

Libby clapped one hand to her mouth to stop a laugh. "You're kidding!"

For thirty years, Kitty Keough had been the elephant in the middle of every table at Philadelphia parties. She reported on weddings and funerals, cocktail receptions and tea parties. She detailed what people wore, ate and said. She had printed more pictures of men in tuxedos than *People* magazine ever will, raised her fork at more sea bass dinners with bulimic girls than a Miss America chaperone and air kissed more wealthy women than a presidential candidate. She wrote clever columns that sent the whole city flipping to *The Back Page* every Sunday to read how she cut the rich and famous down to size.

But she'd also made enemies along the way.

Emma said, "Your life's in danger the minute your name is associated with hers. People hate Kitty Keough's guts."

"Readers don't."

"But our friends do," said Libby. "And what she said about Daddy and Mama!"

"Every word was true," I pointed out.

"So what will you be doing exactly?" Emma asked.

"The job isn't much different than my life used to be," I explained. "I'm invited to the same cocktail parties, banquets and balls. Except afterwards I write up what I've seen and heard. I'll attend parties for a living."

"And Kitty?" Emma propped her elbows on the table, ready to dish. "I bet she was delighted to see you sashay into her territory."

"She hasn't exactly rolled out the red carpet," I admitted.

"It's your name," Libby declared. "The Blackbirds are everything Kitty Keough is not. She's going to make your life miserable."

"And the fact that Rory hired you himself," Emma added with a grin. "That ticked her off big time, didn't it? She hates anybody being more connected than she is."

To be accepted in New York, goes the saying, all you need is money. Lots of money. But here in Philadelphia, it's who you are that counts.

The Blackbirds, a family as old as the city itself, counted.

Kitty Keough did not.

"She seems a little upset about our relationship with Rory," I agreed. "She's send-

15

ing me to some . . . unusual places. Just to teach me the ropes, I'm sure."

"To teach you a lesson," Emma said. "She wants you under her thumb from the get-go."

"Maybe Rory is easing Kitty out." Libby dropped her voice to keep such speculation a secret from the women at the next table. "Maybe they're grooming you to take over. She's been writing the society column for a hundred years."

Emma nodded. "Rory's got you in the bull pen."

"She has no intention of leaving," I said quickly. "If she thought I was trying to replace her —"

"You'd be dead meat," Emma finished for me.

Kitty Keough's work seemed silly to people outside our world, yes, but if you wanted to raise a million dollars for cancer research by holding a black-tie ball, you needed Kitty to sell tickets beforehand and pat the big donors on the back afterwards. If you wanted to heighten the public profile of your company, you sent Kitty an invitation to a party where you gave a dozen computers to an underprivileged youth club. You let her photograph your wife in a ball gown to get a mention for your law firm, investment bank or plastic surgery practice. You needed Kitty's help to build a hospital, save an old theater or feed the homeless.

But for a woman who pretended her father never worked in a steel mill, the climb onto the dais at the mayor's inaugural ball had been a long one. So Kitty relished every minute of fawning, every box of chocolates sent by handsome CEOs, every engraved invitation hand delivered by a personal assistant of society leaders. She dressed like a movie star and splashed her weekly page of newsprint with wit and venom as well as niceties. And readers ate it up. She used her column to slap down social climbers who didn't pay her proper deference. She complained when seated at a bad table or if paired with a dull dinner companion. Her paragraphs gushed with favorite names and high praise for anyone who played the game her way, but sharp put-downs became her best-known comments.

"Lacey Chenoweth's garden looks a little less posh this year," Kitty wrote after one hostess failed to pay her respect. "Maybe the lovely Mrs. C. is letting her lace slip elsewhere this spring."

My sisters absorbed the fact that I now worked for the most feared woman in our social circle.

Emma said, "Well, don't drink from the office watercooler."

"And," added Libby, "don't get pushed down any elevator shafts."

"You're way off base," I said. "It's going to work out fine. My more pressing problem is the tax bill."

I sipped my wine and braced myself to deliver the news I'd really come to tell them. Admitting I'd taken a job as a society columnist had been my smoke screen. My sisters weren't going to take the other news so quietly.

"I'm not going to jail," I said succinctly. "Not because Mama and Daddy didn't pay their taxes."

Both Libby and Emma looked at me with their full attention.

I gathered my courage and said, "This job will help me make payments on the tax bill, but first I have to reduce the debt. So I've sold a few ancestral acres."

I had assumed the Rusty Sabre restaurant was civilized enough that my sisters wouldn't scream bloody murder when I broke the bad tidings. At least I'd hoped they wouldn't.

"You're selling the farm," Emma repeated, as if she couldn't believe her ears.

"No. Just five acres."

18

"You're selling five acres without discussing it with us."

"It's already sold."

Libby dropped her fork, splashing raspberry vinaigrette. "You can't do that. It's been Blackbird land for two hundred years." She put her face in her hands. "Oh, my God."

"Here we go," said Emma.

"I didn't have a choice," I said. "I had to keep the wolf from the door, so I sold five measly acres."

"Without consulting your sisters?" Libby demanded, clearly forgetting we were in a public place. "You just went ahead and threw away our family history?"

"Five acres, Libby, that's all."

"But once you sell land, you'll never get it back." Libby's eyes had actually begun to fill with tears. Her bosom trembled. "You've traded the Blackbird legacy for financial security for yourself."

"There's no tax on *your* inheritance. So what do you know?"

"You can't destroy a national treasure like Blackbird Farm."

"National treasure? The barn is falling down, and parts of the house don't have central heating. I've got weeds twelve feet tall! And neither one of you has set foot on the property since Christmas."

19

Libby clutched the table to gather strength for an impassioned speech. All our dishes and glasses lurched. "Suburban blight has spread too far already. If we keep destroying open land, we won't have any left!"

Emma rolled her eyes. "Oh, for godsake, Lib. Another of your causes."

"It's a valuable cause! A noble cause! We of all people should be doing something about it. Soon every farm in the nation will be paved for superstores and our children will never see a cow."

Emma said, "You talk a good line, Libby, but you never actually *do* anything."

"Take it easy," I said to both of them. "Shouting isn't helping."

"I *am* going to do something," Libby said, wounded but not defeated. "I'm going to stop you."

"Libby —"

"Let her go," Emma said. "She'll start a petition, and that'll be the end of it."

"It will not." Libby trembled with anger. "I'm going to stop you from destroying Blackbird Farm, Nora."

"Oh, good." Emma stamped out her cigarette. "Someday one of our sisterly lunches will end without one of us walking out in a huff. But not today. The record stands."

"Yes, it does," said Libby, spinning around and stalking out of the Rusty Sabre.

"Well," said Emma, "if you've sold land, you can afford to pay for lunch."

And she left too.

My sisters stopped speaking to me, which didn't seem so bad.

I should have known at least one of them was plotting.

It hadn't been easy to part with the family ground. For two hundred years, Blackbird Farm had stood proudly — rich Delaware River bottomland, virgin timber, breeding ground for prizewinning Hereford cattle and some very fine foxhounds, not to mention one of the oldest families on the eastern seaboard.

But in a couple of days, it became a monument to tasteless vulgarity.

A used car lot.

In the presence of two lawyers and a pinky-ringed real estate agent, I had sold the land to Michael "The Mick" Abruzzo, who told me he would put the ground to respectable use. But the infamous despoiler of the New Hope way of life went back on his word faster than my father could spend a dollar. He immediately bulldozed the topsoil, paved it with a quarter mile of asphalt and strung a thousand plastic flags overhead. Then he brought in a dozen jalopies with tail fins, and Mick's Muscle Cars appeared in all its neon glory.

And I had to attend the grand opening.

Kitty Keough sent me on purpose, of course, to cover the debut of Mick's Muscle Cars for all of Philadelphia to read about. To twist the knife, she ordered a photographer along to document my humiliation. I walked over from the house, pen and pad in hand.

The first person to arrive on the scene was my sister Libby, rife with protest placards and a gaggle of her own ragamuffin children.

"What are you doing here?" I asked as Libby rounded the hood of her minivan with a hand-lettered cardboard sign over one shoulder and too much estrogen flushing her cheeks.

"What does it look like?"

"Like you're protesting nuclear proliferation."

"Something even worse."

She had exchanged her hippie sexpot look for one of her suburban mom outfits — beige slacks and matching cashmere sweater set — clothes I knew she could transform from appropriate protest duds into something much more formal with a switch of accessories. She had a bandanna in her hair, a touch she had selected to give herself the look of an experienced social activist. She looked around. "Where's the photographer?"

"Over there, taking pictures of cars. How did you know to come today?"

"It's the grand opening, right? It's a free country."

Behind her, the doors of the minivan burst open, and her four children began to spill out of the vehicle like clowns from a polka-dotted Volkswagen. In their wake came an avalanche of fast-food wrappers and family flotsam, including a large, drooling Labrador named Arlo. The children had been outfitted in tie-dyed T-shirts. Libby put her artist's eye for visual details to good use.

"Libby, what are you doing?"

"We're protesting the desecration of open farmland for suburban sprawl. Go ahead, kids." She pointed. "Set up your picket line over by that hideous yellow car."

Libby's four children eddied around her in confusion. Her nose-ringed son, Rawlins, and the Ritalin-needy twelve-year-old twins, Harcourt and Hilton, were the pictures of their father, who'd been a skinny, longhaired vegetarian long before most everyone else. He'd drowned in the Pacific five years ago after falling out of a Zodiac boat in pursuit of whale hunters.

Five-year-old Lucy, blond and blue-eyed, didn't look anything like Libby's first husband but instead suspiciously akin to a popular young foot reflexologist who'd lived briefly in New Hope.

Little Lucy clutched her placard in one hand and a naked Barbie doll in the other. She looked up at me with the gap-toothed smile of a kindergartner. "You look pretty, Aunt Nora. Are you going to a party?"

"Thank you, honey. Yes, I am."

"Anyone we know?" Libby asked tartly.

"It's not a date. It's an assignment."

"Run along, kids," Libby said. "Just go over by that car and wave your signs while I ask your aunt Nora where this dress came from."

"The attic," I told her as the kids scuffled off in a rainbow of tie-dye. "I can't afford anything new."

"That's one of Grandmama Blackbird's Givenchys."

"You want to protest my wearing it?"

"No," she said grudgingly. "It looks good on you. What about the shoes?"

"They're mine. Last season. I'd have worn

24

my Grateful Dead T-shirt if I'd known you were conducting your campus protest."

Libby whipped her sign around so I could read it: BAN SUBURBAN BLIGHT!

"Oh, Lib."

Her posters were beautifully lettered. A painter by training, Libby had taken the time to make each sign lovely with frolicking cows and smiling ducks.

"Embarrassed?" she asked.

"I could use a little sisterly support, please."

"You've traded away our mutual proud heritage for financial reward. On top of that, I morally object to ruining open land for the purpose of commercial development. And today I'm doing something about it."

"Your first act of protest has to be against me?"

"We could have come up with a creative solution to your tax problem together."

"Like what, a bake sale? Libby, it's a two-million-dollar debt!"

She looked huffy. "You know, it wouldn't be so bad if you hadn't sold to that — that person! Nora, he's the ultimate insult."

"So now we're getting to the truth."

"He's so awful!"

"He paid my price, Libby."

Libby's face flushed. "Wake up and smell

the marinara, Nora. He's an Abruzzo with connections all over Jersey and South Philly. He paid your price with dirty money!"

"That is so offensive," I snapped, finding myself in the awkward position of defending the man. "Do you know how offensive that is? He's a businessman."

She waved her sign at the neon lights. "What he's done to this farm is a crime in itself. Look at this place! Bring in an elephant, and you'd have a circus!"

"He has a perfectly clean record with the Better Business Bureau."

"He probably bribed them. It's a shame you didn't ask a few questions before you got to be his partner."

"He's not my partner. I have nothing to do with him."

"Oh, really?" Libby asked archly. "That's not what I hear."

"What are you talking about?"

"Why don't we ask him ourselves?" she said. "Here he comes."

I had hoped things couldn't get any worse. But I followed the direction of Libby's glare and saw a large male figure ambling towards us from the direction of the river. The setting sun cast a glint on his fishing rod. It could have been a grown-up

Huck Finn coming home from his favorite fishing hole, but only if Huck had turned into an ominous, hulking bruiser with a face that originated in the Brando gene pool and the kind of dark curly hair that is only kept under control by a pair of sturdy scissors or the fingers of an attentive woman.

Michael Abruzzo himself sauntered across the road just in time to see my dysfunctional family in action. It was hard to amble in hip waders, but he managed. He wore a khaki fishing vest that had seen better days, and his jeans were so snug that the faded circle of a snuff can was perfectly outlined on the hip pocket, right smack on the curve of his left buttock. All right, I couldn't see his hip pocket at the moment, but I knew it was there. I'd memorized it.

Under her breath, Libby muttered, "He'd be almost handsome if he wasn't such a thug."

"Stop thinking with your ovaries, Libby."

"Oh, I forgot. You're thirty-one and still come across like a virgin. Well, look out, Nora. I can see that man has unfinished business with you."

I wanted to grab her arm and hold Libby back, but she stalked away, abandoning me to my fate. Within a moment, Michael Abruzzo arrived — a six-foot-four-inch, two-hundred-pound replica of the body Michelangelo studied when he sculpted David. Except with a lazy smile and a slouchy walk.

I raised my emotional defenses and met his gaze straight on.

Chapter 2

"You going off to Cinderella's ball, Miss Blackbird?" The Jersey inflection in his voice dispelled further ruminations on Michelangelo.

I ground my teeth. "Hello, Mr. Abruzzo."

"You're very pretty in pink," he said.

"Thank you." I pulled a small notebook from my handbag with as much professionalism as I could muster. "I'm actually here for your grand opening, and I could use a quote, if you don't mind."

"Grand opening?"

"Yes, this —" I gestured at the car lot and couldn't come up with a euphemism. "Your business. Today is the official opening, correct?"

"Well, yeah, I guess so. Usually I just park the cars and see who stops by. Looks like I got lucky today." He leaned his fishing rod against the nearest car, an enormous seafoam green Pontiac with whitewalls and tail fins. Popping open the door, he said, "Hop in. See how it feels to you."

"I'm not in the market for a car."

He had a grin that must have worked wonders on the Catholic schoolgirls in Trenton in the years before he broke his nose. I was willing to bet that his appreciation for big old cars stemmed from backseat experiences with cheerleaders' sweaters and Bruce Springsteen wailing on the radio. "C'mon," he said. "You need something to write about. Might as well be about the car."

Some people are hard to disobey. They command authority with in-your-face hostility, blatant intimidation or sheer physical size. Abruzzo had a benign smile and a languid demeanor that still managed to scare the hell out of people. A mob boss in the making? A bully who didn't need to prove himself anymore? I decided not to take a chance and did as he told me. I slid behind the wheel.

"What d'you think?"

I looked out the windshield and down the long stretch of gleaming metal at the hood ornament. "It's enormous."

"Well, size is important to some women, I hear." He leaned one hip against the side mirror and rummaged in his pocket. He pulled out a snuff can and proceeded to unfasten a fishing lure from his shirt. He put the lure into the can. "Turn the key in the ignition."

I gritted my teeth, but decided disobedience wasn't going to get me anywhere. I turned the key, and the engine growled to life. The whole car trembled powerfully beneath me.

"Is it good for you?" he asked with that damned grin.

There was nothing I could do but ignore his remark. "Fortunately, I don't need a car. Mr. Pendergast has hired a driver for me."

Which Abruzzo knew perfectly well, since Rory had contracted with his company to provide the vehicle and a driver.

"You must be the only reporter in the country who has a chauffeur."

"He's not a chauffeur. And I'm going to learn to drive as soon as possible."

"Need a teacher?"

Michael Abruzzo was the last person I intended to call when I needed to learn something.

He must have guessed my thought, because he laughed. "Listen," he said easily, "I was thinking maybe if you were starting to get your head above water you might feel like celebrating a little."

"What do you mean?"

He squinted into the distance. "I'm going up to New York in a few weeks. I got a couple of tickets to *The Lion King* and reservations at my favorite steak house. All I need's a little company to make it a perfect weekend."

He had to be kidding.

I clamped my knees together so hard my muscles quivered. I didn't know which was more humiliating — my sister parading around with placards or the fact that the likes of Michael "The Mick" felt he needed to cheer me up after near financial ruin. I made an effort to control myself and said evenly, "I would hate *The Lion King*."

"Classy lady like you doesn't like theater?"

"There's theater and there's *theater*." And going to New York for a weekend with Abruzzo was definitely theater of the absurd.

"I hear the show's really good. My nieces thought it was great."

I took a deep breath and exhaled slowly. "There's no way I would spend a weekend with you, Mr. Abruzzo. Any weekend."

He didn't seem surprised. But he didn't threaten to whack my kneecaps either. "Well, if you change your mind, let me know. Did I give you one of my cards?"

I had thrown it away soon after he'd purchased his five acres, which must have been obvious from my expression.

He laughed again and slid a pack of business cards out of his wallet. They were bound together with a rubber band. He removed one card, and I took it without speaking. MICHAEL ABRUZZO. MUSCLE CARS, MOTORCYCLES, LIMOUSINE SERVICE. And in bigger letters, THE DELAWARE FLY-FISHING COMPANY.

I put the card into my bag without taking note of the various phone numbers. A sick and twisted part of my personality wished he could have acted a teensy bit disappointed.

But he was looking across the used car lot. "Who's the nutcase?"

I looked, too. Libby was arranging people for a photograph.

"That's my sister Libby," I said. "She's protesting your blight on the landscape."

"My what?"

"She objects to suburban sprawl," I explained. "She believes you have defaced open land by paving green space when you promised to put the ground to good use."

"I thought I was giving people jobs, creating economic growth — all that Chamber of Commerce bullshit."

"That's one opinion."

"You agree with her?"

"I'm a journalist now. I'm learning to be objective." Trying not to sound too hopeful,

33

I said, "You can have protesters arrested for trespassing, I think."

He didn't have much enthusiasm for that suggestion. "And who the hell is that?"

The protest grew by one more person when a silver BMW pulled in behind Libby's minivan, parked, and Ralph Kintswell heaved his bulk from behind the wheel. He left the engine running.

"That's my brother-in-law, Libby's husband, Ralph."

"What, is he going to a costume party?"

"No," I said. "He's a Civil War buff."

Abruzzo laughed again. "The war's over, buddy."

Ralph Kintswell, Libby's second husband, was decked out in his usual formal wear — the dress blue uniform of the Army of the Potomac, complete with white gloves tucked into his sash and a sword slapping his thigh. Except the sash had slipped low on his General Grant–style potbelly. Ralph hitched up the sash and launched himself across the used car lot in Libby's direction, his hobnailed boots smartly striking the pavement. The expression on his usually cherubic face was pained.

"He's a very nice guy," I said. "He protects Civil War battlefields."

"With the sword?"

"No," I snapped. "He's a banker. He raises money and helps buy battlegrounds before they are developed into — well, into some kind of atrocity."

"Looks like he's losing the battle with his cholesterol, though," Abruzzo observed.

"It's the wool uniform. It gets very bulky."

"So what is he doing? Heading for Gettysburg later?"

"He wears the uniform to formal occasions. Instead of a dinner jacket. Like some men wear kilts."

Abruzzo looked as entertained as a kid standing along a parade route as the bagpipers marched by. "This is a formal occasion?"

"No, no, there's a party later tonight. He's probably on his way there."

"And people say I have an interesting family. You Blackbirds have us beat in spades."

Usually Libby had my brother-in-law jumping through hoops like a well-trained poodle. He was an amiable, steady guy who obviously loved my sister despite her frivolous temperament and formidable sex drive. But Ralph was the seventh circle of hell at family gatherings. How many times had I endured his incredibly dull retellings of battles fought long ago?

"Hello, Ralph," I called.

He faltered in his march to Libby and waved meekly. "Hi, Nora. Sorry about this."

"Don't worry about it," I called. "Everybody's entitled to an opinion."

He sent me an apologetic smile and continued across the asphalt to his wife.

The *Intelligencer* photographer had been waiting while Libby carefully posed everyone for the picture, but he started to get cranky when Ralph had to be fitted into the tableau and walked over to me. He looked about thirteen years old, wearing a too-large thrift store sport coat over jeans and a Metallica T-shirt.

"Whaddaya want me to shoot?" he asked.

"I don't want you to shoot anything," I replied. "I didn't request a photographer."

"Kitty did. Any way you can speed things up? I gotta be at the Flyers face-off next."

I looked over at my sister's merry band. "Do I get input on this?"

He shrugged. "You're the reporter on the scene."

"Did you take pictures of the cars?"

"Sure. But what about the protesters?"

I considered my predicament. I could ask him not to make fools of my family and myself. Instead, he could take colorful shots of the cars and be on his way to the hockey game. But at last I said, "I'm new at this. Use your best judgment."

I'd surprised him. The kid grinned, apparently more accustomed to receiving orders than having his judgment trusted. "Yeah, okay."

He snapped a few more pictures of the cars and worked his way back over to Libby and company. With luck, the car photos would have more appeal than the protesters.

Still beside me, Abruzzo said, "You could have saved yourself some grief just now."

I shook my head, summoning up what few journalistic ethics I had learned in just two weeks on the job. "It doesn't matter."

"And who's Kitty?"

"Well, she's not Glenda the Good Witch — let's put it that way."

Pictures over, Ralph and Libby headed for the BMW. As I guessed she might, she began to pull the bandanna out of her hair. They obviously had a social engagement this evening. Their oldest son, Rawlins, newly licensed to drive, herded his siblings and the dog into the minivan.

I was saved from further conversation with Abruzzo by the arrival of a sleek black town car that whispered up behind me as Libby's family departed.

"Here's your ride," said Abruzzo. "Where are you headed?"

"Main Line," I said.

The driver of the car got out and proceeded directly to the right rear passenger door, which he opened for me. He waited, unsmiling.

Reed Shakespeare was twenty-two years old, black, studious and with posture as perfect as a Marine drill sergeant's. He was working his way through school by driving cars for Abruzzo, but heaven forbid he tell anyone exactly what he was studying. The first day we'd met, he told me he would not wear a chauffeur's cap.

"I'm not driving no Miss Daisy around in a stupid hat," he'd burst out.

"Nobody's asking you to, Reed," I'd replied.

"Just so you know," he'd said stubbornly.

I wanted to tell him he'd seen too many movies, but Reed was touchy. I was still working on a way to make him smile.

"Hey, Reed," Abruzzo said, "car running okay?"

"Yes."

"You know where you're taking Miss Blackbird now?"

"Yes."

"Looked at a map just to be sure?"

With an edge of testiness this time, Reed said, "Yes."

I noted Abruzzo hadn't had any luck getting the young man to loosen up either.

"Okay, then," Abruzzo said. He turned to me with a sudden and unabashed wistfulness. "You'll call if you change your mind about *The Lion King*, right?"

"Don't wait by the phone," I said.

I got into the car and Reed closed the door. Through the window, I saw Reed look at his boss with something akin to pity.

As the evening cooled, Reed drove me to the Main Line. He did not initiate conversation, drive over the speed limit or flip any rude gestures at aggressive drivers. He did make clear that he wasn't my friend.

In the silence, I took out my pad and pen and wrote up the story about the grand opening of Mick's Muscle Cars. Usually I worked on a laptop, but in the car I found it was easier to write on paper. Later, I'd type my stories into a computer file and e-mail them to my editor.

When the paragraph was finished, I looked out the window.

Philadelphia's Main Line has long been the address of many old American families. One magnificent mansion after another housed people I'd known all my life. Families of bankers, corporate leaders, a few playboys and a lot of inherited fortunes. As the car eased along, I saw that some of the estates showed their age while others had clearly benefited by the surge in the stock market in the late nineties. Those houses had new gutters or sandblasted facades just as their owners sported tummy tucks and dermabrasion.

Rory Pendergast's home stood on a slight rise, forming the crown of the neighborhood. Pennsylvania fieldstone walls and grounds landscaped by Frederick Law Olmsted surrounded a gracious Georgian home that looked like the set for a Katherine Hepburn movie. The intricate wrought iron gates, originally erected to keep out the riffraff, stood open tonight in welcome.

Reed drove slowly through the gates and up the curving drive to the side portico. Gas lamps flickered golden light through the wisteria. Guests anxious to get to the bar had hastily abandoned several sporty cars on the front lawn. Ralph and Libby's silver BMW stood among them. I could see more vehicles parked on the old polo grounds beyond the boxwood hedge.

A wide stone staircase led from the portico up to the side entrance of the house.

Two uniformed valets hired for the evening stood chatting on the steps, oblivious to the grandeur of the home. They wore baseball caps that read MAIN EVENTS, which was the name of a full-service catering company that staffed many social occasions on the Main Line.

I gathered up my notepad and moved to get out of the car. Reed was quicker than the valet and arrived in time to open the door for me.

I got out. "Reed, I've told you it's not necessary to open the door. I'm perfectly capable."

"I heard you," he said.

"Well, thank you. When can you come back?"

Stiffly, he said, "I'll wait. I've got studying to do."

He was taking classes somewhere and used his spare time to catch up on assignments. "All right," I said. "I'll probably stay an hour. How do I look?"

The question caught him off guard. "Uhm. Okay. I guess."

The valet said, "Good evening, miss."

I said hello and started up the steps of the Pendergast house.

Rory Pendergast's family had been relatively late arrivals to Philadelphia — after the revolution — and made their presence known first in get-rich-quick schemes and later through significant charitable work. Rory's father built the house in a wanton spending spree at the turn of the twentieth century. Fortunately, he had the good taste to avoid building a huge, gloomy Victorian pile, and the house turned out to be Jeffersonian in grace and symmetry with rambling interior spaces perfect for entertaining — or playing hide-and-seek.

For the party, the home had been decked out by RickandGabe, Philadelphia florists extraordinaire, in their usual exquisite taste. The double doors at the top of the stairs were pinned open by a pair of Chinese vases containing perfectly trimmed topiary. A copper tub of fresh flowers six feet high stood on the marble-topped table in the center of the entrance hall. A long expanse of Oriental carpet ran from the table down the hallway, punctuated by early American furniture that would render the Antiques Roadshow twins orgasmic.

Before I could reach the top of the steps, however, I heard arguing. Staccato voices, sharp words.

Two people burst out of a side room: a man clutching the elbow of a large, imperious woman.

"I don't care what you think," the woman was saying. "You're a fool."

I recognized Kitty Keough and instantly wished I were invisible. The man scuttling beside her was none other than Stan Rosenstatz, the *Intelligencer* features editor and our boss. "Kitty," he hissed, "you can't go around saying things like that about people. You'll get us both fired."

"If anybody tries to fire me," Kitty snapped, "they'll regret it."

"Kitty —"

"You think I don't mean it?" She threw her car keys squarely into the chest of the startled valet. Then her glacial gaze landed on me.

Stan caught sight of me, too, and stopped dead.

Kitty said, "Well, if it isn't Mary Sunshine herself. What the hell are you doing here?"

"Hello, Kitty. I completed the assignment you gave me." I spoke calmly and smiled, not quite paying homage, but polite. "The story's written and ready for your approval."

She wore a full-length black satin skirt with a frothy white blouse that made her bosom look like the puffed-up breast of an exotic bird. Her very blond hair was upswept and lanced with her signature accessory, a feather. No matter what Kitty wore, she had a feather incorporated into her ensemble somewhere.

From two steps above, she eyed me. "I didn't tell you to come here tonight. What do you think you're doing? Trying to beat me to the story?"

"No, of course not. I'm a guest."

"A guest?"

Her tone was insulting, but I fought my temper down. "Yes, I was invited."

Stan hurried down the steps to me. "Hi, Nora, nice to see you. Lovely evening —"

"Stuff it, Stan." Without taking her gaze from my face, Kitty dared me to lose my good manners. "Don't take sides in this."

"Sides?" Stan forced a laugh. "What are you talking about? Nora's just —"

"I'm sorry, Kitty," I said. "Perhaps I should have told you I was coming." She came down a step and we were face-to-face. I could smell the wine on her breath. She'd had too much, revealed by the glassy look in her eyes. And the scars from her last face-lift hadn't quite healed.

She stiffened as if she knew what I'd noticed. "I know the game you're playing, Miss Blackbird. You want my job, and you think your relationship with Rory Pendergast can get it for you. Well, I've got a few years left, young lady."

Feebly, Stan said, "Kitty, don't be an idiot. This is a team effort. We all work together. Nora's on board to help us improve —"

She swung around on him. "And you — you think you're going to get the managing editor job just because Sweet Knees waltzes into my department?"

"Sweet Knees?" I repeated.

"Kitty —"

She cut off Stan's placating with a sharp gesture. "I'm out of here," she said.

The valet arrived with her car, an aged white Mercedes with a crooked front bumper. Kitty got into the driver's seat and revved the engine before the valet had closed the door. Then she was off, narrowly missing the corner of the portico. Her vanity plate, I saw, read MEOW.

"I'm sorry, Nora," Stan said in the silence left behind like the cloud of her exhaust. "She's temperamental."

"I know, Mr. Rosenstatz. That's what makes her great at her job."

He looked relieved. "You're a good kid. Call me Stan, okay?"

Stan Rosenstatz could have been any-where from fifty to seventy, with a thin frame, nervous hands and tufts of gray hair growing out of his ears. His dinner jacket was a size too large and had been hanging on a wire hanger too long. He looked as if he didn't have much fun.

I patted his arm. "Coming back into the party?"

Stan shook his head and used his handkerchief to mop the perspiration from his forehead. "I've had enough hobnobbing for one night."

"You okay?"

"Sure. Y'know, Kitty's just blowing off steam. And she's had a few drinks. Don't take it personally."

"I'm trying not to. I can't possibly be a threat to her."

"Well, you are," said Stan on a rueful sigh. "But she'll come around. You'll get to like her, I'm sure."

I wasn't the least bit sure, but I knew it would help Stan if I agreed. So I did, and added, "I'll e-mail my story later tonight, okay?"

"Sure. Listen, I appreciate you not coming to the office much yet. It keeps the peace — you know what I mean? But don't think you're out of sight, out of mind. You're doing good work, Nora."

I thanked him. He left, and I went into the party.

A waiter from Main Events caught me just inside the doors. "Glass of wine?"

"Thank you." I accepted a glass and tried to put Kitty out of my mind. I wanted to enjoy myself. "Am I fashionably late?"

He smiled conspiratorially. "People are just getting loose now."

I headed down the long carpet towards the party noise. The strains of a quiet jazz quartet soothed the underlying chatter of human voices. For the first time since my parents took a powder, I plunged into a party.

The throng was a mix of newspaper people and Pendergast cronies, like old Heywood Kidd, the art collector, as well as some of the New Crowd on the Philadelphia social scene. Rory liked to have young people around, so I was well acquainted with many of the guests.

I heard the distinctive laugh of my friend Lexie Paine and turned to see her staking out a corner with several eligible bachelors, probably telling Nasdaq jokes while they breathed her perfume and fantasized about her assets. We caught each other's raised eyebrow signal. We'd meet at the bar as soon as she could get away.

Rory's downstairs rooms looked as if a florist's truck had exploded there. More RickandGabe flowers competed for attention with the art collection, the furniture, the glimmer of crystal and the soft glow of leather-bound books. Someone had matted and framed a selection of newspaper relics that celebrated the long and happy Pendergast ownership of the *Intelligencer*. I avoided the crush in the center of the room and strolled along the display, looking at headlines from long ago when the first Pendergast got bored with selling whale oil and started up a newspaper. In a day when companies were bought and sold within weeks, a single-family ownership of a news-paper — even a slightly tacky one like the *Intelligencer* — for a hundred and fifty years was impressive indeed.

Halfway along the display I heard foot-steps on the main staircase and turned. Peach Treese came barreling down the steps and rammed straight into me. For a woman of unspoken age, she could move like a loco-motive.

"Peach! Are you okay?"

She caught herself on my outstretched arms and looked at me in shock. "Nora." Her good manners kicked in. "Nora Blackbird, how nice to see you."

I put my glass of wine down on a table and held her hands in mine. They were cold and trembling. "Peach, are you all right?"

She wasn't. Although she'd obviously

48

tried to pull herself together upstairs, fresh tears blurred her eyes. Her face was white beneath carefully applied makeup.

Even in tears, Patricia "Peach" Treese looked every inch her role as one of Philadelphia's most-respected hostesses. She'd grown up a child of privilege in the home of her grandfather, the city's mayor back when mayors were dignified and honorable even if social injustice ran rampant. Her handsome husband had died young of a lingering illness, but she'd finished college after his death, raised her children to be community leaders and become a woman of considerable influence in her own right. She had been president of the museum board since forever, and everyone credited her with saving the symphony from its latest financial crunch by her iron-fist-in-the-lace-glove fund-raising efforts.

It was also common knowledge that Peach had been Rory Pendergast's intimate companion for thirty years.

She was the party's unofficial hostess, but she looked anything but welcoming. Her silver Armani suit was impeccable, and her gold jewelry looked spectacular on the simple clothing. But her face was uncontrolled, her expression rattled. The tremble in her hands did not subside.

"Peach? You're really not feeling well. Can I get you a glass of water?"

"Oh," she said, making a visible effort to control her emotions. "No, thank you, Nora. You're very kind. And my goodness, don't you look smashing tonight? And after everything you've been through."

Lightly, I joked, "Better smashing than smashed, I guess, which is more than I can say for some of your guests."

Peach tried to laugh, but I knew she was operating on automatic pilot.

"What can I do to help?" I asked.

She released a broken sigh of exasperation. Or maybe it was genuine anger. "That old buzzard!"

"You mean Rory? Is he giving you trouble?"

"He won't come downstairs again. He says he's had enough for one night. Can you imagine? They're all here to be nice to him!"

"Maybe he's just tired."

"Maybe he's just stubborn!" Peach drew a long breath to calm down. "Why don't you go up and reason with him, Nora? He's so fond of you."

"I'll take him a drink," I suggested. "Does champagne still make his nose turn pink?"

"Yes, pink as a bunny's." Peach laughed shakily. "Thank you, Nora. You're a dear.

Give him a few minutes to calm down first. Then work your magic."

"I'll do what I can. Now go find somebody to flirt with," I advised. "You have a big family wedding coming up. You'll need a date if Rory's being such a pill."

"My granddaughter's wedding, yes. Oh, Lincoln is your nephew, isn't he? By marriage? Well, it's the talk of the whole town, I know, and I wish it were over already. See? Rory's not the only one being a bore."

"You'll recover," I said. "Both of you."

She smiled, gave me an air kiss and slipped off in the direction of the powder room.

I pressed through the crush of men in the dining room to where the bar had been set up. I knew most everyone there and exchanged pleasantries with a few people. Some others saw me coming and subtly turned their backs, making me wonder from whom my father had borrowed money to abscond. Jamie Scaithe, looking tan from his latest trip to his family's Bermuda house, waved. I waved back at the alpha dog of Todd's pack, but continued to the bar. I didn't want to hear Jamie ask again with exaggerated concern how I was coping without my husband.

Just as I reached the bar, a tallish young

man with a shaven head grabbed his drink and spun around. We nearly collided.

"Oh, I'm sorry," I said automatically.

He managed to avoid spilling the drink on either one of us and uttered a surly, "No problem." Then he pushed past me and hastily plunged into the party. I blinked after him. Peach Treese wasn't the only upset guest.

Jill Mascione, whose father had built Main Events into the most relied upon catering service in Philadelphia, was mixing drinks with effortless speed. We'd been friends since the days of the lavish parties my parents threw when they were burning through the family fortune. Jill and I used to play together under the bunted tables. Now she wore a tuxedo-style jacket and ran the bar with cool efficiency while I learned to be a reporter.

"Hey," she said when she spotted me. "What's this? Your Audrey Hepburn period?"

"I raided Grandmama's closet."

"Looks good on you. And I'm not the only one who's noticed." Hands busy, she jerked her head in the direction from which I'd come.

"Jamie Scaithe can take a long swim in the Schuylkill."

"You don't date cokeheads, huh?"

"I'm learning not to be Peter Pan's enabler."

"Atta girl. It's time you were the main event in a relationship."

"Listen to you," I said on a laugh, knowing full well her relationship with her volatile partner, Betsy, was on-again, off-again. "How about lunch some day soon?"

"You're on. I'll call you."

She reached under the table for a bottle of champagne she'd clearly kept precisely chilled in ice water for someone special. "I saw Libby here a few minutes ago. She okay?"

"Just crazy, but what else is new?"

Jill grinned, pouring. "Heard from your folks?"

"A postcard weeks ago. They're having a ball."

She laughed. "I expect nothing less."

"Your dad?"

With another tip of her head towards the kitchen, she said, "Running the show, as usual. He says we're always on the edge of bankruptcy, and he's the only one who can save us." She handed me the champagne.

"Are things that tight?"

"We're afloat," Jill said. "He's too generous with people. If he'd let me take over, we might actually make a profit."

I knew all about parents and money trouble. "I need a glass for the guest of honor, too," I said. "I'm going upstairs to lure him down."

"Good luck." She poured another glass and then wiped her hands on the bar towel. "I took him some supper a little while ago. He's had one scene after another tonight. First Kitty Keough — man, she is just a few rattles short of a snake — and some other guy I didn't know. That bald guy who just ran you over. Weird party. I think Rory's hiding, and I don't blame him."

"I'll see what I can do. Catch you later."

I took two glasses of gently fizzing champagne and left Jill to do her job. I didn't want to draw any attention to my mission by going up the main staircase, so I went slowly through the throng of acquaintances towards the kitchen, chatting my way along.

The back staircase of the Pendergast mansion had been a source of great fun for the Blackbird girls when we were kids. It wound upwards from the kitchen in a series of tight turns. The first landing opened out onto the old carriage house yard — a perfect escape to the outdoors for anyone playing tag.

Standing in the doorway of the landing

was Sam, one of Jill Mascione's lunkhead brothers. He was smoking a cigarette, taking a break from washing dishes. "Hey, Nora."

"Hi, Sam. What's new?"

"Nuthin'." He pointed his cigarette at the cobblestone driveway, where we could see the taillights of a vehicle disappear down the rear drive. "People are starting to get bored and head home. Where you going?"

"Up to see Rory."

I kept going up the staircase and at last stepped into the main corridor on the second floor. The housekeeper's rooms lay to the left, situated over the kitchen. To the right and several yards down the corridor, Rory's study door was open and light spilled out onto the carpet and polished mahogany floor. Music from downstairs floated up the staircase and seemed to fill the space. "Take Five." I could smell Sam's cigarette, too.

"Rory?" I poked my head into the study and raised my voice over the Brubeck tune. "Rory, are you here?"

No answer.

I looked across the room at the beautifully lit painting on the wall. A small van Gogh. My breath caught in my throat at its beauty. I could see why Rory chose to live with it in his favorite room. The colors glowed with life, as if warmed by a constant summer Arles sun.

But it was slightly askew on the wall. I couldn't help myself. I went over and straightened it with one careful forefinger.

The dark paneled study had a pair of plush leather chairs pulled up to a sturdy coffee table with books and papers heaped on it. On another wall two fishing rods were crossed like swords over a framed photo of Rory with a sailfish. I could imagine him sitting in the leather chair wrapped in his green cardigan, floor lamp pulled close so he could read and conduct his business in comfort while enjoying his memories and his van Gogh.

But Rory was nowhere to be seen at the moment.

A small man's dress shoe lay in the middle of the floor, as if kicked off and abandoned. I smiled and shook my head. A lifelong bachelor who'd been looked after by a valet since his teens didn't feel the need to pick up his shoes, I supposed.

The door to the adjoining dressing room was open, so I tiptoed over, glasses in hand. "Rory?"

I leaned inside. "Are you here?"

His suits and trousers hung in neat rows,

surrounded by panels of cedar. Rory was a little man — petite, really — and his dressing room seemed like the playhouse of a wealthy Edwardian child. Crisp dress shirts lined the opposite wall, each hanger perfectly spaced two inches from its neighbor. A jewel-box-like cabinet stood open to reveal carefully stored silk ties, arranged by color. A tufted chair stood in the middle of the room, the perfect seat for a gentleman pulling on his socks.

Rory's bedroom lay through the open double doors to my right. I hesitated in the doorway, not wanting to intrude. "Rory?"

I don't know why I took another step. But suddenly I was in his bedroom and looking down at the crumpled figure on the floor. A small man, on his back, head twisted. His legs were splayed, one shoeless foot bent crookedly. A prescription bottle lay inches from his motionless hand — blue tablets scattered.

"Oh, God."

The next seconds whirled. I called his name. A moment later I was stepping over a pillow and went down on the carpet beside him. I must have dropped the champagne glasses because I used both hands to unbutton his shirt, already torn from his neck, to press his chest, to feel his papery throat for a pulse, to hold his head, saying stupid things, I know, but talking, talking, talking.

A heart attack? A stroke?

I pulled him into my lap and held him tightly, trying nonsensically to will him back to life. His face was smooth, weirdly young again, all personality dissipated. His boneless body was so light, his face so cool that I knew he was utterly gone.

As if a strobe light flashed in the room, I remembered the night Todd died. I saw his body, then Rory's. And I couldn't help either one of them.

My head began to swim, and I knew I was blacking out. That much penetrated the blur. I needed help. Anyone. I stumbled out of the bedroom, through the dressing room and study. I slipped on the steps and fell once, clattering downwards with a black swirling space gushing up around me as I went. I had to reach help before the blackness got me.

On the landing, I ran slap into Sam Mascione. I blundered down the rest of the steps, pulling Sam with me. In the kitchen hallway there was Jill. She was carrying wine bottles and deflected me with her shoulder. "Nora!"

"It's Rory," I babbled. "He's hurt."

"Oh, shit," she said.

"I think he's dead. Call for help."

Jill's voice faded as she said, "You're fainting."

The black swirl engulfed me then and I went down.

Chapter 3

I keep smelling salts in my bag, and Jill must have remembered. I snapped back to consciousness with the stench of ammonia burning my nose and throat.

"Jeez," she said, dabbing my cheek with an icy dish towel. "You faint at the drop of a hat."

"Dammit," I muttered.

"Actually," she said, "it's nice to know you're not as together as you pretend. Does your doctor still think it's psychological?"

"Half a dozen doctors think so. Damn!"

With Sam's help, she half dragged me into the cook's sitting room off the kitchen, and I sat on the settee, periodically putting my head between my trembling knees. Through the door, I could see the orderly mayhem of Main Events staff packing up the party.

"We called the paramedics," Jill said. "And the police are here, too."

I tried hard to make sense of the jumbled images in my head. "Oh, Jill, he's gone."

"I know, honey. But he was old. It's part of life."

I cried, taking the cold towel from my friend and pressing it against my face. She hugged me, and we rocked together. I couldn't breathe, just exhaled all the grief in my heart until I was gasping for air. He'd been a friend. A sweet, gentle man who'd come to my rescue when I needed help. He'd been kinder to me than anyone I'd ever known.

"Miss Mascione?" said a voice.

Jill sat up and wiped her face. "That's me."

"And Miss Blackbird?"

I hiccoughed and nodded.

He was tallish and young, with wet hair combed back as if he'd been summoned from a shower. Blue sport coat, khaki Dockers and spanking clean sneakers. Boy Scout tidy with calm brown eyes. I knew at once he was a cop. A very young cop.

He came into the sitting room tentatively. "I'm sorry to disturb you. I'm Detective Ben Bloom." He pulled a walletlike badge from his breast pocket and showed it to us like an honor student handing over his hall pass.

Jill stood up and shook his hand. I was afraid to try standing.

He pocketed the badge and looked down at me. "How are you feeling?"

"Terrible."

"I'm sure. Do you mind if I ask some questions? I know it's a bad time, but it's best if we do this right away."

"She's not up to a lot of hassle," Jill said.

Bloom ignored her politely and kept his gaze on me. Although I was in shock, I realized why he'd been sent. He was the good cop — the baby-faced one assigned to deal with small children and emotional women in times of trouble.

He asked, "Feeling able to tell me what you saw?"

"I think so."

"You're a reporter, I hear."

"Not really. I help write Kitty Keough's society page, that's all."

He sat on the footstool directly in front of me. Jill sat beside me, one hand across my shoulders. I fished a linen handkerchief from my bag to stop my running nose. Then I leaned forward on the settee, elbows on my knees, feet together and hands clasping the handkerchief to keep them from shaking.

He said, "I'm sorry this has happened. I gather Mr. Pendergast was someone close to you."

I nodded and Jill said, "Nora's family and Rory go back a long way."

Formalities over with, Bloom said, "I'm

also told you went upstairs to see Mr. Pendergast. I'd like you to go through everything you did. There's no rush. Do you understand?"

"Yes. I'm sorry I made a mess. I touched him. I moved things. I know you're not supposed to do that, but I — I hoped he was still alive. I thought I could help him."

"That's understandable," he said, stemming my flood of apologies and giving no hint he was dismayed that I'd blundered all over Rory's bedroom. "We need your help determining what you touched."

"Of course."

"And we'll take your fingerprints."

"I understand."

"Okay. Would you tell me exactly what happened when you went upstairs?"

I tried to think straight. Then, slowly, I told him about talking to Peach, the glasses of champagne, of walking up the back stairs, of speaking to Sam.

"That's my brother," Jill added.

Bloom nodded. "We spoke with him just now. I want to make sure you agree with what he told us. Can you go on?"

"Wait a minute." Jill broke across the detective's next question. "Does Nora need a lawyer?"

Detective Bloom made an effort to look

more official. "That's your right, of course, but this is just routine. We need to know what evidence Miss Blackbird tampered with —"

"Evidence?" Jill repeated. "You think he was murdered, don't you?"

"We just need —"

I said, "I think he was."

Jill and the detective both looked at me.

My heart started to pound again as my recollection of the scene upstairs sharpened in my mind. I said, "There was a pillow on the floor beside him. And he had struggled. He'd lost his shoe and — and I think his shirt was torn. It was, wasn't it?" I looked up at Bloom. "I unbuttoned it," I said. "To help him breathe, but —"

"He was breathing when you found him?"

"No, no." I shut my eyes to remember all the details. "He was dead, but I thought — it was an automatic reaction. His shirt had been torn, and I have the impression now that he had struggled with someone."

"Why do you say that?"

"He looked . . . messy. His clothing in disarray. He was a careful dresser, but the collar of his shirt was ripped."

Rory murdered. I started to tremble all over again. Detective Bloom reached over and put his slim hand on my arm. His grip was strong, but I pulled away and put my head between my knees.

"She does this," Jill explained, rubbing my back. "She faints easily."

"This is the last time," I said to my ankles.

"She can't drive," Jill went on. "We're all afraid she'll wreck the car."

With my head down, I said, "Shut up, Jill, would you, please?"

Jill laughed a little. "And she's always polite."

Bloom cleared his throat.

I sat up unsteadily. "Rory was so frail," I said, almost talking to myself. "A child could have knocked him down. Anyone could have smothered him."

"All right," said Bloom, putting an end to my speculation before it went any further. He dug into the pocket of his sport coat. He came up with a cheap notebook and a Bic pen. "Let's start all over again, shall we? Why don't you tell me the whole story from the beginning? Nice and slow."

I recounted my movements as the detective wrote notes in the small ring-bound notebook. He stopped me twice to clarify my information, but as I gathered my composure I found I could detail the things I'd seen and heard very clearly. I remembered the prescription bottle. I described the angle of Rory's twisted head.

Bloom kept me calm and focused. His own expression was carefully manufactured, but I could see his powers of observation were sharply at work. He watched my hands, then involuntarily let his gaze slip to my legs.

Jill stirred beside me. I knew she'd been observing, too. With her bartender's instincts, I wondered what she noticed. Her reaction to his manner would undoubtedly be different from mine.

"All right," he said when I had finished. "This is very helpful. I'm sure you understand how important it is for us to know exactly what happened here. And the sooner we nail down details, the better our chances for closing this matter."

A uniformed police officer appeared at that moment. "Bloom," he said, "there's a couple of ladies who really want to see you. They're making a fuss."

"I'm coming," Bloom said. "If you'll wait here with —"

He was interrupted by two querulous female voices arguing in the hallway, and a moment later the uniformed officer was pushed into the sitting room by the force of two elderly women, who could not be stopped.

"See here," said the first. "Our brother is dead and we are prisoners in his house because you people —"

"This is our home," the other voice chimed in. "We have a right to know what's going on."

The Pendergast sisters reportedly lived in Palm Beach, having left Philadelphia over some family squabble decades ago. Rumor had it they rarely spoke to each other, let alone their brother. They must have been invited to the party by someone uninformed about the family rift, I realized, and they had come to celebrate their family's ownership of the *Intelligencer*.

I knew most of the main characters in Philadelphia society. I'd gone to dancing class with some, enjoyed country club picnics with others, attended their christenings and weddings and quite a few funerals. As a little girl, I'd had my cheeks pinched by every grande dame in town. Except Lily and Opal Pendergast.

The Poison Gas Sisters, I'd heard my father call them. "Stay away," he'd warned. "They'd probably fry you up with onions for breakfast."

Lily's crusty diamonds matched the hard ice in her gaze. She was tall and ferocious in an expensive black silk dress, and she pointed her ebony cane defiantly at Detective Bloom. "I demand to know what's going on."

Opal had "gone Florida" and her solid, shorter figure was squeezed into a murderous orange track suit with sequins. Her feet overflowed her flat gold shoes with sparkling buckles. Her ear-piercing whine had been perfected by years of complaints. "I don't understand why we're being held like cattle. Our brother is dead!"

Lily said, "We've come all the way from Florida to honor our own family and now —"

"We're exhausted!"

Jill and I exchanged a glance.

Lily's hawklike nose pointed at me, then at Jill. "And who are you? What are you telling him?"

I got to my feet and held out my hand. "Hello, Miss Pendergast. I'm Nora Blackbird. I'm very sorry —"

She narrowed her sharp eyes on me. "Blackbird? One of Charlie Blackbird's granddaughters, I suppose? One of the widows?"

"I'm so sorry about Rory," I said evenly. "We are all — were all — very fond of him."

"Some people were fonder of him than others," she said, but grudgingly accepted my hand. "How do you do, Miss Black-bird?"

"This is Detective Bloom, Miss Pender-gast. He's gathering information about what happened here this evening."

Lily Pendergast allowed herself to be civil to me, but she made no effort to treat Bloom with any such deference. She straightened to her full height and looked at him with dis-dain. "I want you to stop what you're doing, young man. Not another word is to be said until my sister and I are told exactly what's going on."

"I'm afraid it doesn't work that way, ma'am," said Bloom. "I'm from the homi-cide division and —"

"Homicide?" Lily snorted, clearly imper-vious to Bloom's good-cop charm. "Don't be ridiculous. Pendergasts don't get them-selves killed."

Opal snapped, "Roderick died of natural causes, I'm perfectly sure."

"You'd better sit down, honey," said Jill. "Because you're about to get a surprise."

"See here, this is very unpleasant," Lily appealed to Bloom with a gesture to indi-cate Jill. "Obviously, there's no control over who goes where and what goes on. Surely we are owed some consideration from the police on this."

"Yes, some consideration," Opal chimed in. "People are walking in and out, gossiping and — mercy, what about the art collection? Is anybody guarding the art?" She began to fan her face with her handkerchief. "With all these strangers loitering around —"

It was time for someone to take charge, and young Detective Bloom didn't appear up to the challenge of subduing two elderly dragons. I guessed the Boy Scout manual didn't cover all emergencies. I interrupted with a careful blend of obsequious gentility and a dash of Blackbird bossiness. "I think we're all terribly emotional and need time to compose ourselves. Jill, could you get some drinks for everyone? Rory's sisters need time to sit down and collect themselves. And then I think the detective will explain everything to your satisfaction, Miss Pendergast. Does that sound like a plan?"

Bloom pulled himself together. "Yes, that's a good idea. Ladies, let's make you comfortable and I'll be right back to clarify the situation for you."

Bloom drew me into the hall as Jill and the other police officer set about treating the Pendergast sisters like royalty.

Keeping his voice down, he said, "That was quick thinking, Miss Blackbird. You know how to handle these people."

"A lifetime of experience," I replied.

The hall was busy. Most of the Main Events employees had been herded into the kitchen to wait, and I noticed that police officers — both uniformed and in plain clothes — were swarming up the back staircase with cases of equipment.

Bloom put his shoulder against the wall and pulled me out of the path of a burly cop lumbering past with a video camera. "Do you know many of the guests here tonight?"

"Probably all of them."

"And you seem to understand how they should be treated."

"With kid gloves, you mean?"

A glimmer of light appeared in his brown eyes. "Exactly. Look, I'll be honest with you, Miss Blackbird. I'm a fish out of water here. All I know is you stick out your pinkie when you drink tea. Would you mind? You could be a valuable asset in this investigation."

"Does this mean I'm not a suspect?"

"Unless you killed Pendergast in a minute or less, I think we can rule you out," he said. "We'll go easy on you if you pitch in."

"I'll be happy to help in any way I can."

"Great." He took my elbow and pulled. "First, how about introducing me to Peach Treese? Is that really her name?"

Chapter 4

I knew I'd been flattered, but I fell for it anyway. Or maybe I was just trying to find a way to distract myself from the horror of what had happened.

"Rory's sisters are probably right, you know." We moved down the kitchen hallway. "Have you started checking on the art collection?"

"What about it?" Detective Bloom asked.

"The collection is enormous," I said. "I couldn't begin to catalog what Rory owns — owned — but the van Gogh was still in his room. I know because I straightened it."

"Jeez," the detective muttered. "A van Gogh?"

"A small one. But extremely valuable, of course. It was hanging crookedly on the wall. Maybe someone was touching it, and Rory came in."

My theory didn't faze Bloom. He asked, "How do we find out what might be missing? Is there a list or something?"

"Rory probably had a private curator, or

at least an agency who cataloged and took care of things. We could ask his secretary."

Bloom shook his head grimly. "The secretary's on a plane to Los Angeles for a family commitment. He left just after the party got under way. We've talked with him by cell phone once already. He's trying to get back by tomorrow."

"Maybe Peach could help. She knows about Rory's affairs."

"Let's go find her. Scotty," he called to a passing colleague. "Somebody call Levi, the art guy, okay? And keep an eye on things here for a while, will you?"

"Sure," said the other cop. He was snapping his fingers at his side and chewing gum very fast, the only man showing any urgency. A crime had been committed, and all the police moved around us with unhurried purpose. But Scotty betrayed the obvious — the clock was ticking. Around his punished bit of gum, he said to Bloom, "We rounded up all the guests."

"Anyone give you trouble?"

Scotty grinned. "Only the couple fooling around in the bathroom."

The party guests had not been allowed to leave yet but were herded into the main salon, the entry hall and dining room where the mood was somber. The bar was closed and the leftover food had been removed, but Main Events coffee urns steamed gently on the buffet. Most of the guests had china cups and saucers in hand. Police officers were taking names and addresses.

Heads turned as we entered the salon. With a sinking heart, I realized I was a celebrity for all the wrong reasons

Peach Treese sat in a corner in an upholstered chair. She looked far from composed and had aged ten years since I'd seen her an hour earlier. Another detective, a woman in a too-tight navy pantsuit, sat with her.

To Bloom, I said, "Here's Peach. Shall we go speak with her?"

"I'm right behind you."

I led the way through the subdued crowd to Peach's chair. She saw me, and her face crumpled into tears again. I knelt beside her chair and hugged her. She trembled violently.

"Oh, Nora," she said, her cheek pressed to mine.

"Peach, I'm so sorry," I murmured.

"Do you think he suffered?" she asked. "Do you think he was in any pain?" She pulled back to look at my face. "People are saying you found him. Was it his heart? Was he in pain when he — when he — ?"

"I'm sure it happened quickly," I said,

trying to be gentle. I took the handkerchief from her hands and dabbed her tears. "Don't make yourself ill, all right?"

"I won't," she promised, "if those horrible sisters of his stay away from me. They are so hateful."

"They're in shock."

She began to display some of her natural fire again. "They wanted Rory to sell the newspaper — did he tell you that? They've been pressuring him for years, even courted that national conglomerate themselves. And they have the gall to show up here tonight to celebrate everything he accomplished. I should have thrown them out hours ago!"

I soothed her. "Peach, there's no sense getting upset about them right now."

"Oh, Nora, what will I do without him?"

I hugged her again, and Bloom cleared his throat.

I held her a little longer before I had the composure to ask whether or not Rory had a curator for his collection.

"Of course," she said, wiping her swollen eyes. "It was Boatman's. They're in New York. They just began work on the collection. His former curator passed away. Jerry Glickman, remember?"

"Yes. Thank you, Peach."

"Why?" Her face contracted. "The van Gogh? Is there something wrong?"

"No, no, Peach."

Bloom leaned closer. "Mrs. Treese, I know you'll be interviewed more fully in a few minutes, but Detective Wilson mentioned to me that you heard Pendergast on the phone while you were upstairs."

"Yes," said Peach. "He was laughing, I thought. But then he said something — I didn't understand it all."

"What do you think you heard?"

"Rory said, 'Don't threaten me, young man.' I think someone was being cruel. How could anyone threaten Rory?"

"Maybe he was joking," I soothed.

Bloom asked, "You're certain that's what you heard, Mrs. Treese?"

"I told you, I'm not exactly —"

"Please," I said, "she's upset."

Peach clutched my arm. Her hands were freezing. "Why are they asking me all these questions, Nora?"

Bloom said, "When you were upstairs, what were you discussing with Pendergast, Mrs. Treese?"

Her face seemed to flatten out. "It was a private conversation."

"Yes, ma'am, but —"

Peach's color began to alarm me, and I

76

cut across Bloom's next inquiry. "It's all right, Peach. Do you have someone to take you home soon? Can I see you home?"

"No, no. My granddaughter is here. She'll walk me across."

Bloom tried to interrupt again, but I stood, physically blocking him from Peach. I said, "I'll find your granddaughter now, Peach. You shouldn't be alone."

We promised to talk again soon by telephone. I turned away just as young Pamela Treese rushed over to console her grandmother.

As we moved away, I said to Bloom sotto voce, "You don't suspect Peach, for heaven's sake?"

"Why not?"

"She and Rory were closer than anyone else in his life. Surely it's ridiculous to suppose she could — Now wait," I said sharply, seeing his face. "I know the family is always suspected first, but really! It's completely silly to think Peach could have killed him."

"She was the last to see him alive. And she told you herself they argued."

"That's nonsense."

"You'd be surprised how simple these things turn out to be, Miss Blackbird."

Another cop came over purposefully. "Bloom, they're ready for you upstairs."

"Okay," he said, then turned to me. "There's something I need you to do, Miss Blackbird. I'm sorry it has to be tonight, but we don't have another choice."

"You want me to go back upstairs," I guessed, and my heart began to skitter.

"It'll be all right," he said, somehow charming and solemn at the same time. "And I'll be with you the whole time. But it's important for us to know everything about the crime scene. You're the only one who can help us determine exactly how things looked when you found Pendergast."

Inside, I felt a sliver of anger that the detective referred to my friend by his last name. It depersonalized a man who deserved respect and affection.

Bloom must have seen something change in my expression, because he said quickly, "I won't kid you. It'll be hard. But you've been wonderful so far. You can do this."

I didn't want to be coached. I would help because it was dear Rory who had died.

"Let's go now," I said, "while I feel this way."

The questions came rapid-fire after that. Had I touched the railing? Where was I standing when I spoke with Sam? How long had I paused on the landing? What kind of car had I seen leaving the cobblestone yard?

How fast had it been going? When I arrived on the second floor, had I seen or heard anyone descending the main staircase?

Carefully, they guided me along my route. Upstairs, I hesitated in the doorway of the study, so Bloom went before me and asked another question to lure me into the room. The books, the unfinished supper, papers, telephone and paintings were just as I had seen them the first time I entered. I showed them how the painting looked — slightly crooked on the wall.

A knot of cops huddled in Rory's dressing room, murmuring among themselves and pretending to ignore what Detectives Bloom and Wilson were doing with me.

"And here?" Bloom asked, pointing his pen towards the open bedroom door. "This is where you stood when you first saw the victim?"

I stepped into Rory's bedroom. I assumed the body had been removed, but there he lay, covered with a white plastic sheet. It was as if a cheap drop cloth had been thrown over him to allow painters to refurbish the room.

A part of my brain closed down then, as if a curtain had dropped between the intellectual side of myself and the emotional side. The police asked me questions; even some of the men who had kept silent up until that time posed queries. I remember a woman, too, who asked me bluntly about the champagne glasses I had dropped. They were still in place, broken crystal and twin pools of wine soaked deep into the carpet.

I explained what I had seen and done. I explained twice. And after that, they wanted to review their notes. I felt faint only once, but the spell passed when I shoved my emotions behind the curtain again and forced myself to respond to Detective Bloom's relentless interrogation.

I heard one officer mutter, "The kid cop has his big chance. Now look at 'im go."

Finally Bloom and his partner led me out into the corridor.

"The pills on the floor," I said, when we were out of the room. I rubbed my face with one hand and wondered if I would ever think straight again.

"What about the pills, Miss Blackbird?"

"The bottle is a standard prescription container. Were they some kind of heart medication?"

"Were you aware of a heart condition?"

"I knew he'd had a heart attack a few years ago, not a very serious one. What kind of pills were those on the floor?"

The partner said, "I don't think we —"

Bloom interrupted. "Maybe she can help, Scotty."

"You've broken enough rules already," said Wilson. "You want your promotion this bad?"

"For godsake," Bloom said, "the old guy won't mind now."

The two of them sounded like bickering teenagers. "I'm sure it doesn't matter," I said, suddenly snappish, too. "I helped you. Surely you can share this small bit of information? Maybe I can give Peach some comfort if I know what happened."

Wilson turned away.

Bloom took a deep breath. "They were Viagra tablets, Miss Blackbird."

I heard a cop laugh in the bedroom.

"I see."

"It's obvious what he planned to do," said Wilson. "Only he had a fight with the Treese lady instead, so she turned around and —"

Bloom cut him off. "I think we'd better let Miss Blackbird go home now."

"You don't really think Peach could have hurt Rory?" I asked. "Is that what you're trying to do? Convince yourselves she did it, so you can all go home?"

"Miss Blackbird —"

"It's impossible. And you're wasting valuable time."

"We're following procedure," Bloom began.

"She's a kind and caring person. You don't know her. She loves Rory." I felt tears start. "We're very good friends."

The short silence that greeted my last declaration made me realize I had just discounted all my defense of Peach. Naturally I would protect her if we were friends.

I wasn't helping at all. I tried to rub the headache out of my temples. The impact of the night suddenly hit me like a baseball bat to the skull. "I'd like to go home now. Could we find my driver, please, Detective Bloom?"

"Sure thing," he said.

He took me downstairs past the thinning crowd of guests. Even Peach had disappeared. I walked unsteadily beside the detective to the portico entrance, silent and distressed. I tried to formulate another speech to defend Peach's honor, but the police weren't going to listen. They were looking for proof of guilt. Guilt, not innocence.

"Why don't you sit down?" Bloom suggested when we reached the side foyer. "You've had a long night. I'll go look for your driver."

I felt like a senior citizen, but I accepted his offer. "Thank you."

Bloom turned to leave me and stopped short.

Michael Abruzzo took a step out of the shadowy doorway and into the lighted foyer. He wore a brown leather jacket, a black T-shirt and jeans. Over my head, his gaze clashed with Bloom's, and the two of them positively bristled like a couple of dogs defending their territory.

"Abruzzo," said Bloom in a tone quite different from the one he'd used with me all evening. "How long have you been here?"

"If it isn't Detective Gloom," said Abruzzo. "I've been around for a couple of hours. I'm here to take Miss Blackbird home."

"Oh," I said, turning pink for no reason I could imagine. "But Reed's waiting for me."

"I sent him home. It's late."

"What time is . . . ? Good heavens. I had no idea. I forgot all about Reed until just a minute ago."

The two men faced each other and didn't notice me. Abruzzo was bigger and more watchful. Bloom was younger and leaner, but angrier. Somehow they looked evenly matched.

"You know this man, Miss Blackbird?"

"Why, yes. This is —"

"I know who he is," said Bloom. "I'm surprised you do."

Abruzzo laughed.

Bloom said, "Maybe we'd better find an officer to drive you home."

"Don't be silly. Mr. Abruzzo's services have been bought and paid for." I swallowed hard as I absorbed the situation. "By Rory, as a matter of fact."

Bloom raised an eyebrow at Abruzzo. "No kidding? You had a business arrangement with Pendergast?"

"Occasionally I do business with upstanding citizens, yes," said Abruzzo.

"He's dead," said Bloom.

"I heard," Abruzzo replied calmly.

"We'll want to talk to you."

Abruzzo shrugged. "You know how to reach me."

"Is the car ready?" I asked. Any minute the situation was going to become a full-blown pissing contest, and I didn't intend to get caught in the middle. "Can we go now?"

Abruzzo made a sweep with one hand. "Right this way, Cinderella."

I turned to Bloom. "You've been kind tonight, Detective." I put out my hand to shake his. "I only wish I could convince you that you're completely wrong about Peach."

84

"I'll call you," he said, accepting my handshake.

Abruzzo moved aside to let me pass. As the detective watched, Abruzzo slipped one hand under my elbow as I started down the stone stairs in my heels. We descended in silence.

Chapter 5

When we were out of the detective's earshot at the bottom of the steps, I pulled out of his grasp and said under my breath, "You can put away your six-shooter now."

"What?"

"You and Detective Bloom doing your Wild West routine."

"Yeah, I'm his favorite gunslinger."

"Are you?" I asked, perhaps too sharply. There was plenty of room under the leather jacket to conceal a weapon.

"Tonight I'm just your chauffeur, Miss Blackbird." He looked down at me. "You okay?"

We were the only people under the portico. He pulled car keys from his hip pocket and waited for my response. I wasn't okay. But I nodded.

"Rough night," Abruzzo said. "I'm sorry about Rory."

I looked away, nodded again and felt my throat close tight.

With one hand under my elbow again, he helped me into the front passenger seat of a perfectly sedate Volvo sedan and closed the car door. I used the next few seconds to pull myself together. By the time he slid behind the wheel beside me, I had given myself a strong mental lecture and regained my self-control.

I said the first thing that came into my head. "Why aren't you driving one of those parade floats you sell at Mick's Muscle Cars?"

"I like this one. Just don't tell anyone I drive a foreign make, okay?"

I needn't have worried that Abruzzo was going to force conversation after that. He started the car, fastened his seat belt and drove slowly down Rory's curving driveway and through the gates. The car was comfortable, almost cozy. He paid attention to driving and allowed me to think.

I pushed the image of Rory's small, crumpled body out of my mind for fear I might start crying again. The idea of blubbering in front of Michael Abruzzo mortified me into calm. Instead, I leaned back against the headrest and closed my eyes, simply letting impressions float up in my mind.

The Pendergast sisters anxious to keep as many family secrets as possible. Peach weeping quietly for her longtime lover. Kitty Keough making a scene under the portico.

Rory's ties hanging neatly in his closet. Stan Rosenstatz mopping his face with a graying handkerchief. Jill Mascione bristling as Detective Bloom examined my legs as if they were important evidence in a murder case.

Abruzzo drove the Volvo over a bridge, and I opened my eyes. "Rory had fishing rods in his room. Hanging on the wall."

Abruzzo didn't seem surprised that this particular remark came out of nowhere. "Trout."

"I beg your pardon?"

"Rory liked to fish for trout."

I turned in the seat and looked at Abruzzo. "Did you know Rory well?"

"Sure."

"Sure? What does that mean?"

He shrugged. "I took him fishing."

"When?" I demanded, surprised.

"Lots of times."

"Lots?"

"I'm not the usual Pendergast crony, huh?"

"I just — I'm surprised you associated with him."

"I didn't think he'd be safe going fishing by himself these last few years. I was afraid he'd fall in and drown. So I went with him. He showed me all his favorite places on the Delaware."

"Have you known him long?"

He didn't answer for a moment. In the light of the dashboard, I looked at Abruzzo's profile. His blunt nose, heavy-lidded eyes — kept that way, perhaps, to reveal nothing. I wondered fleetingly if he had cared for Rory. What was he feeling now?

At last, he said, "I've known Rory a lot of years. He gave me a start when I needed it, and we were — he was a good guy. I'm sorry he's gone."

"He was murdered," I said.

The news did not startle Abruzzo. "With the homicide cops there, I figured. Who did it?"

"We don't know yet."

He shot a look at me. "We?"

I didn't answer. I wasn't sure why I'd lumped myself in the same category as the police. I looked at the road again. I knew Peach Treese hadn't murdered Rory, that was all. Bloom's automatic assumption that she had made me angry. Peach didn't need to be prosecuted. She needed to be protected.

Abruzzo said, "Looks like I've given your buddy Bloom a new suspect."

"You mean you? Don't be silly." Gathering my courage, I said, "I gather you're acquainted with the detective, too?"

"We spent some time together."

"Oh?"

He shrugged again. "In the juvenile system."

"The juvenile system," I repeated, uncomprehending. "Oh."

"I wasn't an especially well-behaved teenager."

"Neither was Detective Bloom, I gather."

"He wasn't bad. I think his family sent him into the program to — what do they call it now? To get scared straight."

"Is that why you were there, too?"

He smiled, watching the road. "I was a couple of years older, a little more experienced. A judge seemed to think some additional time away from my — from negative influences might be rehabilitating."

"Was it?"

"I don't steal motorcycles anymore," he answered. "I met Rory around that time, as a matter of fact."

"Really? How?"

"When I was ushered out of the state's accommodations, he had just started a mentoring program. I ended up getting paired with him."

"You met Rory when you were a teenager?"

"Yeah. He made me go back to school, get

my GED, take some college classes. And he helped me start my first business."

I sat back in the seat, floored. If Abruzzo had told me Rory raised Siamese cats and gave them to Eskimos I couldn't have been more surprised. I had spent the whole evening showing the police how well I knew Rory Pendergast, and here was information I'd had no clue about. "For heaven's sake. I knew he had strong feelings about teens from troubled — I'm sorry, I mean —"

"It's okay."

"He helped you start in business?"

"He loaned me money from time to time. I didn't want to borrow from my own family, and with my track record I needed a source other than a bank to get started. For a while, I owed him a hell of a lot of cash. I still do, actually."

How many others had Rory helped in the same way? How many young men of questionable background?

Breaking across my thoughts, Abruzzo said, "Why did you say don't be silly?"

"What?"

"When I said Bloom could add my name to his list of suspects. Why is that silly?"

"I don't know," I said. "It just is."

Bloom had become a police detective after his sojourn in jail. And what had Mi-

91

chael Abruzzo become? No, not a murderer. If he took an old man to visit his favorite fishing spots, surely he couldn't be capable of killing him.

But I wondered how Abruzzo's perspective on crime might help figure out who had killed Rory Pendergast. Did he look at murder with a different point of view than Detective Bloom?

"Listen," he said after the moment stretched, "I still haven't had any dinner, and I'm starving. What about you?"

I hadn't eaten anything in a long time myself, and I was genuinely hungry. Spending a little more time with Abruzzo didn't seem like a bad idea just then either.

"Okay," I said cautiously.

"A burger?"

A burger sounded heavenly. "Sure."

"No, wait," he said. "I've got a better plan."

He turned off the highway a few miles later just over the Bucks County line and ended up in a neighborhood of dilapidated warehouses surrounded by acres of broken asphalt and scrubby bushes. The Volvo veered around potholes and nosed through a labyrinth of parked trucks. A tractor-trailer rumbled past. Eventually Abruzzo found a nondescript bar, the Blue Note, standing on the edge of the warehouse district. He seemed to know the parking lot well and slid the Volvo into a space between a Dumpster and a big Lincoln Navigator.

Inside, the place was dim, lit by neon beer signs behind the bar and a television turned to hockey highlights. Three patrons in flannel shirts and baseball caps hunched at the bar and stared up at the television. The bartender leaned on his elbow beside them. At a table, a white-haired gentleman with a much younger woman sipped espresso.

The bartender looked up when we came in and reached for the television remote to turn down the roar of hockey fans. "Hey, Mick, you dog. How's it hanging, buddy?"

"Not bad, Del." They shook hands. "Connie still in the kitchen?"

"Yep. With Scallopine." He kissed his fingertips.

The bar smelled of cigar smoke, and Perry Como crooned on the jukebox. With homey camaraderie, the men at the bar razzed Abruzzo as he threaded me towards the last table along the wall. He took it genially. At the table, he shrugged out of his leather jacket, and in his black T-shirt suddenly fit perfectly into the workingman's hangout.

The bartender tossed drink coasters

down on the table and lit the candle on the table with a Zippo. "What're you? On your way home from a wedding?" His smile was a little loose around the edges, as if he'd been sampling behind the bar. "This young lady looks like a bridesmaid or something. Real pretty."

I doubted the Blue Note had ever seen a Givenchy before.

"She's always dressed for a party," said Abruzzo. "Del, this is Nora Blackbird. Del DeMartino."

"Hi," he said, shaking my hand and grinning. "What can I get you two? A bottle of champagne?"

Abruzzo said, "If I thought you had any, I'd order it. How about the *Vigneto Asinione*, if there's any left." He turned to me, brows raised. "That okay?"

Lifting both palms, I surrendered to his knowledge of the available wines.

"Do you like veal?" Del asked me.

"Yes, of course."

"You ain't had veal like my Connie makes. Has she, Mick?"

"I doubt it, Del."

With a wink I wasn't supposed to see, Del promised to come right back.

We were alone for half a minute before I spoke. "I've traveled past this area all my life

94

and never imagined a restaurant might be here."

Abruzzo nodded, glancing around the hangout. "Well, the ambience is nothing to write home about. But for good food at any hour, it's the best."

"I gather you're a regular?"

"Yeah, I suppose so."

Of course I wanted to know more. I wanted to ask all kinds of questions, but I refrained. Abruzzo had already found just the right weak moment to offer me a substantial amount of money for land I shouldn't have sold, so I knew I should be on the alert around him. But I was tired and hungry and emotionally spent.

The bottle of wine arrived along with an antipasto overflowing with olives, artichoke hearts and perfectly sliced vegetables. Abruzzo removed the bottle's cork himself with an attachment on a well-used pocketknife. He poured, and the liquid flashed like rubies in the candlelight. I took a sip and found the wine dry, but intense. A hint of fruit, a suggestion of Tuscan violets and maybe cinnamon, too. It was not the wine selection of an amateur. My companion drank thoughtfully and reached for a black olive. I felt my nerves relax.

A long dinner of silence stretched ahead,

so I took the initiative and said, "You went fishing with Rory Pendergast."

"Fly-fishing mostly." He sketched the one-handed motion of casting a rod over a stream. "And some shad. We had a good time together. He could get along with anyone."

I said, "Do you suppose everyone would agree with you?"

"I guess nobody gets where he did without making some enemies."

"Enemies who disliked him enough to commit murder?"

"Somebody obviously did."

I sighed. "I can't imagine why anyone would kill a man like Rory."

"He was rich," Abruzzo observed. "Really rich."

"Someone killed him for money?"

"The simple answer is often the right answer."

"That's what Bloom said." I eyed him. "For what other reasons would someone kill?"

He met my gaze. "Why ask me?"

"It's a rhetorical question. I'm just making conversation."

A skeptical smile may have crossed his mouth. "Okay. If money's not the motive, it could be a family thing. Or blackmail. A business deal gone bad, maybe." He gained momentum. "A power struggle. Angry employee. Former partner, a creditor, a borrower, a —"

"Whoa." His list overwhelmed me. Tentatively I said, "Or some — well, a sex thing, maybe?"

"At his age?" Abruzzo grinned. "Well, then, he died happy."

I thought of the Viagra pills, but shook my head to dispel the mental picture of Rory dying during an ardent interlude. Except for his torn shirt collar, his clothing had been only slightly disturbed.

"Whoever it was, it was certainly somebody who attended tonight's party." I touched the stem of my glass and remembered the wine I'd been carrying to him. If I'd gone sooner, I might have prevented his death. I felt the rush of emotion again. "It's so shocking. I can't grasp it. Maybe for you it's business as usual, but for — Oh, good heavens, I'm sorry. I didn't mean —"

He laughed at me across the candlelight, his eyes as blue as struck matches. At that moment I realized why he was called "The Mick." His eyes were an Irishman's blue, startling in his otherwise very Roman face. He said, "Welcome to my world, Miss Blackbird?"

Abashed, I said, "I'm so sorry. I must be more tired than I thought. I didn't mean to be rude."

"Starting to feel different about teaming up with the police? About poking into the segment of society that doesn't wear tuxedos?"

"I'm not teaming up with anyone. I'm just thinking." Tired as I was, my brain hummed. I crunched meditatively on a stick of celery. "It's a matter of finding the right avenue into Rory's life."

"For example?"

"His social circle. Or his art collector friends. The newspaper people were stirred up, that's for sure."

"Over what?"

"Oh, the usual. The features editor wants a promotion. Kitty — my boss, I guess you could say — is upset because of me."

"Because of you?" He looked amused. "What'd you do? Break all her pencils?"

"She thinks I'm out to get her job."

"Are you?"

"Heavens, no. I'm just getting started." I thought about what Peach had said about Rory's sisters wanting to sell the *Intelligencer*. "But there must be people worried about the future of the newspaper. About their jobs. I'll have to ask around."

"Now wait a minute," said Abruzzo. "Who put you in charge of this investigation?"

Our food arrived at that moment. Del balanced two plates on one arm, with a basket of crusty bread in his free hand and a bottle of olive oil pinched between two fingers. "Wait'll you try it," he said to me.

Thin slices of veal with aromatic mushrooms, fresh asparagus, a small serving of pasta in basil and oil. I inhaled the fragrances and was immediately famished. Del fussed over silverware and napkins.

I realized he was waiting for my reaction, so I picked up my fork and cut a small bite of the veal. It was tender, sweet, hearty and spicy all at the same time. The flavors were subtle, yet I could distinguish them all. "You're right," I said with a genuine smile. "It's fabulous. I've never tasted anything like it."

Del grinned down at me. "You'll be back," he predicted before heading to the bar.

I began to eat.

"Look." Abruzzo ignored his meal. "Rory died, and you're upset, I know. But you aren't going off the deep end, are you?"

I swallowed a bite of asparagus. "The deep end?"

"Finding the killer is a job for the police."

I twirled pasta into a bite-size roll. "Detective Bloom thought I could be helpful."

"Detective Bloom is an idiot."

"Your friend was right. The food is delicious." I popped the pasta into my mouth.

"Are you going to let the police take care of this?"

I took my time, avoiding his gaze. I swallowed and sipped the wine. "I think I can help," I said finally.

I knew I could. And what I didn't know yet, I felt sure I could find the right people to ask. I could delve into Rory's life better than anyone. I understood things about Rory's rarefied universe that the police could never grasp. And I wasn't going to start with Peach Treese, for Pete's sake.

Abruzzo leaned forward. "I don't think you get it. This isn't a lightweight newspaper story you can just investigate by dressing up and going to parties. Rory isn't just dead. He was murdered. Killed by somebody who has found it in his heart to shoot a harmless old man —"

"He wasn't shot. He was probably smothered."

He went on, undeterred. "If somebody killed an old man, they're not going to think twice about roughing you up to keep the secret."

"I'm not helpless."

100

"That has nothing to do —"

"I was on the fencing team in college."

He saw that I was teasing, and some of the heat went out of his temper. Wryly, he said, "Great. If somebody comes after you with a foil, you're all set."

"I'm not going to do anything foolish."

"What are you going to do?"

"Just talk to some friends. Now eat your supper. It's really very good."

He gave in grudgingly and ate with steady purpose while I went on about something nonsensical. I wanted to get him off the subject of Rory's death. No doubt I wanted to get myself off that subject, too.

But I couldn't help the detours my subconscious mind took as I sat at that small table. I wanted to know who'd killed Rory.

I needed to know.

Chapter 6

I slept badly that night and woke early the next morning, Saturday.

The world had not changed. Rory was dead, and I wished I could do something about it.

I phoned Peach's house early, but her housekeeper informed me that Mrs. Treese was still sleeping and planned to spend the day with her family. I sent her my sympathy, then sat down and wrote her a long note filled with my own fond memories of Rory. It was difficult to read what I'd written through my tears.

I decided I needed to blow off some steam after that. I took my bicycle out of the barn and climbed on. I headed for New Hope, first passing the split rail fences of Blackbird Farm and then the long parking lot of Mick's Muscle Cars. The plastic flags of the car lot snapped a cheeky greeting to me in the morning breeze. One of the salesmen came out of the trailer that served as their office and gave me a neighborly wave. The Delaware River ran smoothly on my left, shining silver in the sunlight. I pedaled easily, glad to have sharply cool air cleaning out my lungs.

The road ran along the river, past landmarks of Pennsylvania's long history. William Penn had taken possession of his stretch of Bucks County land just up the road from Blackbird Farm two hundred years ago. His friends built farms along the river, too, including the Blackbirds. Our fieldstone house and barn stood on an especially fertile stretch of ground that lay between a curve of the Delaware and the parallel canal. The canal had been used in the eighteenth century to haul Pennsylvania coal south to Philadelphia and Baltimore. More recently, the Park Service had taken over the canal, cleaned it up and promoted it as a tourist attraction. All summer long, mules pulled replica barges full of camera-toting tourists along the towpath past the small communities that lined the river.

The Delaware hadn't seen much action since George Washington gathered up his beleaguered army on Christmas day and crossed over to New Jersey, there to march on Trenton where the Hessian army lay. At least two Blackbird men had gone on that adventure, and family lore had it that one spunky daughter had climbed into breeches and tagged along.

As the morning sunshine brightened, I could see the New Jersey side of the Delaware on my left. On my right I soon began to pass hills that concealed vast neighborhoods of newly built tract houses — all as big as palaces, it seemed, but covered in vinyl siding. Every time I ventured south from Blackbird Farm, those serpentine cul-de-sacs seemed to wind deeper into historic farmlands. Suburbia sprawled farther and farther into Bucks County each week.

Libby was on the right track, I thought. A few protests wouldn't hurt.

I pedaled into New Hope some time later, breathing hard but feeling pleasantly revived in spirit. I passed a line of Victorian houses gaily decorated for spring beneath a canopy of leafy trees. Angelina's restaurant appeared, and I noted a good crowd of cars already parked in the side lot. The Saturday brunch patrons spilled out onto the porch. A couple of art galleries stood alongside an antiques shop. Next came the Delaware Fly-Fishing Company with its tattoo parlor on the second floor. I knew Michael Abruzzo ran the fly-fishing business and wondered if the tattoo parlor was his, too. Which got me wondering where, exactly, he might have his own tattoo.

I shoved that thought firmly out of my head and guided my bicycle to the post office to mail my note to Peach.

Then I rode down a side street to the Episcopal church. Too broke to afford the local health club, I'd found a cheap alternative among the Episcopalians. I dug a lock out of my backpack and locked the bike to the rack outside the entrance to the social hall. Moments later, I was inside the stairwell and trotting down to the multipurpose room.

"Nora!" Eli called. "You're back!"

After the yoga class filled up, I had joined the Saturday morning exercise class at the church. Except it had turned out to be a self-defense class on steroids. Our instructor was Eli — no last name ever mentioned — recently discharged from the Israeli army and delighted to find himself instructing New Hope housewives in the techniques of Mideast commandos.

He left the group of women warming up in the middle of the open floor and came over to greet me.

"Of course I'm back," I said with a grin. "You didn't think I'd cake out after two classes, did you?"

"Marcie did not return," Eli said woefully.

His English was carefully enunciated. "Do you think it was the body slam I demonstrated with her?"

"Maybe she's just late," I suggested, peeling off my windbreaker.

"I will be more gentle today," he promised. "I think Israeli women are stronger, maybe. Not so delicate."

"Oh, come now, Eli. Do your worst!"

"Not to you, Nora," he said, shocked. "You are the most delicate of all."

"That does it," I said, annoyed at being thought a weakling by too many people in less than twelve hours. "Let's get started."

It felt great to throw punches and kick would-be assassins. I pounded the floor and shouted my lungs out with everyone else. I laughed with my partner, Denise Trebicki, a third-grade teacher with a barbed sense of humor and a wicked left jab. Eli provided us with six-foot bamboo poles that we clashed and parried with, playing Robin Hood with gusto. The exercise felt cleansing and energizing.

When the class was over an hour later, I definitely needed a quick shower in the church's tiny locker room. Half of the class disappeared to the parking lot while the rest of us guzzled from water bottles as we took turns in the shower and freshened up.

"Want to grab some lunch?" I asked Denise when we were both combing our hair in front of the mirror.

"I wish I could," she said. "But my daughter's got a T-ball game. Maybe next week?"

"Great."

"You were red-hot today, Nora," she added, going out the door. "You gave Eli a workout."

I drank the rest of my water and took my bicycle over to Angelina's in search of food. The brunch crowd had thinned, and the lunch patrons hadn't arrived yet. I headed to the casual side of the restaurant with its counter service and Formica-topped tables and surveyed the damage the early birds had done to the pastry case. A sole chocolate pecan muffin stood forlornly on a plate and called my name. Feeling virtuous after my workout, I splurged on a caramel mocha latte, too. Comfort food, I told myself.

I took my snack to the next room, winding through the clutter of antiques on sale. Angelina ran a consignment shop in her casual dining room, and every horizontal surface was lined with Depression glass and enough salt shakers to outfit a chain of pancake restaurants. It was all displayed with lengths of lace and pink satin for a frilly Victorian look.

I chose a table between the parlor fireplace and the window, perfect for admiring the view of the canal. It was still too early in the year for the throngs of New Yorkers who rushed into Bucks County on Friday evenings to stay in bed-and-breakfasts and browse the many shops and artist's studios that had sprung up in New Hope and across the river in Lambertville.

I sat down to relax. But as I took a sip of my latte, I looked up at the painting on the wall above the fireplace and nearly choked. The man in the portrait glared down at me with blue-blooded disdain burning in his gaze. I dropped my coffee cup into its saucer with a clatter and a splash.

Half afraid I might be killed by a bolt of lightning, I blotted spilled coffee before cautiously raising my gaze to the handsomely framed portrait. It was the face of Colonel Fitzwilliam Blackbird, who had fought in the Revolutionary War with General Washington, purchased a mahogany armchair from Thomas Jefferson and written scathing letters to Ben Franklin on the subject of consorting with Frenchwomen. His portrait had been done by John Hadley Marsh, the acclaimed American artist.

What in the world was the portrait doing in Angelina's consignment shop?

The steely blue eyes of my ancestor reflected a distinct disappointment in the modern generation of Blackbirds. Although the portrait had hung in the center hall at Blackbird Farm for my entire childhood, I had never noticed before how the artist managed to capture the white-knuckled irritation in the Colonel's aristocratic hands. Even the foxhound — his head laid devotedly on his master's knee — managed to gaze remorsefully down at me from on high.

"Good grief," I muttered. "Emma must need cash."

I was ruminating on the demise of a venerable family when a voice startled me back to reality.

"Hello, big sister."

I almost lost my cup again as Emma dropped into the chair opposite mine. She looked stunning, damn her.

"What brings you out?" she asked. Opening her squashy leather bag, she rummaged around for a moment and came up with a battered pack of cigarettes. She ignored Angelina's NO SMOKING sign and lit up. Holly Golightly with an attitude. Her riding boots and breeches were caked with unmentionable debris, as if she'd been tossed over the head of some excitable young horse already this morning.

"What the hell," I said, "are you doing leaving this portrait in a junk shop?"

"This isn't a junk shop," she replied. "Angelina gets a lot of good trade in here." As usual, Emma dodged the point by throwing a diversion in my path.

I was not sidetracked. "You're selling a family portrait! I can't believe this."

"It's on consignment. I haven't sold it."

"Yet!"

"So?" she inquired archly. "*You* can't believe somebody else is selling stuff? Well, that's the pot calling the kettle ugly."

"This is very different, Emma. I had to pay the taxes on Blackbird Farm somehow. You don't owe a cent on your share of our dubious inheritance."

Emma flicked ashes. "My medical insurance is the pits. If you can sell the farm to the gangster, I can look for a buyer for that portrait."

Almost two years ago, Emma's husband had been killed in a car accident that also broke every bone in her left leg. The damage halted her career in Grand Prix show rings — temporarily, we hoped. I suddenly wondered if her leg was healing slowly because she couldn't afford a good doctor.

More gently, I said, "The least you could

do is take it to a reputable dealer. The portrait is worth a small fortune."

"I don't think I need a family vote to make a decision about something that's mine now. Wait," she said, feigning surprise. "Where have I heard that line before? Why, I believe it was from you, Sis. And Angelina's a friend of mine. She's keeping the portrait for a few weeks until I find an art dealer to take it. She thinks somebody will come along and think they're going to make a killing by picking it up cheap. It'll create some buzz in the art world." She pointed at my muffin with the two fingers that also held her cigarette. "Are you going to eat that behemoth?"

I sat back, unable to argue with her. If a trend had started, I had been the first of my generation to besmirch the family honor. I clenched my teeth. "Help yourself."

She stubbed out her cigarette and tore into the muffin with uncharacteristic enthusiasm.

"Where have you been riding?" I asked at last.

She shrugged. "I was over at Paddy Horgan's this morning. No big deal."

"Has he hired you back?"

"He says he doesn't have room for me, but he lets me help with exercises. I know the bastard's just watching to see if my leg's strong enough."

I felt a rush of sisterly concern and tried to think of a way I could help without pissing off my touchy little sister. "What do you know about the art world?"

"About the same you know about real estate."

"I'm serious," I said. "Do you know anything about art?"

"Just that I've got a bunch of pictures I hate looking at. Except the horse portraits. I'll keep those."

"Is Angelina your only contact?"

She ceased and desisted on the muffin and looked at me. "Why are you asking?"

"Because maybe there's a better way to sell the portrait. And I need some information on an art collection. Not ours. Rory Pendergast's."

Emma put down the muffin and confiscated my napkin to wipe her fingers. "I read the paper this morning. Were you at the party?"

I nodded. "I found him."

"You — !"

"I found his body."

I'd been pretty controlled all morning, and the exercise class had felt good. But suddenly the grief washed over me again, and I saw Rory on the carpeted floor, twisted and dead.

Emma was silent for a long time, letting me pull myself together. Eventually, she said, "I'm sorry. I know you and Libby were pretty tight with him."

Underneath her armored exterior, Emma was just as softhearted as I was. And perhaps more perceptive. Of the three widowed sisters, it was Emma who still wore her wedding ring. Libby's theory was that she wore it to keep men at a distance, but that wasn't Emma's style. I believed she wanted to keep her husband's memory alive.

She said, "Want to split a club sandwich?"

I laughed unsteadily and said yes, so she went over to the counter and placed the order. A few minutes later she returned with two glasses of iced tea.

"Tell me about it," she said.

I told her all about the party and my interview with the police. "Want to hear the strangest thing?"

"Shoot."

"I saw Rory and I saw what happened. I talked with the police for hours afterwards, and now I — Okay, I know I'm being crazy, but I want to find out who killed him."

Emma looked at me steadily.

"We knew who killed Todd," I went on.

"His drug dealer was in jail within hours after shooting him, but this — Em, I don't want to feel the way I did after Todd died. Like I couldn't do anything but bury him. With Rory, it's as if I have a second chance."

She nodded.

"And one person I know I can do something for is Peach. The police seem to be looking for ways to blame her. She was the last person to see him alive and she admits they argued."

Emma gave a snort to indicate how stupid that premise was. "What are you going to do?"

"I thought I'd find out about Rory's art collection first."

"I don't get it."

"Maybe that's why he was killed. His paintings were all over the place. A van Gogh right there in his bedroom! Maybe somebody tried to steal something and killed him in the process."

"Is that what the police think?"

"It's one possibility. And I have to start somewhere."

Emma said, "Like where else?"

"I've been thinking about Harold Tackett. Remember him? A contemporary of Rory's. He lives just up the road from here."

"Isn't he dead?"

"Not even close. He collects all kinds of things, so maybe he can help."

"You want me to drive you up to see the Tacketts? Now?"

"You have something better to do?"

"I want my half of the sandwich first."

I smiled, glad to have one sister who could understand me. She went to the counter and picked up our food.

Twenty minutes later, I heaved my bicycle into the bed of Emma's rattletrap pickup and climbed into the front seat. A heap of sweatshirts and a tangle of bridles made a mess that Emma gathered up and threw into the space behind my seat.

Emma drove very fast. Even a fatal accident hadn't changed her ways. She headed back up the Delaware, whipping past a couple of estates that had been built by signers of the Declaration of Independence. The main houses now functioned as country inns and the grounds of one served as a complex where Olympic-quality equestrian teams trained. Several more large fieldstone houses dotted the high ground that overlooked the river.

At the next curve in the road, and following my instructions, Emma pulled her truck into a shaded lane that wound upward through carefully planted woodlands towards one of the oldest houses in the valley. Maybe Rory Pendergast was a billionaire, but his neighbors were true Old Money. They had bank accounts *and* a pedigree.

As we passed a stone gatehouse built to resemble a Saxon keep, Emma said, "I haven't been up here in years."

In the driveway, I got out of the truck. "Come on. We'll go around the side."

I led the way around the garden wall and ducked under a hemlock tree that needed trimming. A white-faced gray cat slipped out from under the tree, arching his back and meowing.

I said, "Hey, Bruno."

The cat preceded us around the house to the solarium door, which faced the river. Underfoot, the flagstone walkway was crumbling, and ragged bits of wet grass peeked from between the stones. I knew the lack of upkeep wasn't for lack of cash. Something was always falling apart on such a vast property.

The peaceful beauty of the estate enveloped us.

Then a tremendous blast split the air. I yelped as the explosion echoed against the trees behind the house.

Emma dodged behind the gate to escape further gunfire.

But the cat didn't turn a hair. He sat down and placidly licked a forepaw while below us on the lawn, the diminutive figure of Eloise Tackett expertly hefted a shotgun in her small hands.

Chapter 7

"And stay out!" she shouted up at the trees. "Damn crows!"

Brilliant sunlight now dappled the long expanse of lawn that rolled away from the stone balustrade. From that hillside, our view of the river was breathtaking. Eloise didn't appear to notice. She glared into the sky at a flock of retreating crows.

"We surrender!" I called.

Eloise turned and waved. Grinning, she hiked up the lawn towards us, the double-barreled gun cradled in the crook of her arm. "Did I scare you?" she shouted, still a furlong away.

"I thought you were conducting maneuvers up here," I said. "Where's the rest of the army?"

"Asleep inside," Eloise responded cheerfully. "Come in, girls. How delightful to see you both."

Still balancing the gun, she gave me a one-armed hug and rough kiss on the cheek, then the same to Emma. Her hug was hardy, and Eloise Tackett's body looked anything but seventy-two years old. She was dressed in khaki trousers and a man's white dress shirt with the sleeves rolled back over forearms still tight from years of outdoor sports. I knew she'd been a champion skeet shooter in the fifties, but she'd never describe herself in those words. She was the most unpretentious woman I could think of. Untamed white hair that had never been touched by dyes or rinses was caught up in a pink ribbon and framed her lively face. Elflike in stature, she had a strong, athletic quickness to her gait. She sprang towards the door, treating the gun as if it were no more dangerous than an armload of spring flowers.

"Let's go through the porch," she said. "Harold will be thrilled to see you."

The original house was Georgian in design, with flourishes added by later generations. Long ago, the portico had been built, then converted into a solarium, usable year round. Eloise thrust open the door.

"Look who's here, Harold!" she shouted. "It's those nice Blackbird sisters!"

"Heh?" An elderly man struggled to sit up on the wicker fainting couch where he'd been alternately snorting and mumbling to himself beneath the pages of the *Philadelphia Inquirer.* Coming out of his postnap fog of disorientation, he fumbled with a pair of smudged eyeglasses and eventually balanced them on his narrow nose before squinting at Emma and me as we entered. "Oh," he bellowed. "It's the Blackbird widows, is it?"

"Put a cork in it, Harold."

He cackled while his much younger wife hauled him to his feet, protesting that he shouldn't make light of anyone's misfortune.

"It's okay," I soothed. "Please don't —"

"Oh, those Blackbird women," Harold shouted, waving his newspaper at us, "never had any luck with husbands, did they, Ellie? Remember their grandmama? Or was it their great grandmama? That red-haired one with the yappy dog."

"We're all red-haired, you old coot," Emma said.

"That's the way to give it to him." Eloise laughed. "Put in your hearing aids, Harold. I'm finished shooting."

He obeyed, fitting the two plastic aids into his ears. A belt tight and high on his stomach cinched Harold Tackett's trousers, and his still-thick white hair stood up as if he'd been electrocuted. Stiff from napping, he hobbled closer. "Both of you lost your husbands, right?" Harold demanded as he finished screwing the aids in place. "Some kind of drunk driving accident? And yours," he said to me, "was shot in the city, I think? Buying dope? And what about your sisters? What happened to their husbands?"

"There's just one other sister," I shouted back. "And she's remarried. Her husband's just fine, thanks. He's a banker, you know."

"Why would he want a tanker?" Harold asked Eloise.

"Banker!" Eloise yelled up at him, then shook her head. "Oh, you only hear what you want to hear, so why am I losing my vocal cords?"

"Oh, I know which one he is," Harold said. "The Civil War nut. He came up here once asking for money for some crackpot idea."

"Saving a battlefield," Eloise supplied. "A noble cause."

"He'll go bad." Harold looked delighted with his prediction. "All the Blackbird girls marry rascals."

Eloise Tackett finished tucking the shotgun into the open case balanced on a chair and turned back to us, rolling her eyes. "Don't mind this old fool, girls. Take a seat. Don't listen to a word he says. Bruno, don't — oh, just shove that cat onto the floor. Sit down, Harold!"

I said, "We passed the old gatehouse on the drive. I see you're making some repairs."

"Just patching the slate roof," Eloise replied. "With a place like this, there's always something expensive happening."

The solarium was exceedingly bright with sunlight, so it took a moment for our eyes to become accustomed to the glare. I grinned as Emma finally grasped the scene, for the entire room was cluttered with jigsaw puzzles in various stages of assembly. Card tables, breakfast trays, simple slabs of plywood — any flat surface smooth enough to accommodate a puzzle had been pressed into service by the Tacketts, who clearly spent their waking hours moving from one puzzle to another. A couple of office-style chairs on wheels made it easy for them to slide along the tile floor to the next puzzle when frustration set in.

The couple didn't seem to care about the pictures on their puzzles, for I could see Old Masters landscapes, animals, geometric designs and optical illusions. I sat on one of the chairs with wheels and found myself confronted by a picture of a sweaty basketball player going up for a shot while flashbulbs exploded in the stands.

"Wow," Emma said, still on her feet and staring down at a half-finished three-dimensional puzzle of the Eiffel Tower. "All these pieces are the same shape."

"Oh, we like a challenge," said Eloise. "It's even more challenging when Harold starts carrying pieces from one table to the next. He's a pain in the neck sometimes. Would you girls like some lemonade?"

"Get these girls some lemonade, Ellie," Harold shouted, settling onto the other office chair. "Or maybe a piece of that chocolate cream pie you've been hiding in the ice box. How about it, girls? Wouldn't you like some pie?"

"It's too early for pie, Harold! I've got him on a diet, so all he thinks about is food."

"We just had an early lunch," I said quickly. "Please don't go to any bother."

"What brings you girls up here?" Harold asked, rocking comfortably in his chair. "Selling Girl Scout cookies, are you?"

"I was hoping you could help me with some information," I said.

Emma raised her voice, "She's asking around about Rory Pendergast."

Eloise froze in the doorway on her way for lemonade and turned. Harold stopped rocking. Then Eloise said hastily, "Well, it's a shame about old Rory, but I'm sure —"

"It's not a shame," Harold interrupted. "He probably had it coming."

"Now, Harold, no good comes from speaking ill of the dead." She stepped back into the room. "What a tragedy. He was a friend of Harold's once. Well, perhaps not a friend, exactly, but —"

Harold snorted. "You won't see my name on the eulogy list, that's for sure!"

"He was a philanthropist," Eloise argued. "I respect him for that."

"He was a thief," Harold snapped. "A damn thief and a liar."

"Now, Harold —"

"You knew Mr. Pendergast well?" I asked.

Harold grinned at me from under his bushy white eyebrows. "Do I need a lawyer, young lady?"

I smiled, shaking my head. "I'm just asking around. The police detective asked me some questions I couldn't answer last night, and they've been nagging me ever since."

"Well, I've always wanted to be grilled by the police. Call it too much television!" Harold chuckled and began to rock again, looking off into the distance as if to make his recollections accurate. "We went to school together. And played a few hands of cards before I was married. We belonged to the same club in Philadelphia until I retired. How long did I have that membership, Ellie?"

"Forty-two years," Eloise supplied.

"But we didn't associate much." Harold's mouth quirked. "Always looking for a way to make a buck, that Rory. All the Pendergasts were that way."

"Well, they certainly succeeded," said Eloise.

I mused that the Tacketts hadn't done too badly themselves, both being heirs to large fortunes.

"We bought a lot of the same stuff," Harold went on. "We didn't share much of anything, I suppose, except the same taste in pictures."

"Pictures?" I asked. "You mean paintings?"

Harold laughed. "All kinds of things. And anyone will tell you we often competed against each other for items. I've taken to buying by phone now. It's a lot easier that way. You don't have to get all dressed up and go to the city. I just look at catalogs and call my agent — the young man who takes care of the details. In fact, he used to work for Pendergast."

"Do you mind telling me his name?"

"Jonathan Longnecker," Eloise said. "A scamp if there ever was one. Now he works for a museum, though."

I smiled. "He's a scamp?"

"Oh, a pleasant boy, really. Just foxy. He made it easy for Harold to buy. We hate going up to New York now," Eloise explained.

"And you bought the same kind of thing Rory did?"

"If I lost at auction," Harold said with diminishing good humor, "it was almost always Pendergast who beat me. Damned annoying."

Emma said, "What kind of art are you buying? Portraits, by any chance?"

"Oh, hell, no," said Harold, defiantly. "I suppose you'd call 'em dirty pictures."

"Erotica," Eloise corrected.

"Want to have a look?" Harold asked, sharing a grin with my sister.

Emma laughed. "Bring it on, baby!"

"Oh, Harold! You're corrupting these nice girls."

Harold looked far from abashed. "Go get that pen and ink, Ellie. I left it on my desk. The little one."

"It's not necessary," I said hastily. "Really, it's not."

Emma asked, "Rory had a collection of erotic art, too?"

"A big one," Harold replied as Eloise disappeared into the house. "I hope I'll get a crack at buying some of it now that he's dead and gone. I don't suppose those two old Pendergast biddies want to keep it. I've never known women as prudish as those two."

I remembered how Lily and Opal Pendergast seemed anxious to control access to the art collection. At the time, I assumed they were worried about someone stealing a valuable painting. But maybe they were embarrassed by the subject matter instead. I said, "I'll bet you'll stand a good chance of buying from his estate."

Harold's expression was gleefully crafty. "It'll serve him right if I get my hands on the pieces he tricked me out of."

Eloise reappeared with a framed drawing. "Oh, Harold, don't go on so. These girls will think you really hated Rory."

"So I did!"

Emma took the frame from Eloise and looked down at the ink drawing. My sister's grin was broad as she turned the frame this way and that to get a different perspective of the tangled arms, legs and other body parts depicted on the paper. "Why, you scoundrel," she said to Harold. "Can you get yourself into that position?"

"I like trying," he replied, then burst out with a roaring laugh.

"Don't show Nora," Eloise warned just as Emma started to hand the drawing to me.

"I'm sure she's too sensitive for that sort of thing."

"You're right," said Emma. "She's the dainty type."

"Harold," I said, trying hard to get back to my line of questioning, "did you discuss your collection with Rory?"

"Never. But I'd sure like a look at his stuff. Ellie, pick up that newspaper again. Who's the next of kin? Those sisters, I suppose. The old goat never married, although not from lack of ladies. Who do I have to see about getting his collection?"

Eloise rattled the newspaper as she read down through the front page obituary. "Roderick Buchanan Pendergast, publisher of the *Philadelphia Intelligencer*, let's see, la, la, la . . . attended Yale, served in the Foreign Service —"

Harold gave a barking laugh. "Drinking gin with Churchill's pals, maybe."

"Formed the Freedom City Trust in 1956 — let's see — no! Survived by his sisters Lilyanne and Opal Christine, of Philadelphia and Palm Beach."

"A Palm Beach nursing home," Harold guessed. "Those girls must be in their eighties by now."

"They won't be suspects in the murder," said Eloise.

"Oh, I don't know." Harold laughed again. "They still looked like a couple of mean old women last night. And Pendergast was so feeble, why, that cat of yours could have knocked him down."

I was startled. "You were there last night? At the party?"

"Hell, yes," said Harold. "Once upon a time I wrote a financial column for that newspaper. They invited all of us old fogies."

"I didn't see you there," I said.

"We didn't stay long," Eloise interjected. "We left before he was — well, before —"

Emma stopped admiring the drawing and said, "Nora found the body."

That information prompted an exclamation from Eloise and a request for further enlightenment from Harold. I kept it brief.

"You poor dear." Eloise's eyes filled with tears. "You must be so distressed."

"I was," I told her, feeling another wave of grief. "And I can't get it out of my head. I can't help being curious about who killed him."

"Do the police have suspects?"

"I think they're trying to narrow the field at this point."

Harold shook his head sagely. "I bet half the people at that shindig wanted to bash Pendergast's head at least once in his life."

Chapter 8

Later at the farm, Emma hoisted my bicycle out of the truck bed before she remembered why she'd come looking for me in the first place. Out of the heap of sweatshirts, she pulled a canvas bag from Libby.

"I'm supposed to give you this. Libby asked me to drop it off."

I accepted the flowered bag, one of the many we frequently exchanged as we shared books. Looking at it with mock trepidation, I asked, "Do you think it's a bomb?"

Emma shrugged. "It's not ticking. I figure it's a peace offering."

"Feels like a Sears catalog." I turned the bag over in my hands, but didn't open it. Libby and I exchanged books all the time, usually spending a few minutes to give each other a review of our latest reads. She liked weepy romances, but accepted my collection of expat American women who renovated houses in Provence or Tuscany.

"She could have brought it herself."

"I think she's snowed with last minute wedding junk."

Libby's husband Ralph was the father of the groom for the big Treese-Kintswell wedding, and although Libby wasn't a primary player in the festivities, she had some responsibilities, I was sure. Entertaining the bride's prestigious family at the rehearsal dinner was a daunting proposition. The Treese family had expensive tastes and a strict sense of social protocol.

I knew it wasn't the wedding that kept Libby away, though. Still, Emma was kind to pretend our sisterly spat was nothing out of the ordinary. I asked, "Is the wedding going to come off without a hitch?"

Emma shrugged again and climbed back into the truck. "You couldn't pay me to get involved in that ordeal. It's like they're trying to outdo the Windsors."

"Does Libby have a dress yet?"

Emma slammed the truck door and leaned out the open window. "I don't think so. That's only one cause for meltdown. She's got several."

It was Emma's way of telling me to lay off Libby. Although I couldn't risk saying so to Emma, I'd have loved going dress shopping with Libby. If our relationship had been on firmer ground these days, I could have swept her off to New York for a spree at Barney's. Retail therapy.

Emma paused before starting the truck. "You going to Rory's funeral?"

"Yes."

"Need a lift?"

I smiled. "Thanks, Em. Maybe Libby wants to go with us, too."

"I'll take care of it." She started the truck and tore off in a spray of gravel.

I went into the house and found the light on my answering machine blinking like crazy.

"Nora, this is Stan Rosenstatz," came my editor's agitated voice. "Boy, I need you to call me back ASAP. Kitty says she's too upset to go to the Pendergast funeral, and we definitely need your kind of coverage. You know, who's there and what they're wearing. Call me, okay?"

I couldn't imagine what might keep Kitty from attending the funeral of the century as far as the *Intelligencer* was concerned. My radar switched on before I dialed Rosenstatz back. He was away from his desk, so I left a voice mail saying I intended to go to the funeral anyway.

Then the lightbulb went off in my head.

"And I wonder if you could do my a favor, Stan?" I asked. "Since last night's party was sponsored by the *Intelligencer*, somebody must have the guest list. Can you get me a copy? If you could e-mail it to me, I'd appreciate it."

The second message on my answering machine was from my friend Lexie Paine in her best belting-to-the-balcony voice. "Oh, Nora, call me, call me as soon as you can, darling. You must be a wreck — a wreck! Let's go to Peace for a full day — my treat. What you need is a lime pedicure and that Lakota herbal wrap."

A day at Lexie's favorite spa always sounded delicious.

A blur of voices came next. Mostly friends and former friends — Todd's crowd — who wanted to know everything I'd seen at Rory's house and what were the police saying and did I hear that Sam Mascione was a suspect and could I stop in for cocktails tonight before going out?

No, I didn't want to stop in for cocktails. No doubt everyone thought I had an inside track for police gossip. Right now I was the ideal person to provide just enough floor show to make a party memorable.

Then Jill Mascione said, "Nora, the police were here at Main Events all day asking about every move we all made. Dad is spitting nails because they thought Sam did it until Sam admitted he was necking with Julie somewhere. That girl is married and ought to know better. You must have just missed interrupting them, lucky you. Anyway, how are you? Did that baby detective call you yet? Call me about lunch."

The next voice was that of Michael Abruzzo. He didn't identify himself, but allowed a long silence of tape to run before he spoke. The sound of his growling baritone made my insides go squiggly. For a man who was supposed to be a menace to society, he sounded surprisingly . . . sexy.

He said only, "Just calling to make sure you're okay."

And he hung up.

I looked at the answering machine and said, "You're kidding."

I played the message again. No, he wasn't kidding. One sentence fragment.

I tapped my fingers on the kitchen counter.

At last I played the final message, and Detective Bloom's voice filled my kitchen, sounding friendly and even coaxing.

"Miss Blackbird, it's Detective Ben Bloom. I'm hoping you'll call when you get this message. I have a few ideas I'd like to run past you."

With care, he gave his office number, his home phone and his cell number. I wrote down all of them and decided to dial the cell phone first.

He picked up at once. "Bloom."

"Hi," I said. "It's Nora Blackbird."

"Oh, hi," he said and cleared his throat. "Yeah, hi, how are you?"

"Good. What about you?"

"Not bad. I'm glad you called."

Over the telephone line, I could hear phones ringing and people talking. He paused, and I wondered if he was working up the courage to invite me to the malt shop.

I asked, "How's your investigation going?"

"Slow, but sure. Going through a lot of information, setting up timetables. It's a high profile case, national attention. Everybody's being careful."

I had left the house that morning without turning on the news. "National attention?"

"CNN is set up in the parking lot."

"I'm sure Rory's death is a big story. He was a world-class philanthropist."

"Yeah, we've got guys going through his financial records. He was pretty generous from what I understand. Meantime," he went on, "I'm stuck with the timetable. We're trying to place everyone in the house at the time of the murder. Almost a hundred people. I was hoping to go over a couple of things with you."

"I'm happy to help. Rory must have been

killed between the time Peach left him and when I went upstairs, right?" I tried to assume he had eliminated Peach as a suspect. "That was only a matter of ten minutes or so."

Bloom didn't agree. "Well, he was certainly killed sometime between seven-forty-seven, when two employees of the caterer spoke with him, and eight-thirty-five when you came downstairs and the paramedics were phoned. About fifty minutes."

"Can't someone pinpoint the time of death more accurately than that?" I said uneasily. "By his body temperature or something?"

"We can't be that precise."

"So you haven't ruled out Peach," I said.

"We haven't ruled out anybody. Not since we found out about the elevator. Did you see anyone use it?"

I'd completely forgotten about Rory's seldom-used elevator. It was located in another wing of the house near the billiards room, and would have allowed someone to go upstairs without being seen by party guests or catering staff.

"I hadn't remembered it. No, I wasn't near the elevator. Hardly anyone ever uses it, as far I as know."

"The housekeeper says they use it to

move furniture and cleaning equipment, so it's still functioning. Someone could have used it in the fifty-minute window."

"That someone would have to know about the elevator," I guessed. "It's located in an inconvenient place — almost hidden, actually. Rory liked the exercise of using the stairs. It had to have been a person who knew the house really well."

"Yep. Mrs. Treese said so, too."

"Are there any fingerprints in the elevator?"

"Lots. We're looking for matches now."

"And on the painting? The van Gogh?"

"One of yours. Quite a few of Pendergast's. And," he said, "Mrs. Treese."

I remembered the police taking my fingerprints the night of the murder. Funny how details had slipped away while I was so upset. They were just now resurfacing. Why would Peach kill Rory for a painting when she had full access to his house? "I'm sure Peach was in that room a lot. I'm still certain she's not your murderer. Was anything missing elsewhere in the house?"

"Nothing that was hanging on walls. Pendergast's housekeeper checked and walked us through the displayed paintings. Of course, our art guy is working on that angle."

A brilliant idea occurred to me. "Maybe somebody substituted a forgery!"

"Well . . . that's doubtful," Bloom said, as if humoring an avid television fan. "Why bother going upstairs to kill Pendergast if it's easier to steal a painting downstairs and walk off with it?"

I decided to keep my imaginative speculations under wraps in the future. But I wanted to hear more. "How exactly did Rory die?" I asked, switching gears. "Was he suffocated?"

"Like we first thought, he was overpowered and smothered with the pillow."

"Is there any DNA evidence? Something left behind by the murderer?"

Bloom didn't answer for a moment, and I heard paper rustling. Finally, he said, "What the hell, I'm breaking all the rules, but what else is new? We're checking his clothing and the pillow."

"And the Viagra?" I asked. "Was it in his bloodstream?"

Bloom hesitated again. "The label was partially torn off the bottle, so we're checking with pharmacies. Let me ask the questions, okay? We're not going to solve this case unless somebody goes out on a limb, so screw the timetable for a minute. Maybe you know who Pendergast was intimate with. We hear he'd been seeing the Treese woman for years. Were they sleeping together?"

Automatically, I said, "I haven't the faintest idea."

"Anyone else in the picture? Another lover?"

"I can't imagine there was anyone, no."

"No younger women?"

"That seems very unlikely."

"Did Pendergast go looking for partners? Come on strong with you, maybe?"

"My God, no!"

"The Viagra obviously had a purpose. We thought maybe he was seeing somebody younger and, you know, trying to keep up."

The idea seemed fantastic to me. But Bloom was certainly correct in assuming Rory hadn't acquired the Viagra for any purpose but the one for which it was intended.

"I don't know the answers to your questions. Did Rory's secretary get back in town?" I asked. "Surely he has the best grasp of Rory's private life."

"He arrives today. But he warned us that Rory kept his private business to himself. So I'm back to hoping you thought of something else. Or remembered something that's been going on in Pendergast's life lately."

"We were friends, but I was hardly his confidante," I said. "I really don't know what else I can tell you."

"Maybe you could ask around a little?" he said, sounding a little too innocent to be unscripted. "Talk to some of the people in his social circle? Find out what he'd been up to? There's some kind of code of silence among you people, and we're having a hard time making headway."

You people. Well, if gathering gossip meant Peach was in the clear, I was willing to stoop pretty low. I said, "I'm going out tonight, as a matter of fact. Rory's bound to be the primary topic of conversation."

"It'd be great if you could pick up some information for us," said Bloom. "I mean, if you happen to hear something we might find useful. Where are you headed?"

"To a couple of parties in the city."

"You going with anyone?"

I tried to decide from his tone what exactly he was asking. "No," I said. "I'm working."

"Oh." More slowly, he said, "When you went off last night with Abruzzo, I wondered, that's all."

"My driver works for him," I explained. "And he had to go home — the driver, that is, because I stayed so late. So Mr. Abruzzo relieved him. It wasn't anything more than that."

"Uh-huh," said Bloom. "You know who he is, right? I mean, maybe he's not in the family business, if you know what I mean — not that we can prove, anyway. But he sure knows where the bodies are buried."

"Really," I said, "we're barely acquainted."

"I just wondered." He didn't sound convinced. "What time did he arrive at Pendergast's last night?"

"I have no idea."

"Was it before Pendergast died?"

"He came to pick me up. That's all I know."

"Do you know if he had a relationship with Pendergast?"

A sharp pang began to twinge at my conscience. "Why don't you ask him?"

"He's on my list," Bloom said.

"Well, good," I said.

Bloom said, "I shouldn't be telling you this, but considering — well, I just think you ought to know that Pendergast's phone has Caller ID. And the last number that came in . . ."

"Yes?"

"Was Abruzzo's."

I felt my lungs empty. It was a struggle to

summon speech. "The threatening phone call."

"Bingo."

Half a minute might have ticked by. The detective let me digest the information. It stunned me.

So did the fact that Bloom was telling me what should have been classified information. I didn't peg Bloom for an incompetent cop. He'd informed me for a reason. He wanted me to see what I could learn from Michael Abruzzo.

"Well," I said, still absorbing the shock and unwilling to respond to the unspoken request, "I should be getting dressed right now."

"I'm sure you'll look great," said Bloom, almost automatically. Which sealed it for me. His whole friendly routine was just that — a routine. He said, "I'll be in touch, though, okay?"

"Anytime."

"Okay." He lingered another moment. "Uhm, thanks."

"Sure."

I hung up. He was using me, all right. I wouldn't have minded if he hadn't been so obvious. Did he think I was a dolt?

I dialed the number Eloise Tackett had given me for Jonathan Longnecker, Rory's former art agent. It was a cell phone, and the automated recording that picked up told me he was unavailable. I decided against leaving a voice mail and disconnected.

With the handset still to my ear, I considered calling Abruzzo. He had threatened Rory Pendergast perhaps within minutes of Rory's death. What was that about?

I chickened out and hung up the phone without dialing.

Promptly at five-thirty, Reed Shakespeare arrived at my door. I had dressed carefully in another one of Grandmama's couture dresses, this one lemon yellow with a wide obi-style belt in a slightly more vivid hue. It had a stand-up collar, no sleeves and a low back. Elegant, simple. Chanel. I carried a beaded bag I'd also dug out of a trunk that must have come from one of Grandmama's Caribbean tours.

Reed took one look at the ensemble and blanched.

"You don't like it?" I asked, turning so he could get the complete view.

He shrugged and opened the rear door of the town car, looking off into the distance. "Not for me to say."

The hell with him. Maybe I was a fashion throwback to Jackie Kennedy, but I wasn't comfortable in the belly button flash of teenybopper fashion or the hard-edged sex of the stiletto feminists. I felt pretty and that's what counted when going off to a party.

I got into the car. While he drove into the city, I started writing the pieces I needed to turn in at the newspaper that evening. Stan and Kitty would review my work in the wee hours of Sunday morning and choose what would be published on *The Back Page*. Kitty's pieces would be our lead stories, of course. She attended the A-list events. My pieces would fill in here and there, since I covered the less exciting side of the social scene. Photographs of beautiful people attending important parties usually balanced out the space.

Tonight, I knew, Kitty was scheduled to attend an event at the Ritz-Carlton. Hundreds of the city's most moneyed and influential people were paying a thousand dollars a ticket to enjoy cocktails, dinner and entertainment while rubbing elbows with an aged movie star who would make an after-dinner speech about his long movie career. His speech would be full of anecdotes about other actors, directors and celebrities, giving the appreciative dinner crowd an impression they were tight with half of Hollywood. Afterwards there would be dancing and opportunities for the locals to have their picture taken with the movie star. After paying the actor and the hotel, the sponsoring organization donated the rest of the ticket money to a local school for the arts. A good cause and fun for many people, but it would have been Dullsville for me. I knew Kitty would lap it up, though, and her column would include an interview with the movie star.

I didn't mind being sent across town to a warehouse where a Philadelphia law firm was throwing a party to kick off a weekend of wheelchair racing. They'd taken up the cause after one of their partners had been injured in a car accident and ended up a paraplegic.

"I don't do wheelchairs," Kitty had told me.

Fine. I did.

The party was a humdinger, and I knew it as soon as I got out of the car. New Orleans zydeco blasted me, and I decided no music was more danceable than zydeco. Reed held the car door open, but goggled at five extremely beautiful girls in hot dresses dancing in front of the warehouse doorway. One girl in cornrows spun a wheelie that flipped her skirt up over a lovely pair of knees. She caught Reed's eye with an enticing laugh.

"Better give me an hour," I told Reed. "Want me to get your hand stamped so you can hang around?"

"No," he said, although he shot a longing glance at the dancers. "I've got studying to do."

"Okay, but the good times are gonna roll without you, Reed."

I slithered my way through the mob, unconsciously bobbing to the music and happily wishing Kitty a good time with the senior citizen movie star. This party was definitely more my style. A local microbrewery had partnered with the law firm, and free beer flowed from kegs set up strategically around the warehouse. I could smell spicy food in the air and saw guests eating red beans and rice from paper plates. The crowd was mostly young and definitely stunning — all dressed with sass and panache appropriate for a hot good time. At least one of the Philadelphia 76ers stood head and shoulders above the other guests, graciously signing autographs.

I found my contact, the law firm's PR director, who gave me a kiss on the cheek and asked me to dance. As we two-stepped, he filled me in on the particulars.

"We invited two hundred guests, plus the race entrants and their families," he shouted over the music. "Carmella's did the food, and you can talk to Jerry about the beer. Want to meet some of the racers?"

"Of course! And Tom Nelson, too."

Tom had been an acquaintance of mine from a preteen ballroom dance class, and although he was confined to a wheelchair after his accident, he could still dance, I was delighted to see. He spun me around for a few turns, while I clumsily tried to get the hang of dancing with a seated partner. He didn't seem to mind my stumbling, but we soon quit and I interviewed him in a relatively quiet corner.

His accident and resulting physical changes had done wonders for Tom Nelson, I decided after we'd talked for a few minutes. In the past, he'd basically been a jerk with no time for anybody but his drinking buddies. Now he seemed more relaxed, more witty, more focused on other people. I was glad to meet his new wife, too, a charming young woman with a glint of pride in her eyes when her husband talked about the upcoming races and the competition the firm had started for teens.

"Racing has been fabulous for Tom," she said when I asked her for a quote. "It's given him back his edge — not just his edge for work, but for his whole life."

It was a terrific quote and I could have left the party then with sufficient information for a great story, but I needed to wait around for the photographer who'd been assigned to the event. When Jason arrived, I asked him to take pictures of the Nelsons and some of the racers, who cheerfully posed with the brewmaster and the pretty girl in the wheelchair. Jason wrote down names and left for his next assignment, but I wanted to enjoy the evening a little, so I had some fiery jambalaya and a Dixie longneck with a trio of racers and chatted with a few friends who'd come out for an evening of fun.

Then Tom came over to talk again.

"How are your parents?" he asked.

"I haven't heard from them in weeks," I reported. "But I assume they're alive and well."

He grinned up at me. "I'm not trying to track them down, honest. I was just asking. I heard you were at the Pendergast party last night."

I nodded. "It was awful. We're all going to miss him."

"Not everyone," he replied wryly. "First thing this morning I got a preemptive phone call from one of his sisters. What do you know about them?"

"I only met them last night, actually. They were upset, of course."

I could say no more without gossiping, and he couldn't say anything else without violating attorney-client privilege, so that was the end of it. He changed the subject and left me wondering why the Pendergast sisters were contacting lawyers. Had they started to divide up the estate already?

The party was still going strong when I left. I congratulated everyone on the success of the bash and wished several racers good luck. Then I went out to find Reed and the car.

Half an hour later I walked into my second event of the evening, another of Kitty's rejects. Usually Kitty grabbed the chance to attend parties on Society Hill, but Hollywood's call was stronger than politics.

Society Hill was one of the city's poshest addresses, with leafy streets, beautifully preserved architecture and millionaire neighbors. The townhouses were packed snugly together, and the families were equally tight. It was said that any couple who dated from outside a two-block area were contemplating a mixed marriage.

Political fundraisers weren't my cup of tea

either, but I knew many of the guests who milled outside the townhouse of Molly Irwin and Jack Hardy. Molly wrote a liberal-minded column for the rival newspaper in the city, and her lawyer husband, Jack, often helped local Democrats load up their war chests. Their house sported a large American flag that waved from a second-floor window.

Upstairs in the beautifully decorated second-floor living room, the party hummed with excitement. I had arrived just moments after the mayor, I realized, and he was holding court in front of Molly's Waterford and Wedgwood-laden breakfront.

The mayor hadn't been out in public for weeks. The whole city had speculated he'd been contemplating a big career change as a result of an unusual political blunder — a flat denial of bribery in his office just days before subpoenas were delivered. He was a flamboyant man, given to drinking a little more than he should and making statements in public that were better off left to his prudent PR staff. I had overheard reporters in the *Intelligencer* coffee room wondering if his fondness for alcohol had begun affecting his previously uncanny political instincts.

I met Molly's gaze across the room. Her

brows shot up; then she immediately frowned. She murmured an apology to the mayor, who kept on talking to the other guests as she slipped away from the group.

"Hi," I said as she shook my hand. "I'm Nora Blackbird."

"I know. Molly Irwin. We met at the library benefit at Easter."

"That's right. Listen, I'm here for the *Intelligencer*. Since you work for the other paper, I thought you —"

"Yes, it's nice of you to come." She wasn't delighted to find her paper's lowbrow competitor standing in the middle of her party at exactly the wrong moment, but she had the good manners to fake a welcome. "You have a photographer with you?"

"She'll be here in ten minutes."

"The mayor may be gone by then." She looked relieved at the prospect. "How about pictures of Jack and some of the big donors instead?"

"Sure. And you?" I asked with a smile. "Care to have your picture in the *Intelligencer*?"

She laughed. "My boss wouldn't be too happy."

"Is he here? Maybe he'd like a photo with us, too."

With a forced smile, she guided me towards some other guests, pointedly avoiding a meeting between the mayor and me. "Why don't I introduce you around?"

I knew most of them anyway, but Molly did the honors, and someone brought me a glass of wine. Molly was soon called away and within a few minutes, despite our hostess's best effort, I found myself chatting with the mayor himself.

In his rumpled seersucker suit and clutching a gin and tonic in one hefty fist, he was the picture of an Old School pol. His ruddy face was already flushed with bonhomie . . . and gin.

"Oh," said the mayor, recognizing my name when I introduced myself. "Isn't your family friends with Roderick Pendergast? Damn shame about what happened."

"Will you be attending the funeral?" I asked.

"Of course, wouldn't miss it," he said. "Pendergast gave a lot to the city of Philadelphia. I only wish there was something we could give back."

He launched into a politician's nonsense that immediately made his entourage tune out. They must have figured they had a minute of off-duty time and simultaneously edged for the bar, leaving the mayor safe in the hands of a citizen who presumably wanted to talk about Rory Pendergast, nothing important.

I only had a minute, I knew, so I cut across his speech and asked, "How's the investigation into his murder going?"

"Very well." The mayor looked down at me with some surprise at my interruption. "I get updates every hour direct from the chief of police. I'm told they have some very promising leads."

"Any truth to the rumor that his sisters might sell the newspaper?"

The mayor gathered his brows in an expression that had served him well in front of the evening news cameras while he gathered his political wits. "I can't comment on that except to say the city is making every effort to keep the *Intelligencer* locally owned and operated. We must take the long view. A world-class city needs two vital newspapers to keep the lifeblood pumping. We hope we can convince Pendergast's family."

Which told me that indeed the Pendergast sisters were already looking for a buyer. With an encouraging smile, I asked, "Do you plan to be around long enough to help do the convincing?"

He laughed. "What's a pretty girl like you asking that for?"

"I'm from the *Intelligencer*," I began, wanting to be sure he knew he was talking to a reporter. "And I —"

But the mayor leaned close enough that I could smell the Beefeater on his breath. "Sweetheart," he said, "if it ain't me, it'll be my own son. Don't you think he'd make a fine mayor?"

"Well —"

"And maybe I'll run for governor if they don't hustle me off to dry out first."

If he'd planted a big wet kiss on my cheek I couldn't have been more surprised that he'd chosen me, of all people, to slip that information to.

"Can I quote you?" I asked, returning his smile.

"Sweetheart, a girl as easy on the eyes as you can do anything she likes," he said loudly. "How about a drink?"

His entourage came scrambling back, but the deed was done.

Sara Jane, the photographer, showed up just then, and while Molly was still distracted, I asked for a few quick pictures of the mayor as he spoke with one of the evening's big donors. Sara Jane sensed that I had a big scoop and quickly snapped the photos. Then we hit the street. I snatched my notebook from my handbag and hastily wrote down what the mayor had said to me, making sure I got every word right.

"This is my last stop tonight," Sara Jane told me when I finished writing. "I'll drop off the film right now."

"Great. Can I borrow your cell phone?"

She lent it to me, and I vowed to acquire one as soon as I could manage the financial commitment. I dialed Stan Rosenstatz's desk at the *Intelligencer*.

Bless his heart, he answered. I quickly told him what I'd learned from the mayor.

"You sure about that?" Rosenstatz barked. "He said his son is considering a run?"

"I have it in my notes."

"And he might run for governor himself?"

"If he doesn't go to rehab first."

"What a break," Stan crowed. I had never heard him so excited. "I bet his staff is spitting nails! I'll tell the news desk right away. They'll want to use your information for the morning edition."

"This feels funny to me," I said before he could hang up. "I'm not a trained journalist, Stan."

"What are you talking about? Did he know you were a reporter?"

"Yes, but —"

"Did he tell you it was off the record?"

"No —"

"Honey, it's the deal with the devil. Politicians use the press for their own reasons. But they can't choose when they *don't* get coverage. For guys like the mayor, this is their business. He's looking for PR!"

"But —"

"There's no Pulitzer for party reporting, honey. This is your big chance for fame and glory."

"I'm just not sure he knew what he was saying."

"Nora," said Rosenstatz firmly. "We're the eyes and ears of the city. What the mayor said to you, he said to everybody. Breathe easy, kid. You did the right thing. Besides, we've been printing nothing but the Pendergast murder, and this will be a welcome change. Now give it to me again."

I dictated what the mayor had said to me, and Rosenstatz wrote down every word, then repeated it back to me for accuracy.

"Great," he said. "Thanks, kiddo. You don't know how big this is, but believe me, it's gonna do us both some good. Too bad the old man isn't around to give us our promotions."

"I'm glad you're pleased." While I still had him on the line, I rushed on, "Stan, did you get my e-mail? About the guest list for the Pendergast party?"

"Yeah," he said, distracted by the story. "Check your e-mail."

"Thanks."

"You're gonna be a star, kiddo!"

Chapter 9

After midnight, I plugged my laptop computer into the phone jack in the kitchen and chewed a Tums while I typed up my notes and sent the party stories by modem. After the pieces were filed, I checked my e-mail and received a message from Rosenstatz with the Pendergast party guest list as an attachment.

I opened a Diet Coke and read through the list. It was a very highbrow crowd, I noted. The city's most prominent citizens hardly ever gathered in one place for an occasion, but they had definitely been invited to fete Rory. Since the *Intelligencer* had thrown the party, lots of the names on the list were employees, board members, top advertisers and business connections. I recognized many names, of course, and noted how many I had not actually seen. Of course, I'd arrived late, and the party had begun to wind down as guests went off to dinner engagements in the city.

The Tacketts were on the list. So were many of my old friends and new colleagues from the newspaper.

Halfway down the list were the names Ralph and Elizabeth Kintswell. I remembered seeing Ralph's car parked in front of Rory's house, but I hadn't seen them later, when the police were taking names. They must have left with the other early birds. I felt a pang of longing for the opportunity to hash over the murder with my sister.

I paused, puzzled. Why had Libby and her husband been invited? Oh, yes, Ralph served on one of the newspaper's advisory boards. They must have driven directly from Mick's Muscle Cars to the party. Ralph had been dressed in his uniform as if prepared to attend a big event, and Libby must have exchanged her bandanna for jewelry.

Until that moment, I'd forgotten about the bag from Libby. With the laptop screen still shining at me, I kicked off my shoes and pulled the canvas bag towards me across the kitchen table. Usually I looked forward to Libby's offerings. She made a production out of selling each book with gushing reviews. Opening the bag without her there to tell me what she'd brought made me feel oddly frustrated.

Inside was not a book.

I unwrapped the pillowcase that enfolded the object. Then I sat staring at it.

It was an ancient leather folio with heavy metal hinges and a decorated clasp. It weighed as much as a five-pound bag of sugar and the leather was crumbling.

A folded note fluttered out and fell to the floor. I put down the folio and picked up the note. Unfolding it, I saw my sister Libby's handwriting.

"This came from Rory," she had written. "Can you return it without letting anyone know? It's important, please. Libby."

What the hell? I stared at the note. That's all she had to say to me?

I opened the folio and stared at the work of art painted on the first page of thick, dry paper. It was Asian, no doubt, with human figures contorted in a sexual act. The eroticism hit me in the stomach.

Erotic art. Part of Rory's collection.

What was Libby doing with it?

Hands suddenly unsteady, I put the first page on the kitchen table and began to look through the other drawings. The pictures were luminous, expertly drawn and lovingly enhanced with the lightest touches of paint. They were profoundly beautiful. Naughty, yes, but so exquisitely rendered that I knew I was looking at the work of a gifted artist. Candlelight glowed on the upturned buttocks of a laughing young girl. Her pigtailed companion glistened with the perspiration and exhilaration of a heightened sexual moment. The threesome in the next drawing seemed to shout with breathless abandon. Yet there was wit, too, in details like the little pug-faced dog that peeped laughingly from behind a curtain at a pair who coupled like animals on a silk cushion. Their skin gleamed with the sheen of pearls and their expressions were voracious, but the dog wore the most lascivious of grins.

"My goodness," I said, transfixed.

I was struck by the blending of eroticism — both playful and dark — and the artist's amazing command of technique in depicting the details of each encounter. As I lifted one page after another, I counted dozens of drawings, yet each picture seemed to discover some small nuance not manifested in the ones that came before. The artist conveyed an unashamed fascination with all things sexual, a sense of adventure and sport. Of fun. It was impossible to look at them without smiling.

Each of the drawings was accompanied by a paragraph of faded, feathered script in traditional Chinese characters. I bent closer to read them. I had suffered through a long and difficult year of modern Chinese in college in which we'd skimmed over the basics of the ancient version of the language. I recognized some of the old radicals. I would need some review and further study before I could accurately decipher the text. I knew the folio was centuries old.

It was a masterpiece.

My hands shook harder then ever.

I couldn't imagine why in the world Libby would send such a thing around New Hope in Emma's truck, wrapped in a canvas bag. What was she thinking? And why did she want me to return it?

I checked my watch. It was after midnight — too late to phone Libby's house.

How in the world did Libby imagine I was going to return something to Rory's house, which was now completely sealed off as a crime scene? And why the big secret?

I looked at the pictures again. I could understand why Rory enjoyed the blend of delicate beauty and witty sexuality. He'd led a secret life. Viagra and now this.

I smiled. Then started to laugh.

I found myself carrying the folio to bed with me. Maybe there were parts of my life I wanted to keep to myself, too. But just because other people didn't see them didn't mean they didn't exist. In bed, I spent another hour looking at the drawings on those enticing pages.

I didn't often miss my husband anymore. Nearly two years had passed since I'd become a widow. Kind friends, including Rory, had pulled me out of the long slough of depression that followed Todd's death. But looking at those pictures in my bed that night, I felt more alone than I had in a long time.

Maybe Todd hadn't been much of a husband, and maybe his murder at the hands of his cocaine dealer was his just desserts according to certain moralists. But I had loved him despite his weaknesses. For better or for worse, we'd said. I'd meant it.

He would have gotten a kick out of those pictures.

I closed the folio and lay back in bed. I didn't cry, though plenty of tears had flowed over the last couple of years. I had counted on Todd for lots of things. Okay, so maybe he'd been a terrible narcissist and his moral compass had pointed mostly at his own nose, but he'd been spontaneous and clever and loved Venice and sushi and Lalique glassware as much as I did. I thought we'd be borrowing his cousin's boat to sail on the Chesapeake until we were too old to manage the lines. I thought we'd have children. Lively kids with many interests and lots of laughter.

The Pendergast folio with its pictures of

lusty young lovers made me think of my youth — what was left of it — and my chances for a family of my own going to waste because Todd couldn't keep up the payments on his drug habit. I had survived a time of being furious with him, but not anymore. The folio portrayed sex as a primal urge, a joyous life force I'd shared with my husband — who hadn't held up his end of the bargain.

Chilled, I put the folio aside and pulled the coverlet up to my chin. Then I realized I wasn't cold, but trembling.

Okay, sometimes I was scared. No husband. No children. No parents. One sister was a nutcase and the other was my polar opposite. And I was so far in debt that I couldn't even joke about it. I was thirty-one and still hadn't found a life for myself.

Aloud, I said, "Good God, is it time to join the DAR?"

In the morning I decided to bike over to Libby's house to talk face-to-face. I needed to know exactly what was going on. I put the Pendergast folio back into Libby's book bag and stashed it in the basket of my bicycle. It fit neatly into the space. As long as it had survived in Emma's truck, it would last a few miles in my bike basket.

I pedaled easily along the river for several miles, took a turn west and spun smoothly along a stretch of two-lane road densely lined with pines on either side until I reached Libby's barn-shaped mailbox.

I noticed the box was stuffed with mail, the door even ajar because the protruding envelopes were too much. Libby must have forgotten to pick up her Saturday mail. I'd do her a favor and carry it up to the house.

In handfuls, I pulled out envelopes, advertising flyers and catalogs. The pile of mail grew on top of the canvas bag and eventually spilled to the gravel driveway. I reached down to retrieve the fallen envelopes and saw return addresses for some of the causes Libby and Ralph supported — everything from Meals on Wheels to a couple of animal rights groups. A Save the Battlefields newsletter landed on top of the heap.

Libby gave money to every cause on the planet. It was a good thing Ralph had similar altruistic interests.

My sister had begun looking for a new husband weeks after Bob died. She attended a bookstore signing by an author of Civil War books. Libby had never indicated any interest in the Civil War before, but she must have known what kind of customer hung out at those events. Sure enough, she'd met Ralph at the bookstore and started dating him only a few weeks later.

Ralph Kintswell was an easygoing older man with grown children who liked Libby's kids and the idea of raising a second family. Although he never said so, I suspect the real reason Ralph married Libby was the cachet of our family history. In addition to our revolutionary relatives, a Blackbird had accompanied General Grant to Vicksburg, information that sent Ralph diving enthusiastically into family journals and letters. Our Civil War connection sealed the marriage.

The farmhouse sat on a high meadow with a distant view of the Delaware and an old sheep pasture out front. On three sides, however, modern housing developments had sprung up like mold on an old cantaloupe. Hundreds of huge tract houses dwarfed the small lots landscaped with too-small bushes and no trees. As I walked my bicycle up the steep drive, I could see a boomer neighbor's swimming pool.

The gravel driveway looped around the farmhouse, and I went around to the back door rather than the front entrance with its fanlight doorway and quaintly painted porch. Several hundred yards behind the house stood the barn. Ralph's silver sports car was parked inside, visible through the open barn door. There was no sign of Libby's distinctive minivan.

Libby's Labrador, Arlo, came out from under a shady tree, his tail wagging gently. I patted him, but when I didn't produce any treats, he ambled back to his napping spot and flopped down again.

I put the straps of the canvas bag over my forearm and carried the bundle of mail over to the back door of the house. It hung open on its hinges, as if somebody had just breezed inside and forgotten to close it. Life with kids.

Today they were surprisingly quiet.

I entered the house. "Hello?"

No answer. I shouted, "Hello!"

Libby was not a fussy housekeeper, but I was surprised by the mess around me in the entry hall. A pile of boots, shoes and clothing had been abandoned on the floor at my feet. Several days' worth of newspapers lay in a heap by the back staircase along with a clarinet case and a baseball glove. Ralph's Civil War uniform hung on a hanger from the doorjamb as if waiting to go to the dry cleaner.

I hugged the mail to my chest and looked around in surprise. "Wow."

I headed for the living room where Libby worked on her various artistic projects. "Lib? Are you home?"

Inside the doorway stood her work table where she sometimes drew or painted in the patch of sunlight that streamed through the nearby uncurtained window. Her brushes stood, bristles upright, in a glass frog used for flower arranging. Various tin pots and palettes lay overturned as if to dry. Small jars of premixed paint stood in lines like little soldiers ready for duty. Although her house was a mess, her work space was scrupulously neat.

Libby also dabbled in other art forms, primarily to encourage her four children to be artistic. Pencils, sketch pads and jars of beads were lined up along the bookshelves. A tub of modeling clay sat under the table.

With some relief, I noticed that the Blackbird family furniture had not been hauled directly to Libby's house and left in her less than scrupulous care. Maybe her husband had prevailed and stored the exquisite desks, tables and upholstered pieces in a safe location.

The silence of the house was almost creepy. Usually kids were everywhere, playing their music, bouncing their basketballs, and shouting for their mother to come check their homework or find a sock. The quiet was unnatural.

I went back down the hallway to the kitchen. In the doorway, I stopped dead.

The dishwasher door hung open, and the machine was stacked full of dirty plates. The countertops were cluttered with more dishes, crusty pots, greasy utensils and a couple of used Jiffy Pop pans. Filthy water filled the kitchen sink.

A large tiger-striped cat sat on the counter, ignoring me and sniffing at two lone Cheerios drying in a bowl. Someone had spilled a sack of cat food, and the contents were scattered across the already well-tracked floor. Bits of squishy kibble had already attached themselves to the bottoms of my sneakers.

"Nora?"

The raspy voice behind me sounded like Hannibal Lecter on a killing spree. I gasped and spun around. The mail went flying.

It was Ralph. He was dressed in sweatpants, scuffed slippers and a T-shirt emblazoned with the logo of a children's softball league and the word COACH stamped on the chest. His hair stuck out in tufts.

"Oh, Ralph," I said on a nervous laugh. "You scared me! I'm sorry. I must have awakened you."

"S'okay," he said with a sleepy smile, running one hand through his mussed hair.

"I'm so sorry. Really." I bent down to gather up the mail. "I didn't realize — I — well, is Libby around?"

"Libby? No, she isn't here." Ralph made an effort to wake up. He helped me gather up the envelopes and put them on the counter.

I handed him the last of the mail, and he noted the battlefield newsletter. I thought he blanched before tucking it under the rest of the heap and ambling towards the radio on the kitchen windowsill. He snapped it on. Classical music instantly filled the air, very loud. Over it, he said, "I think she's — Oh, she's probably taking the kids to Sunday school."

"Oh." Of course. I should have thought of that.

"Coffee?"

While he opened the cupboard, I shifted the canvas bag from one arm to the other. I debated whether or not I should ask Ralph about the folio.

Ralph rummaged in the cupboard and came out with a can of coffee. "Sorry about the mess," he said over the music. "We've been so busy with the wedding arrangements, plus Harcourt's got a cold. Nobody's had time to clean up."

The mess didn't seem to faze easygoing Ralph. I wondered if Libby had become equally accustomed to the war zone created by her family. I asked, "How are the wedding plans going?"

Ralph managed a rueful smile as he disassembled the coffeemaker. "Sometimes I think the invasion of Normandy must have been easier to organize." He headed for the sink to rinse out the glass pot. "When Libby and I got married, we went to the magistrate, and it was over in ten minutes. Even my first wedding wasn't anything like this is going to be."

"I'm sure it will be beautiful." I leaned against the counter, careful to keep my hand off the sticky mess of spilled liquid that had dried there. I raised my voice over the radio noise. "The Treese family loves a good wedding."

Ralph sighed. "Yeah, well, they can afford it. I'm taking out a loan just to pay for the rehearsal party."

I knew then that I'd awakened Ralph from a very deep sleep indeed. It was unlike him to complain about money matters.

"How's Lincoln handling it?" I asked, half tempted to go turn down the blare of music. "Is he ready to kidnap his bride and elope?"

Ralph began measuring coffee with a

spoon and dumping it into the coffeemaker. "I've told him he can have cash and a ladder, but he says he's going through with the wedding."

I thought Ralph sounded genuinely unhappy. "A lot of people will be disappointed if he doesn't. I think half the city is invited. It's going to be the wedding of the year."

"Yeah, thanks to Kitty Keough's coverage."

I didn't want to talk about Kitty. Casually, I said, "I noticed your name on the guest list for the Pendergast party Friday night."

Ralph filled the glass pot with water from the tap. "Yeah, we went. After Libby got finished with her protest thing at the used car lot, we drove over to the party. I'm sorry about that, Nora. Even the kids were embarrassed about the signs and everything."

"It's okay. I know how Libby can get. I didn't see you at the party."

"I'm glad we left before the excitement started. I hear people were kept awfully late while the police talked to everyone. But we wanted to get home to Harcourt."

"So you weren't at the party when Rory was killed."

Ralph slid the glass pot into the coffeemaker and flipped a switch. "No, thank heavens. Libby would have been a wreck."

"Did you see anyone else leaving when you did?"

"Why do you ask?"

I smiled ruefully. "I guess I'm trying to figure out who killed Rory."

He smiled, too. "Oh, yeah? Any luck?"

"Not yet. Can you remember anyone outside the house when you left?"

Ralph began to go through a cupboard like a bear foraging for honey. "Sure, lots of people. The party had started to fade, so people with dinner plans were taking off. What a terrible tragedy. Rory was a wonderful man. Are you really playing detective?"

"Not really. I just wish I could do something. For Rory, you see."

Ralph came over and put a brotherly arm across my shoulders. "You're a nice person, Nora. But I'm sure the police will take care of this in no time."

"I hope so." I almost gave Ralph a quick hug. Although Ralph and I rarely exchanged more than pleasantries, his kind words touched me. But I slid out from under his arm, telling myself I wasn't ready to be demonstrative with any man. "Will you tell Libby I came by? And ask her to call me when she returns?"

"You don't want some breakfast?" he asked.

I suppressed a shudder at the thought of eating anything out of that kitchen, but said a polite no-thanks and good-bye over a blast of Vivaldi.

Chapter 10

I should have left the canvas bag and the folio with Ralph, but I absentmindedly carried them back out to my bicycle, deciding to take them home rather than go back into the messy house.

Back at Blackbird Farm, I hid the folio in my underwear drawer.

Libby, damn her, did not call me.

I knew my sister could be stubborn, so on Monday I phoned her first thing. No answer. Kids were in school already, and Ralph at work. I hung up in frustration. Where was she? Sitting there at home and knowing it was me calling and choosing not to answer? I bit back a shriek of sisterly frustration.

I phoned Stan Rosenstatz next and thanked him for adding my byline to the story about the mayor considering a run for the governorship. The story had run first in the Sunday edition of the *Intelligencer*, not in our competitor's paper.

"You deserve the credit," Rosenstatz told me. "The guys on the city desk want to buy you a beer. I think you should hold out for a case of champagne."

"Tell them I'll take the beer," I said with a smile.

"The competition is playing catch-up in today's issue. Have you seen it?"

"Not yet."

"They had to scramble on Sunday, but they got the mayor to admit he's studying campaign strategies for himself and his son. But we broke the story first, thanks to you."

"I'm not used to this," I admitted. "I feel sneaky. I hope I didn't ruin his political career."

Stan laughed. "Somebody once said the only two things that can ruin a politician's career are a dead girl in his bed or a live boy. He'll survive this and probably flourish, so don't worry."

I hesitated, then took the plunge. "How did Kitty take it?"

Rosenstatz sighed, and his enthusiasm died. "Just be glad you weren't in the office yesterday."

"I see."

"And don't be surprised if she shows up at the funeral. She won't be able to resist going now that there's a real competition between you."

"But there isn't."

"Kiddo," said Rosenstatz, "you bet there is."

I spent the rest of the day sorting through the dozens of invitations the newspaper received for social events. Arranging my calendar had become a job requiring constant vigilance and delicate negotiations. I returned phone calls to hosts and hostesses, sending regrets to some and a promise to bring my notepad to others.

Periodically, I dialed Libby but did not reach her.

I spent the following morning searching through my closet for something appropriate to wear to Rory Pendergast's funeral. I ended up with a charcoal sheath dress under an old black Calvin Klein jacket.

Emma phoned early and arrived in my kitchen at the appointed hour.

She wore a sedate gray wool jacket over a pair of black leather pants that managed to look both sexy and suitable for a funeral. I suspected she wasn't wearing a bra under the jacket. I decided she looked like a dominatrix dressed for church.

"Have you reached Libby?" I asked, offering her a Diet Coke.

"Nope, sorry." She grabbed the can and drank directly from it.

"When was the last time you actually talked to her?"

"When she gave me the book bag on Saturday morning."

I frowned. "I haven't been able to reach her."

"Maybe she's planning another protest." Emma didn't seem very concerned. She put down the soda can and jiggled her keys. "Shouldn't we be going?"

"Did you know what was in the bag Libby sent to me?"

"No. Did you lose it?"

"Of course not. I just — I'm wondering what she's up to, that's all. She asked me to put something back in the Pendergast house, and I don't know what to do."

"Ask her."

"I would," I replied tartly, "except I can't reach her."

"Well, she'll probably be at the funeral. And we're going to miss the kickoff if we don't haul some ass, Sis."

I followed Emma outside and got into her pickup truck. We headed down the gravel drive at high speed.

"Nice byline in the paper," she said as we hit the road. "I didn't realize you were moving up in the world so fast."

"I'm not," I told her. "I was in the right place at the right time."

"Well, that can't be bad for your career, can it?"

"I doubt the mayor will ever speak to me again."

"No loss," said Emma. "He pinched my butt once."

Like any self-respecting local girl, Emma took a circuitous route of back roads over the countryside and ended up at the mouth of the expressway just before it funneled into Philadelphia. Once on the four lane, she drove very fast, dodging around lumbering trucks with the agility of a gazelle in a herd of wildebeests. One tractor-trailer dared pull in front of her, and she blew her horn hard and long until he pulled back into his own lane. As we whizzed past the cab, my little sister flipped him off. We arrived at the cathedral in plenty of time.

Emma left the car in a parking garage a couple of blocks away, and we rode a slow elevator to the street. We walked up past the Four Seasons to the church. A light rain began to fall, so we hustled.

The cathedral was one of Philadelphia's most stunning landmarks, and I suspected that Rory Pendergast might have financed some part of its restoration. He had been able to afford being generous with all races and creeds. One stained glass window depicted a voluptuous Eve before the fall, and I smiled, wondering if Rory had paid for that particular window.

The steps of the building were crowded with an odd mix of photographers and priests, who parted like the sea when a town car pulled up to the curb and disgorged the monsignor with his entourage. The photographers jostled as if he were Tom Cruise.

We went into the cathedral and found ourselves in a knot of people who had not yet made their way past the temporary metal detectors and into the nave. Most of them seemed to be a security team — men and women with earpieces and cold stares.

"Yo," Emma muttered, taking off her sunglasses and nodding toward a sallow-faced man in a very expensive suit. "The senator."

"Talking to the mayor," I murmured. The mayor happened to look over the senator's shoulder and spotted me in the crowd. He quickly averted his head.

Emma looked bemused. "Looks like you don't have to worry about getting pinched."

We edged around the politicians and their flocks of assistants. I looked for Libby, but she was nowhere to be seen. I saw the

Weymount family — all world-famous artists who painted at their old Pennsylvania family estate called Trundle.

Emma saw the Weymounts, too, and whispered to me, "I remember a rumor that Pendergast was their patron. Must be true if they're here today."

Since the Weymounts were all known for their penchant for female nudes, I understood Pendergast's interest in their work. "I went to school with Audrey."

I suddenly thought that Audrey might be able to help me understand if Rory's art collection might have anything to do with his murder. I took Emma by the arm and pulled her with me. "Come on."

The Weymount family wore grief well. They had practiced for years, starting when Jack Weymount ran off with a male lover, with whom he flung himself off a bridge in California. Forever the grieving daughter, Audrey looked like one of those rail-thin and huge-eyed urchins that used to be painted on greeting cards. Her brother, Connor, came off like Heathcliff, exquisite and handsome in a huge black coat and with a stormy expression on his brow. Their mother, Yedita, endeavored to be mistaken for a Jewish Yoko Ono — short-cropped hair, big glasses, grim expression. She was obviously dying for a cigarette. The tension showed in her tight mouth, rigid shoulders and the way she toyed with a silver cigarette case.

Emma once said, "I bet Jack jumped off that bridge so he wouldn't have to come home and face Yedita."

I gave Audrey a kiss on her pale cheek. I'd gone to Miss Porter's with her, and she hadn't altered since then. She was still petite and very shy.

"How nice to see you, Nora," Audrey whispered. "I'm sorry it's under these circumstances. How dreadful about Rory, don't you think?"

"Just dreadful," I agreed.

I had stayed with Audrey a few times at Trundle and would always appreciate the glimpse she gave me into the work of an artist. I'd gone through a period of wanting to be a painter like my sister Libby, but even Audrey hadn't been able to overcome my lack of talent.

Audrey was considered the lowest rung on the Weymount family ladder of success, however. And the family worked at keeping her there. She clung to my hand as I turned to her mother.

"Hello, Yedita." Then to Audrey's brother, "Hi, Connor. Have you met my sister Emma?"

Emma and Connor locked glowering stares, and I realized they knew each other well indeed.

Yedita always did the talking for the family, and she didn't fail us.

"I'm desolate," she said, waving the cigarette case. "I can't believe he's gone. Such a dear friend. What will we do without him? Are you coming to our exhibit at the Center City gallery, Nora? Rory underwrote it. I'll be sure you get an invitation to the opening. It's going to be a Weymount retrospective. We're even using some of Jack's pieces. And Connor's stuff is brilliant these days. Just brilliant. I love what Audrey's doing with collage now, too, of course, but it's not my thing at all. You must come. I'll see that you get an invitation. And you're writing for the newspaper now, aren't you? You'll appreciate the work. You have such a good eye."

"Thank you, Yedita. I'd love to see it. Especially Audrey's things." Audrey gave my hand a conspiratorial squeeze.

"Bring your sister," Yedita urged, watching as Emma and Connor continued to size each other up in heady silence. "I'd love to paint her. So would Connor, I'm sure. Does she pose? What wonderful bone structure. And she has beautiful breasts. Connor, dear, wouldn't you love to paint her breasts?"

"I already have," said Connor without tearing his gaze from Emma.

I heard my name being called then, and we all turned to see Eloise Tackett making her way through the crowd with Harold in tow. Harold looked kingly — tall, with his distinctive white hair under control. Eloise had him by the arm, and her pert face was as lively as ever.

"Oh, I'm so glad we found you, Nora," Eloise cried. "We were afraid we wouldn't know anyone."

"All our friends are dead," Harold announced. "It's good to see some young people. And you, too, Yedita."

Yedita Weymount let that one pass. "Hello, Harold. I have another painting for you to see."

Harold's hearing aid must have given out, because he looked confused. Eloise answered quickly. "Oh, we don't need any more paintings, Yedita. We have far too many already."

Harold caught on. "There's always room for more art, if it's good."

"Well, it's hardly art," Eloise said tartly. "Sorry, Yedita. All those naked women get a little dull. Just once I'd like a pretty picture of a lake or something."

Yedita looked far from offended. "I was just about to deliver my most recent piece to Rory when he passed away. I wonder if you'd like to see it, Harold? It's just your kind of thing."

Harold looked quite interested. "I'd love to see it. But I don't get around very easily anymore. Maybe you'd bring it out to me sometime?"

Yedita must have seen dollar signs dancing like sugarplums, because she took Harold aside and they huddled together.

To me, Eloise said, "He's incorrigible. But I guess it doesn't do him any harm, collecting those pictures. It never affected our sex life, you know. He's still frisky."

Faintly, I said, "How nice."

Eloise changed the subject cheerfully. "Have the Pendergast sisters shown up?"

"I haven't seen them yet."

"I have a bet with Harold," Eloise confided in a conspirator's whisper. "I say they'll surely come to their own brother's funeral. Harold says they're too mean to make the effort."

"Maybe they plan to have a private ceremony."

Emma turned to us, suddenly eager to put some distance between herself and Connor, who had switched from brooding Heathcliff to something more aggressive. "Shall we go inside?"

People had begun to move through the metal detectors into the main body of the cathedral. Our small group flowed with the crowd past the security checkpoint. We accepted printed programs from two young ushers in altar boy robes, then proceeded down the center aisle.

We had barely traveled ten yards before a loud voice echoed in the cathedral behind us.

"Break out the grenades," Emma cautioned. "Miss Kitty has landed."

I glanced back and watched Kitty dress down one of the ushers. I couldn't hear her words, but I gathered she wanted an escort to her seat.

"Down front," she demanded, voice rising. "I need to be close, dammit."

The young usher looked confused, but put his arm out. Kitty latched onto it like a piranha and started down the center aisle with the velocity of a guided missile. Mourners dodged out of her way.

Emma nudged me, and we slid into a pew to avoid being run down. The Weymounts slipped into the row in front of us, with Harold and Eloise beside them. Kitty sailed by.

Emma said, "Somebody throw a net over her."

Right behind Kitty came none other than Detective Bloom with his partner. Bloom saw me and came over to shake my hand.

"Miss Blackbird, you remember my partner, Scotty Wilson?"

I shook Wilson's hand, too, and introduced my sister to them. For an instant they were both struck dumb by the perfect fit of Emma's leather pants.

I said, "I'm surprised to see you here, Detective. Is coming to the funeral part of your job?"

He looked solemn. "We're here to pay our respects to Mr. Pendergast."

The detectives moved off and Emma said, "You've been holding out on me, Sis."

"I don't know what you're talking about."

"Since when did you make nice with young detectives?"

"Don't start," I warned.

"How old is he?"

"No idea."

"Does he ever crack a smile?"

"I haven't seen one yet."

We sat down just in time. Suddenly the aisles seemed crowded with men in nearly identical black suits, all wearing transmitters in their ears. The reason for all the heightened security became clear.

"It's the Vice President," Eloise murmured in front of us. "Can they spare him in Washington today?"

Sure enough, the Vice President of the United States strode out of a side entrance and into the cathedral with an entourage of enough middle-aged white men to constitute the board of General Motors. The security team cleared the way so the Vice President could be seated with the other honored guests. Kitty Keough was unceremoniously bumped to the end of her pew.

Next Peach Treese came in surrounded by her family. As if commanded by a signal, every head in the cathedral turned her way.

Peach wore a small black hat with a veil that came down over her nose, concealing most of her face. Her gait was slow and shaky. Pamela Treese, the soon-to-be bride, held her grandmother's hand.

Peach did not weep. Not in public.

I understood entirely, but I wondered how Detective Bloom would view her lack of public grieving.

I couldn't imagine Peach hurting anyone, let alone Rory.

My brain took a totally inappropriate segue and I wondered guiltily about Peach's sex life with Rory. Had he acquired the Viagra with her in mind? Or was Bloom correct in speculating Rory had other women, too?

A Motown diva got up then and joined a large gospel choir in front of the cathedral. As their voices swelled with the lyrics of the gospel favorite "Deep River," the last few dignitaries took their seats.

I noted many of my own family friends in the crowd, too, and received a few nods — mostly from the over-sixty crowd, the people who remembered my grandparents fondly. A few of my parents' contemporaries, on the other hand, pretended Emma and I were invisible.

Kitty Keough sat stiffly upright near the front. Was she thinking of Rory? She'd been angry with him the night of the party. Had she been furious enough at Rory to murder him? Had my arrival at the newspaper caused her to go crazy?

And Libby. Where in the world was my flighty older sister? She would have attended Rory's funeral come hell or high water. Where *was* she?

An Episcopal priest approached the pulpit and began to read from the Book of Common Prayer. I remembered the lines from my grandfather's funeral. I had gone home and looked them up afterwards, in fact, to read the words for myself.

My heart was hot within me
And while I was thus musing
The fire kindled and at the last
I spake with my tongue.
Lord, let me know mine end
And the number of my days;
That I may be certified how long I have to live.

My grandfather's funeral had not been so well attended, perhaps, but he'd been a respected man in his day.

The Blackbird clan had not traveled in such rarefied circles since his death fifteen years ago. Still, there were the Warringtons, my mother's peculiar cousins. Although lunatics when it came to fox terriers, they looked completely respectable lined up together in a pew near the front. Nearby sat the O'Keefes, who partnered with my grandfather in some lumber ventures, then went their own way in building ski resorts in the Poconos. The Largent daughters, hardly as prim and proper as they looked, had invited me to their Maine house over a few summer breaks but were now both taking AA very seriously, or so I'd heard. Several rows over, I recognized the broad shoulders of the Cooper brothers, whom I had dated in my teens. Now they all worked for their family's aircraft manufacturing corporation — even Flan, who had been a great kisser at nineteen. I'd slept in his Penn crew T-shirt for years after he'd left my turbulent waters.

"Hmm," murmured Emma as the priest yielded the service to the choir, yanking me out of a steamy memory. "I wonder if Pendergast knew he had this many high-powered pals when he was alive. Except that maniac woman from the newspaper. I can still hear her yakking up there."

I looked for Kitty, but my gaze skimmed right over her to a side door. Suddenly the rest of the crowd vaporized as I clapped eyes on the last person to slip into the cathedral.

It was Michael Abruzzo, almost unrecognizable in a suit and tie.

I saw Detective Bloom's head snap around, and his stare bore into the back of Abruzzo's head like a flaming arrow launched from a crossbow.

Quickly, I faced the front of the cathedral. Of course, Abruzzo had a perfect right to attend Rory's funeral. They'd been friends. Business associates. It really wasn't the least bit strange that he'd come to pay his respects.

But I knew Bloom had another theory.

Coming out of one of the private chapels, Abruzzo passed through one of the secret service checkpoints and stole up the side aisle behind the row of pillars until he found an empty seat almost opposite us in the cathedral. I watched as he genuflected, crossed himself, then went into the pew. I couldn't quite see him after that. I wondered if he was saying a rosary as the choir sang. A minute passed. At last he sat back.

The monsignor mounted the pulpit, and the service took on a greater solemnity. Hankies came out and muffled weeping began.

Emma leaned over and hissed, "Who's the stud?"

"What stud?"

"The guy over there by the nuns. He's looked at you twice."

"Never mind." I pressed my handkerchief to my cheek.

"Ooh," said Emma. "It's the Abruzzo guy, isn't it?"

"Emma —"

"What's he doing here? Is he stalking you?"

"Of course not."

"Then what the hell's he up to?"

"Whatever it is, it's bound to be trouble."

Chapter 11

Mozart's *Requiem* thundered on the cathedral's massive organ, making conversation thankfully impossible as we inched our way up the aisle after the service. The Vice President had been efficiently whisked away after the removal of the casket, but the rest of us took nearly another half hour to vacate the cathedral. We had been told the family preferred a private interment at Laurel Hill cemetery. I used the time to gather my composure. Life seemed rife with losses. At last I tucked my handkerchief into my bag and fastened the catch, wishing I could lock up my emotions just as neatly.

Finally we made our way outside. Dusk was gathering, and many large cars clogged the street. My ears still rang with the noble words spoken by our eloquent senator, a few industrial magnates and one weepy woman who represented a foundation Rory had funded.

I felt dull, as if beaten into exhaustion by their words. Or maybe I was thinking of Todd again. I had known Rory Pendergast

193

well, loved him like a grandfather, and I respected what he'd done with his life. He'd left the world a better place, whereas Todd — well, he'd left his mark in a different way. In bruises on the people who'd loved him. I let Emma drag me down the cathedral steps into the milling crowd outside.

Michael Abruzzo was waiting for me. The other mourners gave him space, as if he were a Brahman bull in their midst, but he looked unaware of the apprehension rippling through the people who parted around him.

"Hello," he said, hands thrust into the trouser pockets of his dark suit.

I gathered my wits. "You seem to pop up everywhere these days."

He shrugged. "I was going to grab an early dinner. You want to come?"

"Hi, handsome," said Emma, sticking out her hand. "I'm Emma Blackbird, Nora's sister."

"Nice to meet you." As he returned her handshake, he appeared not to notice her leather pants. I gave him points for self-control.

"I'm starved," she declared. "Did I hear something about dinner? The Swann Cafe in the Four Seasons is just across the street."

I didn't know what Emma was up to, but I

was sure I didn't like her plan. She skewered Abruzzo with a smoldering look that had surely frightened lesser men.

He didn't panic. "Why not?"

But we were interrupted by the arrival of Detective Bloom and his partner.

"Abruzzo," Bloom said, "I wonder if you'd be kind enough to join us at the station?"

Abruzzo looked down at the detective, amused. "What for?"

"We'd like to ask you some questions. It's an invitation," Bloom added. "Not an arrest."

Emma's interest sharpened as both men eyed each other.

Abruzzo shrugged. "I'm happy to help the police whenever possible, Detective. Unfortunately, I'm busy at the moment."

"We'll wait," said Bloom. He did not look at me.

"How about this?" Abruzzo proposed when it became clear the police wanted to speak with him at once. "I come when it's more convenient or I call my lawyer right now and turn this into something completely different."

There was no aggression in his voice. But his polite manner defied argument. How did he do that?

Bloom's partner opened his mouth and looked on the verge of making a hasty comment, but Bloom cut him off. "Okay, sounds good. Tonight?"

"Tomorrow morning. That soon enough for you?"

Bloom shrugged. "Sure. See you then. Good night, Miss Blackbird."

When they moved away, Emma said, "My, my, what was that about?"

"He wants to know when I got to Pendergast's house on Friday night."

"When *did* you get there?" I asked.

"Still playing detective?"

I ignored the question. "Reed was supposed to take me home, but you were there instead."

"Reed had studying to do," Abruzzo said mildly. "I told you that. I took over so he could go home early. I arrived around ten."

Or half an hour earlier? In time to have slipped upstairs after the angry phone call? What had he discussed with Rory on the night of the murder? We looked at each other and waited.

Emma broke first and glanced between the two of us. "We going for dinner?"

I thought for an instant that we shouldn't associate with Abruzzo. He was obviously a suspect in Bloom's investigation.

But the crowd jostled around us just then, and Eloise Tackett appeared beside me, an energetic elf. "Nora, I found that young man art dealer we talked about. Come on, dear, let me introduce you."

"Certainly," I said to Eloise, glad to escape. Then, to Emma, "You two run along to the Swann. I'll catch up. Only be careful, Em. He's sneaky."

Abruzzo laughed.

So did Emma. She took hold of his tie. "C'mon. Let's get acquainted."

I waved them off and plunged into the crowd to follow Eloise Tackett. I wasn't annoyed with Emma. Not much, at least. And Abruzzo could do whatever the hell he pleased and it wouldn't affect me at all. Not remotely. But I was furious just the same. Must have been the funeral that put me into such a foul mood.

Eloise didn't notice my temper. "Nora, dear, this is Jonathan Longnecker, a young man we've known for a long time. Jonathan, this is Nora Blackbird. Nora was a friend of Rory's."

It was the bald man who'd elbowed me out of his way at the bar at Rory's party. He was in his late thirties, I guessed. Like so many youngish men who found themselves going bald, he'd shaved his entire head and put a tasteful diamond stud in one earlobe. His suit was a two-year-old Hugo Boss; I knew, since my husband had favored that designer. Longnecker had updated it with a steel blue shirt and a dark blue tie beneath the perfectly cut lapels. Arty, yet butch, I decided.

I shook hands with him and smiled. "I've seen you before."

"I think I'd remember if we'd met."

"Rory's party," I reminded him. "We passed at the bar."

Longnecker poured on the charm with a practiced smile and good eye contact. "You have a good memory for detail."

"I've just spent a lot of time thinking about what I saw that night."

"That's understandable." Longnecker continued to hold my hand after we'd shaken. I recognized the technique — Step One in coaxing rich women to entrust their money to him. "We're all in shock."

I remembered how agitated Longnecker had appeared at Rory's party. His face had been a mask of anger when he shoved past me. Had Jill said something — what was it? — about his having an argument with Rory?

"Jonathan used to be a freelancer," Harold explained, voice raised. "Brought me some pictures for my collection.

Pendergast's, too. Now he's respectable, though. Just took a job with a museum in California. If you can call that respectable!"

General laughter.

I asked, "Are you still freelancing?"

"It doesn't hurt to keep my hand in."

"That's interesting," I said. "I wonder if you could tell me more about how your business works?"

He kicked his flirting up a notch. "I'd love it."

"Now?"

He laughed, looking pleased. "You mean this minute?"

Smiling like a matchmaker who'd completed her mission, Eloise said archly, "Come on, Harold. I hate driving in rush hour, but I hate driving in the dark a lot more. We'd better get going."

"Lead the way," said Harold. "See you soon, I hope, Nora?"

The Tacketts tottered off, and I was left with Jonathan Longnecker.

"Would you like a drink?' I asked, determined to see my plan through as long as I didn't have to be alone with him. "The bar at the Four Seasons is open, I hear."

"Perfect. But let's make it my treat."

We dashed across the street in a light, misting rain, dodging the last limousine that departed from Rory's funeral. As we reached the opposite sidewalk, I glanced back at the cathedral. It looked dark and empty already. Rory Pendergast was gone.

Jonathan Longnecker held the restaurant door open for me. The diamond in his ear-lobe winked.

Subdued and clubby in atmosphere, the Swann was out of the way for most of the downtown crowd, but tonight it bustled. It felt safe. As we stepped inside and made our way into the bar, I saw a lot of people who'd attended the funeral. The men grabbed single malt scotches and were relieved enough to laugh, and the women took off their Saint John suit jackets, revealing bare shoulders underneath. The lights were soft, the upholstery was plush, and candlelight suffused the polished length of the bar. The waiters were all over fifty and quietly efficient.

We ended up at one of the small marble-topped tables, escorted there by a hostess who managed to find a seat where I couldn't see the bar. I caught one quick glimpse of Emma lighting a cigarette from a match Abruzzo held. Of course, I didn't intend to spy on them. It was only sisterly concern that made me glance their way now and then.

Longnecker put his Palm Pilot on the table beside his cell phone and ordered a Grey Goose martini. "Did you know Rory all your life? Or did you just meet him lately?"

"He was a friend of my grandfather," I replied, trying to decide on a plan of attack. "What about you?"

"I worked with him for about two years. I'm surprised we didn't bump into each other."

"Me, too."

He smiled warmly. "Are the Blackbirds as old and powerful as the Pendergasts?"

"Probably older," I replied. "But no power whatsoever."

He leaned closer across the table, getting chummy as quickly as possible. "Have you met the Pendergast sisters? Can you believe they didn't come to their own brother's funeral?"

"I'm sure they were devastated."

Longnecker gave an exaggerated shiver. "What a couple of battle-axes! They act like czarinas. Off with my head! I really am afraid of them."

"They can be demanding."

"I just hope I can deal with them."

"Deal with them?"

"When it comes time to sell the estate.

I'm sure they won't want to keep Rory's collection, and I'd love to have some of those pieces for the museum I work for."

"Surely they'd be foolish to part with the paintings."

"Oh, I don't mean the paintings." Longnecker waved his hand dismissively. "They'll keep the Impressionists forever. No, I mean Rory's other stuff. Things that are very hip right now. Very collectible. They're going to go through the roof, and I'm anxious to get in while the museum can still afford good pieces."

I waited.

Longnecker leaned closer. "You know what I mean. The X-rated things."

I shook my head. "Frankly, until recently, I didn't know Rory's collection leaned in that direction."

"And how did you become aware of it?"

"Harold mentioned it."

"Oh? I thought maybe it was your sister."

He caught me by surprise.

Longnecker smiled as though he'd just found a rabbit in his trap. "He gave it to her for refurbishing, didn't he? He told me it needed some touching up, and I said it had to be done by experts. I know just the firm to do the work properly. But your sister — Rory was determined to throw some work her way. Of course, she wasn't up to the job. She's an amateur, really. Just a hobbyist."

Faintly, I said, "I don't know what you're talking about."

"Okay," he said, with a positively voracious grin. "Tell the truth. What did you think of the Zhejiang Folio when you first saw it?"

Chapter 12

The effort to keep my face blank caused a spasm in my right cheek. "The what?"

"The Zhejiang Folio. You've seen it, haven't you?"

I've never been so happy for a waiter interruption in my life. He put our drinks on the table while I regained my composure and madly tried to think how this man knew I had the folio.

Longnecker ignored his martini while I gulped a fortifying slug of Chardonnay. He said, "It's beautiful, isn't it? And sexy as hell. I fell in love with it instantly. I was with him in China when we found it, you know."

I knew Rory sometimes traveled, but I'd had no idea he'd been to China in the recent past.

Longnecker went on enthusiastically. "The color! The condition! The sex! I almost came in my pants when I first saw it. But what did you think? I'd really like to know."

His crude enthusiasm made me want to

get up and leave. But I had to know more. "Mr. Longnecker —"

"You must call me Jonathan." He planted his elbows and linked the fingers of both hands like a schoolboy. "I know Pendergast gave it to your sister for repair. She's done all his black-market stuff. Half his collection came from disreputable dealers, of course. When paintings are stolen out of museums, who do you suppose buys from the thieves? Not museums. Guys like Pendergast keep the black market thriving. I doubt your sister realized what she was working on."

He enjoyed shocking me. He was taking great pleasure in telling me that Rory hadn't been pure as snow. But most of all, I was suddenly angry that he thought my sister Libby was a fool.

He went on pleasantly, "He gave her the folio a few weeks ago. That's when it disappeared."

"I don't know anything about this."

"Oh, now, don't keep up the charade," he chided playfully. "Your sister has it, but it belongs to the Reese-Goldman Museum."

"Really —"

"I'm here to take it back," said Longnecker. "It's not the sort of thing we can ship UPS, is it?"

"If this folio belongs to your museum, why did Rory have it?"

"He paid for it." Longnecker took a drink of his martini and dug out the lemon twist with his fingers. He popped it into his mouth and said around it, "At least he paid for the China trip. He bought the folio for us with the understanding that he could keep it for a little while. I suppose the dirty old bastard wanted to show it off. But then he started talking about repairing it! I knew he occasionally sent hush-hush items to your sister for that sort of thing and God knows I tried to talk him out of using her."

"Have you spoken with my sister?"

"Not yet. I came east to discuss things face-to-face with Pendergast. But then — well, he died, and I've been trying to rethink my game plan. I figure it's going to be hell trying to pry the folio out of the Pendergast biddies, so I was hoping to go directly to your sister to get the folio. When the Tacketts said you were looking for me, I assumed you'd been elected as the go-between. Am I right?"

Not even close, I thought, sipping my wine.

He went on, "I'm creating a whole exhibit around the folio, and we're scheduled to open in July. You can understand my eagerness to get the folio back to California. I've been a wreck worrying about it floating around. It's probably worth six million dollars."

The spasm in my cheek tightened into a full-fledged cramp. A six-million-dollar work of art lay under my lingerie in a drawer back at the farm.

"So," he said, "what's the deal?"

I sighed with as much regret as I could put on. "I wish I could help you, Jonathan, I truly do. But I don't believe Libby has your folio."

He stared at me. "She has to. He gave it to her."

"I haven't heard that from Libby."

He loomed forward again. In the background, soft jazz piano music began — a weird counterpoint to his cold expression. "Look, Miss Blackbird, that folio never belonged to Pendergast in the first place. He bought it for the museum, and we want it back. You and your sister can be charged with any number of crimes, you know, including fencing stolen goods, if you don't give it up."

"Mr. Longnecker —"

His smarmy demeanor totally evaporated. "I've heard about the Blackbird family, you know. Your parents are crooks. There's been one scandal after another. You can barely keep your heads above water. But if you think you can get away with selling the Zhejiang Folio, you'd better think again."

"I wasn't —"

"No self-respecting institution in the world will buy it from you, and the black market would eat you alive."

"I think this discussion is —"

"You don't know what you're mixed up in, lady. You think it's a game? An easy way to pay off your credit card bill?" His voice rose and I feared the whole restaurant could hear him. "You have no idea what kind of people you'd be doing business with. Know what? I don't even think you'd live to see the money."

I stood up from the table. "We're finished, Mr. Longnecker."

"We haven't even started," he snapped. "Think it over, Miss Blackbird. Do you and your sister want to get out of this alive?"

I stepped backwards and collided with a tall, male body. One of his arms came around my waist, and behind me Michael Abruzzo said, "Everything all right here?"

"Yes." I was glad to hear my voice sound steady when all I wanted to do was run screaming into the night.

"No, it's not all right. This woman thinks she can swindle the Reese-Goldman."

Abruzzo said mildly, "That something you take penicillin for?"

"Who the hell are you?" The words were out of Longnecker's mouth before he looked up at Abruzzo and saw something that frightened him.

"Nobody you want to know," said Abruzzo. "Ready to leave, Nora?"

I picked up my handbag. "Yes, please."

"This is far from over, Miss Blackbird."

Abruzzo steered me out of the bar without a word, and we arrived in the hotel lobby before I could summon speech.

Even then, I sounded pretty shaky. "Where's Emma?"

"She had to go check on a horse. That make sense to you?"

"I — Yes. Yes. She has a job at a stable."

The Swann's door opened and I jumped, thinking Longnecker had come after me. But it was just the hostess putting out the evening menu board. She glanced from me to Abruzzo and back again as if the picture didn't quite look right. She edged back inside the bar.

Abruzzo said, "How about if I take you home?"

"Are you taking over for Reed again?" I tried to laugh and sneaked a look up at him.

"Not today." Quieter, he asked, "You okay?"

"Fine. Yes, I'm fine."

"That character threatened you."

"It was nothing."

"Are you in some kind of trouble? Maybe we should call the police."

"You really want to do that?"

He shrugged. "I don't mind. Maybe Detective Gloom should know what just happened with your drinking buddy."

"It was nothing."

I cleared my throat and tried to think straight. Libby — what was she mixed up in? I needed to get in touch with her right away.

"You want me to do something about him?"

"My God, what does that mean?"

"I could talk to him." He smiled a little and loosened his tie. "Nothing painful."

I gulped. "No, please. I — Listen, I need to stop at my office. I'm supposed to write the story of Rory's funeral for tomorrow's edition." Plus I wanted to get to a phone as soon as possible. "You should go. I'll call a cab when I'm finished there."

"I can wait."

"No, really —"

"I'm not going to slug anybody, if that's

what's scaring you. I'm not leaving you alone like this. Let me drive you to your office."

There was no arguing with the man. And I was starting to feel foolish. "All right," I said.

We left the Four Seasons and walked to the parking garage. I set a brisk pace to prove myself. He had brought his Volvo again. I gave him the address of the Pendergast building. Within ten minutes, I left him at the curb with a warning that I might need half an hour.

"I'll wait." He pulled a newspaper out from under the seat and ignored the No Parking Here to Corner sign.

I rushed through the revolving door and spoke to the uniformed security guard who examined my *Intelligencer* ID before allowing me through the lobby. The elevator shot up through the Pendergast building, which housed many offices for Rory's various business ventures. The top four floors were newspaper offices.

On the ninth floor, one of the night cleaning crew pushed a roaring floor buffer right outside the elevator.

I thought the features department would be empty, but a young man I recognized from the style section came toward me, shouldering a leather briefcase. He was the always-spiffy men's clothing expert, a black man with a ready smile and a penchant for red licorice. A piece of the candy dangled from the corner of his mouth as he dug into his trouser pockets for his car keys. "Hey, Nora," he said, sidestepping when I nearly crashed into him. "Great job on the mayor's story. Everybody's impressed as hell."

"Thanks."

"You're the talk of the newsroom."

"Is that good or bad?"

He laughed. "Very good, believe me. See you around, huh?"

"Yes, of course."

He pushed the elevator button and disappeared with a wave, leaving me alone with the cleaning crew. Around me were empty desks and blank computer screens.

My desk was tucked into a corner, wedged between that of a jolly food writer who heaped her desk with samples sent to her by cookie companies and the acerbic restaurant critic who kept her desk scrupulously neat. Getting closer, I saw mine was covered with pink message slips and a vase of cheap carnations. I flipped through the notes and found them all amusing atta-girl messages from my new colleagues. I smiled as I leafed through the memos. Maybe I was going to fit into the camaraderie of the newsroom better than I thought.

No time to really enjoy them, though. I stuffed the papers into my handbag. I needed to talk to Libby before I could gather my thoughts enough to write about the funeral. But I didn't want to make a phone call with the floor buffer roaring nearby.

Stan Rosenstatz's office was a cramped, windowless cubicle located near the cluster of desks where most senior features columnists worked. I figured I could use his telephone.

But Stan wasn't sitting behind his desk.

It was Kitty Keough.

I stopped short in the doorway.

There was no escape.

She looked up from the sheaf of papers she'd been reading on Stan's desk. A red pen was poised in the claw of her right hand. Her face registered my arrival without surprise. In the harsh fluorescent light, her skin had no color. Her black suit glittered with sequins, looking like snakeskin. Her hair spray had begun to lose its grip on the helmet of her hair, but she looked coldly in control otherwise.

"Well, hello, Sweet Knees." She put down

her pen. "What brings you here tonight? Need a place to freshen up before a hot date?"

"No —"

"Come to write up the funeral? Yes, Stan told me he asked you to do it."

"I suppose," I began again, "since you were there, you'd prefer to write it yourself."

Her dark eyes radiated dislike. "You think you can do it better?"

"Of course not. I only —"

"Because you can't," she said, and picked up the papers from the desk. I could see red ink slashed through whole sentences. "Stan printed this out before he left. It's your stuff from yesterday's edition. And it sucks."

It was time for a showdown and I wasn't ready. But Kitty didn't frighten me with her nasty brand of bullying. I didn't like schoolyard taunts and belittling tactics. They only made me stubborn. Evenly, I said, "I'm sorry you don't like it."

She threw down the pages. "It doesn't matter what I like. Stan says it's fine. I'm just showing him the error of his ways. I suppose you're invited to the Treese-Kintswell wedding."

So that was it. "Yes. I'm related to the groom."

"Yes, by your sister's marriage. And I suppose you'll write up the wedding afterwards."

"If you'd like me to, of course."

"I'm not invited," she said, almost sneering. "Peach Treese made it very clear she doesn't want me there. But my readers will want to hear about it."

"I'll do the story. But I'll write it my way, Kitty. They're my family, after all."

Her face tightened. The little black feather she had worn like a pin on her lapel looked like a small dagger she could snatch off her bosom and use on an unsuspecting victim. "You don't like me, do you?"

I did not respond.

"You don't have to," she went on. "You only have to respect me. And you will. Right now, you're supposed to do what I tell you to do."

"I know."

"Stan can try making an end run around me, but it's what I say about you that counts. Now that Rory's not here to protect you."

"I'm still learning the protocol," I said. "If you'd like me to send my work to you when it's written, I'll be happy to —"

"Don't be so damn polite! That really pisses me off!"

I took a breath. "Do you want me to write

215

up the funeral, Kitty? Or would you prefer to write it your own way?"

"Go do it," she said abruptly. "Do it now. You can use one of the computers out there." She aimed her pen at the desks outside the office. "You have ten minutes."

"I'll need some time to gather my thoughts."

"You didn't think of what you wanted to say while you were sitting in church?"

"No," I said. "I guess I was thinking about Rory."

Big mistake. Kitty stood up from the desk. "You thought about Rory," she repeated. "What did you think? About happy days gone by? The good old times? Did he bounce you on his knee when you were a little girl?"

"I don't think this discussion does either of us any good."

She cut around the desk and forced me out into the darkened newsroom. The floor buffer roared behind me, and I took comfort in that sound. It meant I wasn't alone with her.

Because the look on her face suddenly worried me. She looked capable of murder, all right.

She said, "You weren't the only one who knew Rory well. Don't go parading around here like you're the widow or the daughter or whatever the hell you were to Rory. You and your sisters — all of you practically his family while the rest of us took all the shit he dished out."

"Kitty —"

"We made this paper what it is, and he fought us every step! But somehow he managed to make us all love him for it. You think he knew anything about journalism? Let me tell you something. This paper is great in spite of Rory Pendergast. And now his stupid relatives are going to sell it out from under us! We worked our butts off while he went out and hired pretty faces with empty heads — as if people like you could learn to write by osmosis!"

Did I see tears in her eyes? From rage? Or grief?

I turned away. "I'll go write the funeral now."

"The hell you will," she shouted after me. "I've changed my mind. I'll do it myself. This is one piece that'll be done right. Now get out of here!"

I left. I tried not to run. When I reached the elevator, I hit the button hard. From across the room, Kitty watched me as the doors slid quietly toward each other. Judging by the look on her face, she wasn't finished with me.

Chapter 13

When I got into the car beside Abruzzo, he held up his newspaper. "You have a more exciting life than I figured. You're even chummy with the mayor."

The headlines were Rory and the mayor, both with photos. "I'd like to forget about my career in journalism right now, if you don't mind."

Agreeably, he folded the paper and started the car. Tuesday rush hour was long over, and we zipped out of town in light traffic while I tried to regain my wits. As the car wove across the streets and then got onto I-95, I tried to replay Kitty's crazy tirade in my mind. Exactly why had she been so furious? Was she mad at me for getting hired behind her back? At Rory for his management of the *Intelligencer*? Or because the newspaper might soon be sold and she'd lose her job? Not to mention her claim to fame?

I must have moved restlessly in my seat because Abruzzo said, "Want to tell me what happened back at the restaurant?"

"Not really, no." I rubbed my forehead.

He glanced over at me. "Indulge me for a minute. You knew that museum guy?"

"I'd just met him. Really, it was nothing."

"He seemed to think you had something that belonged to him."

"We were discussing Rory's art collection."

"That means you're still snooping around for Rory's killer."

"I'm not snooping."

"Okay," he said placidly. "I'm starting to wonder, that's all, if the murder has something to do with your sister Libby disappearing."

I said a word that didn't usually cross my lips. "What do you know about Libby?" I demanded, turning in the car's seat. "How do you know she's missing? Which she isn't, by the way."

"She isn't? Your sister Emma said you've been trying to reach her for a while. I call that missing."

"You're wrong," I argued, ridiculously upset all over again. "I just haven't been able to get in touch with her."

"How long have you been trying?"

"Since Saturday."

"You've talked with her husband?"

"Of course. I went over to see her, but he

said she had taken the children to Sunday school. Except she didn't call me back. And," I added, more to myself, "she didn't come to the funeral today."

"So what do you think?"

I sighed and gave up trying to keep my business to myself. "I'm starting to think she's missing."

"Check with the husband again," Abruzzo advised, guiding the car off the exit ramp. "It's usually the husband."

I shook my head. "He doesn't have anything to do with it. Ralph has his peculiarities, but he's a rock. Libby, on the other hand, has been known to be an idiot from time to time."

"Un-huh," he said. "What's she done now?"

"I don't — Look, this is my business, really."

"Is she in trouble?"

"Oh, I hope so," I said fervently. "Because she deserves to be drawn and quartered for putting me through this."

"What does Emma think?"

I looked over at him. "You think her opinion counts?"

"Sure. She seems smart."

"Not to mention attractive." Tartly, I asked, "Did she seduce you?"

He smiled at the road. "She didn't have quite enough time."

I'd seen the look on Emma's face when she'd taken Abruzzo off to the Swann. I knew she wanted to find out about him. And what Emma wanted, she usually got.

"Look," he said, "I'm not interested in your sister."

"I'll tell you what I'm interested in," I said, feeling ornery. "What you and Rory argued about Friday night."

"What?"

"You phoned him. And you threatened him."

Sharp, he said, "Did your pal Detective Gloom tell you that?"

"He's not my pal, so don't try changing the subject. You lied to me."

"I didn't lie."

"You lied by omission. That's the same thing. Come clean, Michael."

It may have been my use of his first name that startled him into silence. Or maybe he was trying to figure a way to spin the truth into something he wanted me to hear. He was quiet for a long, tense moment.

At last he said, "All right. We argued about you."

"Dammit, can't you be honest with me?"

"I am being honest. We — He — Oh, hell.

You weren't supposed to find out."

"About what?"

"Don't," he said, hearing the fear in my voice. "Don't be frightened. It's not bad, it's just a thing we intended to keep a secret until it all shook out."

"A secret from me?"

"Yes, it's — Well, you're going to think the worst, I suppose, and Rory's gone, so what does it matter?" Explosively, he said, "I didn't buy that ground from you. Rory did."

"Rory?"

"He knew you were in trouble when you asked him for a job. He also knew you'd never get out of the tax hole no matter how much he paid you in salary, so he came up with the idea of buying some of your farm to give you breathing room. He didn't want you to know he was bailing you out, so he put this deal together."

"What deal? I still don't understand."

"I needed a place to put the muscle cars, and you needed cash to make a payment on your taxes. And since I'd already mentioned your name to him, Rory lent me the money to buy as many acres as you'd part with. You know, like a front."

"What do you mean, you already mentioned my name to him?"

"I asked him about you. A few months

ago, I was looking for a way to meet you."

"You're kidding, right?"

"Friday night I called him to say I wanted out. I didn't want you believing I had saved you from —"

"You think you saved me?" I started to laugh. "Oh, God, do you know how funny that is?"

"Why?"

"Because two minutes after I sold that land, you immediately destroyed two hundred years of — Oh, why get into that now?"

"How was I supposed to know it's practically a sacred burial ground? This is what I do — I create businesses. This was just supposed to be another one. Except it turned out to be a lousy way to start with you."

"Oh, heavens." I put my forehead against the car window.

"Listen," he said. We'd somehow driven through New Hope and only had a few more miles before reaching Blackbird Farm. "I know I came on too strong at first."

"Don't," I said.

"I'm sorry about that," he went on.

"Please don't."

He said, "Seeing you with those people at the funeral today, well, you fit in with them. Maybe you belong with them. But I get the feeling you've done your time."

"Please, please, don't."

"You're ready for something else."

I put one hand over my eyes and tried not to laugh. Or cry. It had been a long, long day and I was too drained, too weak to resist even the most clumsy effort at romance. "You're going to have this discussion now?"

"You can tell me to buzz off, if you like," he went on, undeterred. "But I won't — I'm not trying to get something out of you. I saw you at the New Hope post office once last winter. You dropped a yellow umbrella. And you were crying all by yourself. Jesus, Nora, you broke my heart right there in front of the stamp machine. And then one day in February you came out of the Episcopal church in some kind of exercise outfit, and you looked so spectacular that I — well, I asked around. When somebody said Rory was your friend, I gave him a call. He thought it was pretty funny that I was mooning around after you, so he —"

"You have no idea how colossally bad your timing is."

"I wish it hadn't happened the way it did. You know what I'm saying? I'd like to start again. Put the past behind us. I know we're different, but — well."

He finally gave up trying to explain himself.

"What did you mean," I asked again, "that I'd done my time?"

He didn't answer right away. In a moment, he said steadily, "I think you're finished with those people, those guys in the suits with the Palm Pilots and the coke on weekends. You've played with the little boys long enough."

He pulled the Volvo into the farm's long drive and parked near the back door. It took me a moment of fumbling to unfasten the seatbelt and gather my bag. By the time I did, he had come around and opened the car door for me. I got out into the darkness, and he didn't move. He seemed taller, more substantial and more thoroughly masculine than ever. Wearing that suit, even with the tie loosened, he could have passed for a blue-blooded banker or a law-abiding stockbroker. But he wasn't either of those things.

"Nora," he said, his voice soft and intense.

Like an idiot, I let him kiss me.

Chapter 14

Okay, I should have known it was coming and done something to stop it.

But it felt good to hold on to those shoulders and let something besides murder and my sisters consume me. I just plain forgot what I was doing and with whom. And in another minute the kiss escalated from a first move into something more steamy. He wrapped one arm around me and pulled my whole body tight against his, then ran the other hand into my hair to hold me for a long, slow, deliberate kiss that melted my reluctance into a hot cauldron of hormonal soup.

Fortunately my brain didn't totally self-destruct. I knew I'd better call a halt or we'd be upstairs, sprawled on a pile of discarded clothes, in the next five minutes.

Which would not have been a good idea.

Really.

So I broke the kiss and let out a long, shaky breath.

"This is not good," I said, somehow unable to let go of him.

"Feels great to me."

"Trust me, it isn't."

"I disagree." He slipped closer to try again.

"For one thing, I can smell Emma's perfume on you."

"Oh, damn," he said, laughing.

I pushed past him, feeling more scared than annoyed. This definitely was not the way I'd planned my evening. I got out my keys to unlock the back door.

"Nora —"

Except the door was already open.

I must have said something, because he was beside me again in an instant.

"Wait here," he said, sounding very different. He went inside.

Of course I followed. I turned on the light.

A tornado had gone through my house. The destruction took my breath away.

My knees wobbled, and I sat down on what was left of a kitchen chair. "This has not been a good day."

All but two of my kitchen chairs had been smashed against the stove. A bag of oatmeal was spilled on the floor with splintered chair legs and the contents of all my cabinets. Pieces of dishes mingled with broken jars of homemade applesauce. Through the doorway, I could see that the dining room floor was ankle deep in books. Even my Audrey Weymount paintings had been torn off the wall and thrown on the floor, their frames broken.

Libby's mess had been simple slovenly living, but this was the systematic work of vandals.

Abruzzo headed for the rest of the house and said over his shoulder, "Stay here. And I mean it this time."

An out-of-body experience took over. My physical self seemed to stay in the chair and my consciousness floated up to the ceiling to absorb the destruction and the silence. The house was very cold and I hugged myself, shivering. I heard Abruzzo take the stairs in leaps and I sat listening to him go through the rooms overhead. When I could manage, I got up and ran some water from the tap into my palm to drink. But my hand shook so badly that the cold water ran down my elbows into the sink.

"You okay?" Abruzzo was back. He grabbed my wrist.

"Give me a minute. Is the rest of the house — ?"

"Just like this, torn apart. I'll call the police."

Louder than I intended, I said, "No, wait!"

Abruzzo swung me around. His face was

228

very different. He was a man I didn't know, an angry one who looked capable of slugging anyone he chose. "Now, look," he said. "This isn't funny."

"I just need a minute to think."

"Jesus Christ. This is something you shouldn't be handling without the police."

"I just —"

"What the hell are you hiding?"

"Nothing!"

"Then you're protecting somebody."

"Who would I — ?"

"Dammit, Nora, this has gone too far. What if you'd been here when this happened?"

"It's just vandals. They wouldn't have come if I'd been here."

"You need help, for godsake."

"Not from the police!" I shouted.

He let go of my wrist. The house was absolutely silent.

"Now that," he said very quietly, "calls for some explaining."

"Please," I begged. "Let me figure out what's happening. Just give me time to think."

"All right," he said, calmer. "Maybe you better take a look around to see what's missing."

"My laptop is still here."

The computer sat undisturbed on the kitchen table. We both looked at it blankly.

"Any self-respecting thief would have taken that first thing," he said.

I nodded. My heart began to throb.

"Anything else you want to check on?"

"Y-yes." But I couldn't seem to move.

"You want me to look for you?" he asked.

"No," I said, gathering myself with tremendous effort. "But I have to go upstairs."

He saw that I was afraid to be alone. He said, "Okay, let's go. I'm right behind you."

In my rush, I caught my foot on the books scattered on the dining room floor. I knelt and found the three precious first editions I owned — a book of Whitman poems, a Dashiell Hammett and a rare volume of Richardson's *Pamela*. I carried them, hugging the books instinctively.

In the sitting room, more books were all over the floor, but the CD player was still in its cabinet with all of Todd's jazz collection. A group of Libby's early watercolors had been thrown on the stairs in a shower of broken glass. The sight of my sister's paintings damaged gave me my first boost of angry adrenaline. On the upstairs landing, the linen cupboard shelves had been emptied onto the carpet.

Behind me, Abruzzo walked carefully, on alert.

In my room, my jewelry box still contained the meager collection of costume jewelry and the few family pieces I owned. Even Grandmama's sapphire ring was there. My bedclothes had been ripped off, and the mattress was askew on the box springs. Nervously, I leaned closer to see if some weirdo had left his calling card. But the bedclothes were clean, thank heavens.

Abruzzo stepped into the room and spotted the small rabbit-eared television on my dresser. "What about jewelry?"

"It's all here."

I took a deep breath and opened the second drawer in my dresser. In my lingerie drawer, I had left the folio wrapped in a black lace slip buried under a collection of pastel bras. By some miracle, the vandals hadn't dug down through the bras to find the prize.

With trembling hands, I lifted out the folio and unwrapped it. The slip floated to the floor at my feet.

"What is it?" Abruzzo asked at my shoulder.

"It's Rory's," I said.

Unsteady again, I sat down on the bed.

Abruzzo sat beside me and gently pried

the folio out of my hands. He thumbed the latch and the leather case opened.

Everything started to get murky, so I put my head between my knees again. I said, "Your self-respecting thief was probably looking for this."

"What is it?" he asked.

"Rory collected erotic art."

"Oh, yeah?" Abruzzo leafed through the pages. "He didn't mention this hobby down at the boys' club."

"It's very valuable," I said. "It's what Jonathan Longnecker asked me about this afternoon."

"How come you have it?"

I sat up again as my head cleared. "I have no idea."

Abruzzo continued to look through the pages.

I said, "Libby sent it to me. She wanted me to return it to Rory's collection without telling anyone. It's such a stupid idea that I can't imagine what she was thinking. Except . . ."

"Except?"

"Maybe Libby is doing work that's not entirely legal. Obviously she wanted to keep her connection to this folio a secret. She didn't want anyone to know she had it — and I have to assume that includes the police."

Abruzzo didn't appear to be listening. His attention was fully engaged by the pages in front of him. "Uhm," he said.

"So I can't tell the police yet. And I can't report this break-in until I've figured out what Libby wants me to do and why. I don't want her going to jail."

"Uhmmm."

"On the other hand, I don't want to get myself in trouble either." I looked down at the writhing figures depicted on the lustrous page between us. The man's erection was huge. I blinked, and my brain snapped back to reality, which was me sitting on my bed with Michael Abruzzo while he looked at erotic pictures. I said, "Maybe I'm panicking. Maybe this really was just vandals."

"Mmmm," he said.

"Kids, perhaps."

"Brave kids to break in here in broad daylight."

"Well, it could have been teenagers looking for excitement."

"They didn't find it," Abruzzo said, turning to the next page.

I sat on the bed and looked at the wreckage of my bedroom. My eyelet sheets had been ripped to the floor, and my down-filled pillows thrown to opposite sides of the room. My slip was on the carpet, too. I wondered if Abruzzo had noticed it.

He seemed pretty absorbed by something else at the moment.

I reached for the folio and took it from him. I began replacing the pages into the leather covers. I heard myself saying primly, "I think you've seen enough to get the general idea of Rory's taste in art."

He leaned back, hands braced on the bed behind him. "If that's art, I'll give museums a second chance."

"Rory had a very specialized collection."

"He sure did, the old dog."

I hastily snatched the black lace slip off the floor and used it to rewrap the folio. I was clumsy, though, and he reached to help. "I can manage," I said.

"You could have put this in a safety-deposit box, you know, but you've kept it up here in your bedroom." His smile made me think about kissing him outside in the dark. "What are you doing? Looking at the pictures before you go to sleep at night?"

"I thought it was safest here," I said, ridiculously prim, and stashing the folio back in my drawer. "Turns out I was right, Mr. Abruzzo."

He rose to his feet and let his gaze sweep over the bed, the eyelet lace, and my pillows on the floor. "You called me Michael before, you know. It wouldn't hurt to keep on doing it."

Somehow, using his first name in that particular location didn't seem like a good idea at all.

He turned and slouched against the door, waiting.

I couldn't meet his eye. "Thank you."

"For?"

"Not making me call the police."

"No problem," he said.

"And I shouldn't have told you about the folio," I began. I tried to find a way to say more.

When I looked up, he smiled somewhat wryly. "You don't have to worry about me. I'll keep your secret."

"Thanks."

"But you're in danger. It doesn't take Sherlock Holmes to see that."

Maybe I was, but just then it didn't feel like vandals were going to give me the most trouble. Suddenly I didn't want Abruzzo anywhere near my eyelet sheets. The good news was that he wasn't treating me like a hysterical child. The bad news was that I wouldn't mind being treated like a grown woman just then.

Caution won. I said, "Let's go downstairs."

"Just one second," he replied. "What are the chances Libby did this herself? Maybe she was trying to get this thing back."

"No, she'd never make a mess like this." I was thinking of the watercolor paintings torn off the walls on the staircase. "She wouldn't destroy things."

He shrugged. "Just a thought."

He stood aside and let me precede him out of the room.

On the way down the stairs, I picked up the three framed watercolors that Libby had painted. Looking at them, I used the phone in the kitchen and dialed Libby's number.

Ralph answered. Although it was late, I could hear the kids arguing in the background.

"I'm sorry to call so late," I said, "but, Ralph, I really need to talk to Libby."

"She's not here," he said placidly, despite the shouting near him. "She went to New York."

"What?" My voice cracked. "What for?"

"To look for a dress."

"A dress," I said. A huge crash resonated over the phone line.

"Lucy, cut that out, please. Leave your brother alone. You know," Ralph said to me, "for the wedding."

"She's shopping," I said stupidly.

"Yeah, I think she'll be back in a couple of days."

"Listen, Ralph, do you know where's she's staying? What hotel?"

The children's altercation turned into a brawl. I could hear shrieking, but Ralph said calmly, "She's with a friend. At her friend's apartment. Sylvia somebody. I don't have the number, though. She usually calls home to check in."

"Okay," I said steadily. "It's important that she call me, Ralph. I really need to talk to her. As soon as possible."

"Sure," said Ralph. "I'll tell her. Is there anything I can do? Are you okay?"

"I'm okay," I said. The last thing I wanted was anyone else dragged into the quagmire. And it sounded as though Ralph had his hands full with the kids. "Just ask Libby to call me soon — it doesn't matter what time."

"Will do," Ralph promised before signing off to deal with Libby's wild animals.

I phoned Emma next. She listened to my story and promised to arrive in twenty minutes.

While we waited for her, I cleaned the broken glass out of the picture frames and looked at the small watercolors Libby had painted when we were still in school. Even then, her technique had been beautiful, out-shone only by her flare for capturing a moment of action and figure with simple brush strokes. She had sketched all three of us one evening when we'd gone skinny-dipping in the river and added paint later. She'd even managed to insert her own, fuller frame between Emma's and my own, the three of us laughing in the half-light — natural girls teasing each other into showing off our teenage bodies. My throat clogged as I looked down at those three sisters bound by countless such evenings together. We hadn't always gotten along or been happy, but nothing kept me more grounded than my bond with my sisters.

By the time Emma arrived, I was angry. Someone was trying to break that bond.

Chapter 15

Emma stared at me when Abruzzo had fled — apparently not wanting to be in the same house with two women he'd kissed on the same night. Emma said, "Are you nuts?"

"What have I done now?"

"Why did you bother calling me when you had the gangster studmuffin here?" She wagged her head in despair. "Some day, Nora, you're going to explode from all those pent-up hormones."

I looked at her askance. After the funeral she had changed into jeans and a sweatshirt. The shirt was smeared with something that could have been dried horse slobber, yet my sister still managed to look like a sex kitten. I asked, "Did you have a good time with him?"

She grinned. "Can't blame a girl for trying. I jumped him when he walked me to the parking garage. He cooperated, but his heart wasn't in it. Did you have better luck?"

"My house has been vandalized, Em."

"I get it. No time for nooky. Okay, tell me what's going on."

Blasé as she pretended to be, Emma actually became solicitous and made us one of her trademark margaritas to share. Then we went upstairs and made my bed while I spilled the whole story. I showed her the folio along with the note Libby sent me.

"And now she's gone dress shopping in New York," I added, running my finger along the rim of the glass for the salt. "And Ralph doesn't have her phone number."

Emma curled up on the bed with the folio and became as engrossed in the pictures as Abruzzo had been. "So? The wedding is next weekend. She needs a dress."

"But, Emma —"

Emma turned another page. "She's shopping for clothes, for Pete's sake. You know the whole Treese family will look like they've been to Paris. Libby will want to look just as good."

"I'm so sorry Libby has to obsess about her wardrobe! Dammit, Emma, I'm going crazy. She dumped this on me and skipped town! Did she say anything when she gave you the folio?"

Emma looked up from the folio at last and blinked. "I thought it was a bag of books. She didn't say what it was. So I took it and left."

"Back up. Did she call you to come get it?"

"No, I stopped at her house on my way to Paddy's barn. I take doughnuts to the kids on Saturday mornings. A little sugar jazzes them up. Sometimes I think those kids need to cut loose."

"Was Libby okay?"

"Of course. I mean, she was her usual self, if that qualifies as okay. Maybe she was a little upset, I guess. Jill Mascione was there."

"Jill? At Libby's house? What on earth for?"

"She was talking to Ralph about the menu for the rehearsal dinner. Ralph was angry and Libby ran outside to talk to me while he argued with Jill about chicken or something."

"Ralph was angry?"

Emma shrugged and went back to the folio. "As angry as Ralph ever gets. I certainly didn't hear him shouting. The whole wedding has gotten out of hand, I think. It's expensive. Ralph was looking for a way to cut the cost."

"And Libby promptly went to New York to buy a dress?"

"Nobody ever said Libby is sensitive. Remember, she was the one who upstaged you at your own wedding by going into labor."

"Hardly her fault."

"She could have kept the screaming to a minimum until the minister finished."

I sighed. "I want to shake her right now."

"Get in line."

I sank down on the bed and put the empty glass on the nightstand.

"We'll find her." Emma kicked me gently, which was as supportive as my younger sister ever got. "But not tonight. You look like you've been wrung out like a towel. Is this what sex does to you? Because I can see why you avoid it if —"

"I did not have sex with anyone."

"Too bad," said Emma. She lay back on the bed and noticed the horse slobber stain on her shirt. She picked at it. "You should give him a chance."

I flopped back on the bed and looked at the ceiling. Too much adrenaline had exhausted me, but I knew who she was talking about. "Libby says he's a criminal."

"Consider the source." She gave up on the stain and stretched out her stiff leg. Then she looked at the ceiling, too. "I thought he was kinda sweet. An Old World sort of guy, who'd maybe kill a man for touching his woman, you know? A little macho. But sweet."

"Sweet?" I had not considered him sweet when for an instant I thought he was ready to beat up Jonathan Longnecker on my behalf. The possibility had horrified me. "No, he's not sweet."

"Lighten up. He's trying to be nice. He's trying to take care of you. And from the looks of this place, you could use it."

We continued to gaze at the ceiling. Some water damage was starting to show in the corner. Before winter, I'd have to do something about the roof.

I said, "Why do people feel I need to be taken care of? I'm not a pushover."

"You're — I don't know — feminine. That automatically gives people the impression that you're helpless."

Looking over at my sister in her riding clothes, I decided nobody would ever mistake her for a helpless female. Yet I knew she was as soft on the inside as a woman could get. I made an inner vow to start exuding more self-confidence. Or buy myself a pair of riding boots and a slobber-stained shirt.

Emma said, "I've got to get up early and run over to Paddy Horgan's place. Dibs on the first shower. When I get back, we'll go look for Libby. Meantime, quit worrying. Libby might be a twit, but she's not stupid."

On Wednesday morning, I started putting the house back together and listened for the telephone. I willed Libby to call. She could explain everything, I was sure, and tell me what she wanted me to do. Meanwhile, I swept up glass and filled garbage bags with the broken rubble smashed by the vandals.

My collection had been scattered all over the floors. It needed a good thinning, I knew, but it was hard for me to part with books of any kind, even to a good cause like a library sale. Some of my shelves had been broken, so I stacked volumes on the kitchen table and in some of the cardboard cartons left over from my move to the farm.

Libby didn't call.

I took a break from cleaning to phone Detective Bloom. I figured he might have learned something about Rory's art collection by now. Surely the police had their hands on an inventory. It was only a matter of time before they discovered the folio was missing. And Jonathan Longnecker would point them straight at Libby.

I planned my questions to pry the most information out of Bloom without arousing his curiosity. But he was away from his desk, and his cell phone didn't answer.

At noon I brewed tea, and worked up my courage to phone Abruzzo. I found his business card with his various phone numbers. I tried them all, but he didn't answer.

Of course, I remembered. Abruzzo had

made arrangements to meet with Detective Bloom that morning. I hung up. No wonder I couldn't reach either one of them. They were probably slugging it out at the police station.

Around one, Emma returned with Wawa hoagies, a local delicacy that provided most of Emma's weekly calorie intake.

"I should go out this afternoon," I said. "I have an assignment for work. But I hate to leave the phone. What if Libby calls?"

"I'll stay here," Emma said, eating her sandwich as she poked through the pile of books on the table. "I can clean up a little. If you want, I'll haul this trash and broken furniture out in my truck. And I'll try phoning some of Libby's PTA pals, too."

"Good idea." It felt good to have an ally at last.

"I wonder," she said, pulling the onions out of her sandwich, "if maybe Libby and Ralph had a spat. Maybe she's just off sulking somewhere. It's her style. And Ralph may be too embarrassed to tell us the truth."

That didn't explain someone breaking into my house. We both looked at the mess again.

I said, "Maybe you shouldn't be here alone this afternoon."

"I'll be fine." She dusted the crumbs of

her sandwich onto the plate and carried it to the sink. "Paddy Horgan has some puppies right now. You should take one."

"What would I do with a puppy?"

"It would grow up into a dog." She saw my scowl and shrugged. "Just an idea. Where are you going today?"

"I have to cover a tea for the flower show fund-raising committee."

She leaned against the counter, folded her arms and gave me a wry look. "Wow. Take your smelling salts. The excitement may be too much to handle."

"I want to talk to some people about Rory's murder," I said. "And the tea party may be just the right place. It's at Peach Treese's house, and she's first on my list."

"Go for it." Emma came over and shuffled idly through the books on the table again. She fingered Michael Shaara's *The Killer Angels*. "What are you going to wear?"

Her oh so casual tone raised my suspicions. "Why do you ask?"

She grinned wickedly. "I think I can do something about your tendency to look like a nun no matter what you have on."

We raided Grandmama's dress collection, and Emma dragged out a lavender satin skirt with hundreds of tiny flowers that had probably been appliquéd by French nuns.

"You could probably sell this on eBay for a small fortune."

"On the other hand, I need something to wear this afternoon."

She studied the skirt with a critical eye. "Got any scissors?"

"You're kidding, right?"

"You could use a little sex appeal, Nora. Get me the scissors. It'll be fun."

I couldn't watch. My grandmother had traveled to Paris every spring to buy new clothes for her worldly lifestyle. Her taste wasn't always perfect, but she had shown a certain spunk in her selections that criss-crossed various couture houses. I loved the pink silks, the beautiful bias-cut dresses and the slinky bathing suits meant for Cannes. I even liked her Grace Kelly period of the wasp-waisted dresses with the flouncing skirts. Most of the pieces were still pristine. When I'd first started attending parties for the *Intelligencer*, desperation had driven me to the cedar-lined closets where the exquisite clothing had been packed in delicate paper or hung on padded hangers.

But Emma had no reverence. She hacked, studied, hacked again. "Now try it on and let me see how it looks."

I did as I was told. The skirt came to my

midcalf, but was now slit up to my thigh. I received a fashion thumbs-up from Emma. She selected an eggplant-colored tank top for me to wear with the skirt. The thin straps meant no bra. Usually I wore a sweater over it, but Emma stopped me.

"But —"

"Don't argue," she ordered. "Put on some Band-Aids if you want to go modest."

As I slathered on sunblock, she asked, "Do you have a gardening hat?"

"Oh, Em, people will think I'm the Queen Mother."

"Trust me," said Emma, working magic with the hat by punching it a few times. "You won't look like the Queen Mum."

She finished me off by hauling a pair of very high heels out of my closet. "There."

I looked at my reflection. I wasn't accustomed to seeing quite so much bare skin. Or my own coloring so heightened by the combination of hues Emma had put together.

"For a garden party?"

"You bet."

Dressed and made up, I took one last look at myself and decided I needed Emma every time I got dressed. But I could also use some of her chutzpah to carry it off.

Reed arrived with the car and looked me

over more carefully than before. He made no comment, of course, but drove me into the Main Line neighborhood.

The Philadelphia Flower Show, the biggest event of its kind in the world and still a success thanks to a wonderful mix of creative minds, hard work and big money, attracted some of the city's most interesting people to its leadership. I enjoyed their company and looked forward to writing about their fund-raiser in the newspaper. I just needed a clever hook for my story.

The horticultural society had chosen the garden of Peach Treese for the fund-raiser long before Rory Pendergast's death. Her estate adjoined Rory's. Peach kept a beautiful rose arbor, but the centerpiece of her magnificent landscape was the peach orchard. The rest of the grounds had been manicured to perfection, I knew, in preparation for the upcoming wedding, but the orchard was her triumph. She had been generous enough to allow the society to use the garden for their event, and I respected her for encouraging it to continue so soon after Rory's death.

"Peach couldn't join us this afternoon," said one of the ladies who greeted me at the gate, discreetly fending off inappropriate questions. "I'm sure we all understand.

Aren't we lucky to have this wonderful sunshine today?"

I checked my disappointment. I'd come to see Peach, but she was in hiding.

In my high heels, I stayed on the stone walkway and strolled around the side of the house to the upper gazebo. From there I could see the full vista of the garden spreading away from the house to the orchard. The rose arbor bisected the lawn, and I knew it provided a covered walkway almost the whole distance between Peach's back door and Rory's conservatory. Today, however, long tables of refreshments had been set up beneath the arbor. The roses were just starting to bloom. In a few days, they would be exquisite for the wedding. I took a moment to appreciate the beautiful landscape and the hard work it required.

"Nora!"

I turned. Coming towards me up the slope, Eloise Tackett waved her empty champagne glass. The breeze ruffled the tips of her white hair that blew out from beneath the brim of her straw pith helmet. She looked as if she'd walked out of darkest Africa by way of Sissinghurst. I gave her a kiss and a hug.

"Where's Harold today?"

"At home working on a puzzle," Eloise

said, not even slightly out of breath after climbing up the slope. "Don't you look wonderful today, dear. So artistic."

"I have Emma to thank. She's my new wardrobe consultant."

"Put her on the payroll," Eloise advised.

I laughed. "Are you on the fund-raising committee?"

"Not this year." Eloise leaned closer and whispered, "They kicked me off the team. I didn't bring in my quota last year. Harold is furious with them, but I thought I'd come today and hold my head up high."

"You have every right to. You've been a mainstay of this organization for years."

"Don't say how many years," she cut in, smiling. "But you don't want to hear about horticultural politics, do you? Some of these old bats are still pouting about your mother and father, aren't they?"

"I can't blame anyone. Mama was an awful leech. I don't think she picked up a lunch tab for ages. And she didn't keep her promises, either."

Eloise nodded. "I know. She pledged money to the committee and reneged. There's no faster way to get yourself black-balled than not paying the piper. But you can hold your head up, Nora. Besides, some of these people need to get a life. Who said it? Women ought to raise more hell and fewer dahlias."

I laughed. "You go, girl!"

Eloise linked her arm through mine and we started to stroll down into the garden where other guests mingled.

I decided to take the bull by the horns and said, "Eloise, have the police questioned you about Rory's death yet? I know they're talking to everyone who attended the party."

"Why, yes. A nice young man came to see us yesterday. Detective Bloom. He wanted to know where Harold and I were during the party. And he asked a great many personal questions, which I found highly inappropriate. What a shame such a nice young man has such a tawdry job."

"Hmm," I murmured.

"I thought it best to profess complete ignorance. That's the way to stay out of trouble. Especially at my age. People just think I'm dotty if I don't remember. And poor dear Harold was worried they might confiscate my gun."

"Your gun," I said. "You mean your shotgun?"

"And this one, too." Eloise opened her handbag to show me. "I never go anywhere without it. It's such a comfort to both of us, you know. Once you get to be a certain age, Nora, you become a target for all kinds of crime."

Nestled between Eloise's snowy white handkerchief and her neat Gucci wallet lay a small silver handgun with a pearl handle. I recoiled from the deadly weapon as if it were a snake.

"Eloise! My God, is it safe to carry such a thing?"

She snapped her bag shut, pleased to have surprised me. "My dear, I've been carrying weapons more lethal than this little pea-shooter since before you were born. Harold finds it very reassuring. He'd be so upset if the police took it away from me. But I think the detective was more interested in people than weapons."

"What people?"

"Well, that Treese woman, for one."

"Bloom asked you about Peach?"

"Yes, but I didn't tell him a thing." Eloise tilted her chin bravely. "I may not like the woman much, but I'm certainly not going to blab to strangers about her. The same for Harold. They asked him about his days at the newspaper, but he didn't tell them anything. What could events of thirty years ago tell the police about Rory's plans for the *Intelligencer*?"

"I don't know. But if the paper were being sold, a lot of people would be affected."

"Well, what does that have to do with us? Honestly, Nora, we live quietly and don't interfere with anyone, and we like being treated just the same way."

Her tone made me reconsider my plan to ask more questions.

Instead, I said, "Eloise, thank you for introducing me to Jonathan Longnecker."

"Oh, did you enjoy meeting him? Isn't he charming?"

"We had a good discussion. He seems to know his business," I said diplomatically. "And he's passionate about it."

"Oh, yes. He and Harold hit it off from the start for that very reason." Eloise clapped one hand to her chest in rapture. "Look at those wonderful *Iris sibirica!* One of my favorite flowers. Look at the color!"

"They're lovely. Eloise, did Jonathan Longnecker help Harold build his collection?"

"Well, he led Harold in the right direction many times." She waved at an elderly friend across the lawn. The friend squinted, leaning on a cane, but didn't wave back.

"I gather Harold and Rory's relationship hadn't been friendly for a long time."

Eloise walked a few paces in silence.

Then, voice lower, she said, "They hated each other."

"Do you really think so?"

"I know it," she said. "Oh, I'm sure everyone thinks Harold is an easygoing sweetheart, but he has his moments. And Rory was so cruel to him sometimes."

"Cruel?"

"Yes, rubbing Harold's nose in his failures. Puffing himself up sometimes. Just a year ago they were bidding on the same piece, an exquisite thing, but Rory pulled some strings and got it for himself. He didn't play fair. And then there was —" She caught herself. "Well, now he's gone."

"Yes."

"I'm sorry, Nora. I know you were fond of him."

"I'm sure he had his faults. Everyone does."

"He was a nasty old man," Eloise said firmly. "And I should know. I'm glad he's dead."

Distressed, I began, "Oh, Eloise, I know you love Harold very much but —"

"I'd do anything for my Harold. I should have filled Rory Pendergast full of buckshot when I had the chance, but I didn't. Now I — well, I only hope Harold can have a few years of peace now that Rory isn't around to spoil his small pleasures."

I wanted to hear more, but there was no way to question Eloise without upsetting her, I could see. Tears sparkled in the corners of her eyes, and she turned abruptly way from me.

Two women from the committee came up to us then, and Eloise pretended to be examining a brass plate at the base of one of the trees while I engaged the women in a banal conversation about the garden.

"This is so much better than last year!" cried the first woman.

"Oh, and remember the year we had the party at the Smythes'? Hundreds came because they'd never seen the inside of that wonderful house? Except on the day of the party, the Smythes locked all the doors and even made everyone use those horrible porto-potties and nobody got so much as a peek inside!"

They laughed.

"It's too bad Peach couldn't be with us today," said the first woman. "I'm sure we could have lifted her spirits by admiring her beautiful handiwork here."

"I hear she's very upset," the second woman murmured. "Taken to her bed with grief."

I heard Eloise give a huff of derision and said quickly, "It's probably for the best that they're planning a wedding. I understand it's going to be here on the grounds."

The ladies brightened. "Yes, and the bride is here today. She's so pretty. But so thin! I suppose she's dieting to get into her wedding gown. But won't the garden be an exquisite setting for a nuptial celebration?"

I decided I had my story idea. "Eloise, I think I'll go look for Pamela. Would you like to come along?"

Eloise straightened briskly and smiled. "Thank you, Nora, no. I'm on my way home to Harold. I promised I'd stop and buy him a Big Mac for his dinner tonight, and I want to have it on the table at five-thirty sharp."

I said good-bye and went off in search of Pamela Treese, the bride-to-be.

Chapter 16

Instead I found Jill Mascione pouring tea under the arbor. "Good grief," I said. "No wonder you never have time for lunch with me. You're always working."

She looked up from refilling china teapots from a large tank worn over her shoulder. In her right hand, she held the nozzle of the hose. Her face was damp from steam, and her black hair more flyaway than ever. "This is our second event today, and we still have a cocktail party to do tonight on Boathouse Row."

"Who's having the cocktail thing?"

"Some museum people. The art crowd. It's at Lexie Paine's place."

I had received an invitation myself and forgotten about it. Lexie lived in a wonderful little pad on Boathouse Row, and she gave terrific parties. Parties that would be bursting with art connoisseurs. And maybe Jonathan Longnecker.

"Say, Jill, Emma said she saw you at Libby's house on Saturday morning."

"Saturday?" She replaced the lid of a

freshly filled teapot. "I don't remember."

"Did you go to see Ralph Kintswell? Something about the rehearsal dinner?"

"Oh, right. Yeah, I was there. Dad sent me to go over details with Ralph."

"Did you see Libby?"

Jill frowned. "For a minute, I guess. She was around. Why?"

"She went away for a couple of days and I can't reach her. I wondered if she said anything to you, or maybe you heard her speak to Ralph?"

"About what?"

"I don't know. Anything. I'd like to find her."

Jill kept moving down the table. "I didn't pay attention to her, I guess. I was having it out with Ralph."

"About the dinner."

"Yeah, he wanted some last minute changes. We can't do that kind of thing, you know. We already bought the food. We're barely breaking even anyway. Ralph can't switch on us just because his budget got tight. Listen, I've got to fix these trays."

"Of course. I'm sorry to interrupt. I'm looking for Pamela Treese."

"The bride? She just went inside. Probably to throw up."

I raised my eyebrows. "Something wrong with the food?"

"Nothing except the calories," Jill retorted. "No, I think she's checking on her grandma."

"Peach is here?" Automatically, I looked up at the bedroom wing. Curtains had been drawn upstairs, I noticed. "I thought she might be staying at her daughter's house while everyone was here today."

Jill shook her head, moving away. "I took her some tea and scones half an hour ago. She ate like a truck driver."

"Think I could sneak inside and see her?"

Jill shrugged. "Fine by me. Use the kitchen entrance."

I followed the flagstone walk around the side porch and slipped past a waiter who emerged from the kitchen bearing a tray of watercress sandwiches. Not an inspired menu, I thought, although Main Events had clearly done a beautiful job of preparing and stylishly serving the boring menu selected by the committee. Kitty Keough would find a way to make that snide observation about the committee in the newspaper column. But who did cutting remarks serve?

The kitchen was orderly. I ducked past Sam Mascione slinging plates into the dishwasher. I waved. If not for him, I might be a murder suspect myself.

I had been in Peach's house twice in my life and knew to push through the swinging kitchen doors, pass through the butler's pantry to a narrow hallway and finally go through a heavy paneled door to end up under the archway that led to the foyer of the grand house.

I stopped under the archway. The paneled door swung shut behind me with a sharp noise.

"Dammit, I won't have that woman on my property!"

I froze, recognizing Peach Treese's voice above me on the staircase. Her words cut across the noise of the door. But I was caught in the age-old eavesdropper's dilemma. I could either stay and listen now that the door prevented me from making a silent escape, or I could announce myself and risk the embarrassing consequences.

"Grammy, please. Let's go upstairs and —"

"Why is she here?" Peach shouted. "Just to torment me! She's out there parading around like she owned him!"

I had hesitated too long and now my curiosity kept me where I was. The argument continued on the stairs.

"Please don't be upset," Pamela coaxed.

"Well, she didn't own him," Peach bellowed, sounding far from the sedate, composed woman I knew. "She might have enjoyed his company from time to time, but he was mine! Mine!"

"I know, Grammy."

"He shouldn't have kept her a secret! If I'd known about her, I'd never — I wouldn't — I can't believe the old goat thought he could get away with having two mistresses! And for godsake, she's *old!*"

Then Peach burst into tears and I heard her rushing footsteps go up the stairs. Five seconds later, a door slammed on the second floor.

I heard Pamela curse indelicately, and then she came down into the foyer. She saw me and stopped on the marble floor, twelve feet away.

"I'm sorry," I said. "I didn't mean to eavesdrop."

Pamela Treese, very young and so painfully slim that her eyes looked like they'd been drawn by a Disney cartoonist, sighed and came towards me. "She hasn't been herself, you know. She's very upset about Rory."

"I know."

"She didn't mean anything just now. It's just that Eloise makes her furious."

Eloise Tackett? Eloise and Rory?

"Rory's death was horrible," Pamela continued, "and now my wedding — it's just such a terrible strain on everyone." Big tears welled up in her Bambi eyes and she began to cry.

I barely knew Pamela, but I gave her a hug. Putting my arms around her, I realized she was beyond thin. She was hardly more than brittle bones and creamy skin. I patted her bony back and recognized a champion vomiter. "It's okay, darling."

"N-no, it isn't," Pamela cried. "Grammy has gone crazy, and I — I'm supposed to be on my best behavior and it — it's just t-too hard. I can't wait for the wedding to be over!"

I pulled her into the sitting room, and we perched on the edge of a silk-upholstered Chippendale sofa. A huge longcase clock towered over us, ticking sonorously. I gave Pamela the linen handkerchief from my handbag, and she snuffled prettily into it for several minutes while I placated her with nonsense.

"Just give her a few more days," I said. "She'll calm down, and the wedding will be beautiful. It just takes time."

Pamela sniffed and looked hopeful. She stopped twisting the handkerchief between her bitten-down fingernails.

"Is your dress ready?" I asked, hoping to

divert her. "And the flowers ordered?"

Pamela nodded. "We decided against releasing the doves. Lincoln kept joking they were, like, going to crap on the guests."

"Well, he's a sensible young man like his father," I said.

"So we're having a shower of rose petals instead. I just hope they don't smell like compost."

"And your honeymoon?" I asked. "Are you going away?"

"Two weeks in Italy," Pamela said, beginning to perk up. "Then we're moving into a house on Delancey Street. It's being painted while we're traveling."

"It sounds as if you have everything beautifully planned," I soothed.

She looked a lot like her grandmother, despite her complete lack of body fat. Very straight with a natural elegance that would, unfortunately, be ruined by osteoporosis by the time she was fifty. Perhaps she didn't have Peach's intelligence, but a few years of good books and sensible friends might do the trick.

Pamela smiled fetchingly at me. "Can I tell you a secret?"

"Well —"

"We found our surrogate!"

"Your — ?"

I must have looked completely blank, because Pamela laughed. "For our baby! I haven't had a period since I was fourteen, so we're using a surrogate. She's the sweetest thing — from Norway, blond genes, you know — and I think it's going to work out wonderfully. Our lawyer is closing all the loopholes now. We want to be sure she never sees the baby, of course."

I had no clue what the proper response should be to such a revelation. "How nice," I managed to say, abandoning the hope that even graduate school could help Pamela.

"Do you think I need to go back to the party?" she asked, as empty-hearted as a junior-high cheerleader. "I'd really rather skip the tea. The sight of all that food makes me nauseous."

I patted her hand. "Everyone will understand you must look after your grandmother."

"She's beside herself," Pamela confided. "She found out Rory had a girlfriend and went ballistic."

"It must have been a terrible shock."

"Yeah, but, like, what did she think? She wouldn't sleep with him, so of course he went looking for someone else. Men are such pigs."

"All those years with Rory, she never — ?"

"Not once," Pamela said proudly. "And who could blame her? I mean, he wasn't exactly gorgeous. Or even very clean."

I thought Rory looked perfectly sanitary, and I was willing to stack my judgment up against anybody's — except perhaps that of Pamela Treese, who now that I looked more closely, appeared to have scrubbed her hands down to a new layer of pink, scaly skin.

"So who cares if he slept with Eloise Tackett?" Pamela went on. "Let her have him! It's what Grammy had with Rory that counts. Public respect. Dignity. But she's gone postal about it. I'm so glad we don't have a gun in the house."

"You don't think Peach would harm Eloise?"

"Who knows? It must have been humiliating. When Grammy found that drug in Rory's hand!" Pamela shuddered in disgust.

"The Viagra?"

"Right, and then she figured out that the Tackett woman gave it to him, well, you can imagine how manic she got."

"How did Peach discover Eloise gave Rory the Viagra?"

"She interrupted them discussing it. She was so furious! I thought maybe she had — Well, no, she wouldn't hurt Rory."

Wouldn't she? I tried to remember the way Peach looked as she came down the staircase that night. She'd been distraught over her argument with Rory. Or had she killed him? Were the police right in their pursuit of her after all?

Stunned, I managed to say, "I'm sure she's glad to have you here."

"Thank you." Pamela stood up. "I'd better get back to her. You've been very kind."

"I'll find my own way out," I said.

She went upstairs, and I staggered back through the kitchen, wondering if Harold Tackett knew his wife had been having an affair with Rory Pendergast. Or had Eloise successfully diverted Detective Bloom's questions with her blunt denials?

Outside, I found the *Intelligencer* photographer waiting for me under the arbor. It was Sara Jane, the same young woman who had snapped the pictures of the mayor. I felt as if we'd bonded that night, and she obviously agreed. We conferred with the committee chair and decided on the photographs. I suggested a backdrop of the rose arbor, which might come in handy with the article I intended to write about Pamela's wedding. I thought readers might like a prewedding peak at the garden.

The committee chair was a birdlike woman in a huge straw hat and short white gloves with daisies embroidered on the wrists. Her hands fluttered nervously as she talked. "We invited the Pendergast sisters to come," she explained. "They were supposed to plant a peach seedling to honor Mrs. Treese, but they didn't return my calls, and I'm sure they don't intend to come so soon after their brother's funeral, but I do wish they'd phoned because I could have made alternative plans, so now I just don't know what to do!"

"We'll take a few general photos of everyone else," I said. "Some candid shots of your guests enjoying themselves will be wonderful."

"Well, if you think so," she whimpered, then walked off mumbling anxiously.

The photographer enjoyed snapping pictures of beautifully dressed women against the backdrop of the lavish garden. A few men in ice cream suits and straw boaters lent just the right air of charm and civility to promote the flower show. I began to hope the photos would be so pretty that nobody on the committee would miss the Pendergast sisters.

My mind flew back to the news that Rory and Eloise Tackett had been lovers. I

268

couldn't believe it. Eloise seemed so devoted to her husband. Had she strayed from her marriage? With a man her husband made no bones about despising? A man she obviously disliked herself?

Did the police know where the Viagra came from?

I wondered if Jonathan Longnecker could tell me about the Tackett-Pendergast relationship since he had worked for both families.

I found Jill again behind the tea tables. "The party you're working tonight at Lexie Paine's. Did you say it was going to be for museum people?"

"That's what I was told. We made sushi. God, I hope Dad didn't make them too early. He doesn't pay attention to that kind of detail sometimes."

I made a mental note to avoid the sushi.

Just as I was about to leave, I noticed a small entourage come through the gate that bisected Rory's boxwood hedge. The group entered Peach's garden and began to make a majestic procession along the rose arbor.

"It's the Pendergast sisters!" an awestruck bystander whispered near me. "They've been supporters for years."

"I never thought they'd come today," murmured another voice.

Lily Pendergast wore another black dress — this one covered with floating bits of chiffon that gave her the look of a haute couture scarecrow. Her shorter sister was decked out in yet another extravagant tracksuit with a matching baseball cap decorated with flowers. I decided to keep my distance as they were greeted by a flock of committee members.

Someone dragged out a potted peach tree, and someone else began to make a garbled speech. The photographer took pictures of everyone. Lily and Opal Pendergast each accepted a gold-painted shovel.

It was only a ceremonial shovel of dirt, but I watched as the sisters each hefted their garden tools with surprising strength for their ages.

My mind was full of adultery and sexual conquest among the elderly. I mused about fratricide as the Poison Gas Sisters dug into Peach Treese's flower bed. Had they spent their years wishing they had control of the family money while their brother trotted the globe, bought extravagant art and gained influence among powerful people?

No, it seemed unlikely that they had murdered their brother for his fortune. They looked pretty well-off to begin with. And I assumed they had inherited a cut of their father's estate. They lived in comfort in Palm Beach, after all.

But now that they had the whole fortune in their clutches, would they want more? Did they plan to sell Rory's newspaper and put me out of a job before I had really sunk my teeth into work? Maybe the idea of running a newspaper — even from a civilized distance — was too much responsibility for two ladies to handle at their ages.

Well before Rory's death there had been rumors that he was considering selling the paper. But could the possible sale of the paper have driven some employee to murder?

I thought of Kitty Keough's rant about the *Intelligencer.* I remembered the look on her face as she shouted at me. She might have been so terrified of losing her hard-fought social position that murder seemed the only way she could keep her job. Except, I reasoned, if she'd killed Rory, her plan had backfired. The Pendergast sisters might well destroy Kitty's raison d'être.

"Tch, tch," said another committee member. "They look happy as larks, don't they? And their dear brother barely cold in his grave."

Chapter 17

My friend Lexie Paine knew how to throw a party. First of all, she had a great time herself.

"Darling!" she cried, throwing her arms around me. "You poor dear, what a trial. A trial! You must have a drink. What will you have? Anything but red wine. Somebody always stains my carpet when I serve red wine, so I've sworn off. Name your poison. Please don't make me drink alone."

"You're having Perrier, aren't you?"

"Well, yes." She waggled her empty martini glass. "But I have to keep up appearances. Are you totally whacked, sweetie? If you are, it doesn't show a bit. Not a bit. You look absurdly gorgeous. Love the duds."

Lexie, of course, looked deceptively delicate in a black slip dress that matched her sleek black hair. But her square shoulders belied hours of paddling her kayak on the river, and the warrior's gleam in her eye bespoke a keen intelligence that made her a financial whiz. Good thing, too, since she'd inherited a truckload of money when her investment banker father passed away a decade earlier. She'd made partner in her father's old financial firm by age thirty and looked to be on her way to running the show when his contemporaries cashed in their portfolios. The museum had begged her to join their board, and she had the right combination of money smarts and good taste to help lead that institution to even greater heights.

Plus she was a hoot.

She linked her arm with mine and ducked her head furtively close. "I hear you're taking no prisoners as Kitty Keough's protégée. Is it kill or be killed? Pistols at dawn? Death by — oh, heavens. I'm sorry. What am I babbling about?"

"It's okay. A little gallows humor is just what I need."

Lexie lived along Boathouse Row, the stretch of picturesque Victorian boathouses built by private rowing clubs that still sculled the river in shells and conducted colorful regattas. The turrets and gables of the old houses were almost as picturesque as the scads of handsome athletes who decorated the riverscape on weekends and evenings. A lover of the water, Lexie bought a boathouse that had fallen into disrepair and she was living on the upper floors in renovated splendor. She had swooped into Pottery Barn one afternoon for simple, disposable furniture, but the walls were adorned with truly beautiful works of art from the collection of her mother, a woman of discerning taste and double fortune after remarrying an Argentinean named Helmut.

My favorite painting in the boathouse depicted a black-haired woman who had thrown herself in naked abandon on a heap of golden pirate treasure and luxuriated in the riches.

Lexie said, "I want to hear about everything. The rumors are rampant, darling. Did you really find poor Rory? Are the police using rubber hoses? And what's this about a man you're seeing? I mean, finally, dear! Finally!"

"What man?"

"Someone saw you with a veritable blacksmith, sweetie. A linebacker. A longshoreman! Shoulders out to here." Lexie threw her arms extravagantly wide. "I can't wait to hear the gory details."

"There is no gore, especially not in public," I said, glancing around the crowd that lolled on her sofas and eyed me with frank curiosity over their drinks. "It's not nearly as exciting as you imagine. In fact, it's a little scary."

"Oh, how delicious."

"Listen, Lex, I need to find somebody tonight, and I thought he might be here with your museum friends. Jonathan Longnecker. Do you know him?"

"Know him? Not in the Biblical sense, of course, since he's purely the other persuasion." Lexie popped her dark eyes wide in mock despair. "I hope he's not your blacksmith. He hardly qualifies."

"No, no, I just need to talk to him."

Lexie saw my expression and got serious in a hurry. "Why, honey, are you all right? What's wrong?"

My friend's immediate concern caused my throat to clog up. "It's Libby. She's done something stupid, and I'm trying to figure out what before she ends up — well, you know Libby."

"Yes, I do," said Lexie. "She's done some work for the museum, you know. She has a talent for restoration. I think she'd have a future in the biz if she weren't such a ditz."

"I know. She's created a real mess this time."

"Can I help?"

Lexie, with her connections to the museum, had a lot to lose if she became entangled in a scandal. I said, "I'll talk to Longnecker first. Maybe he can tell me what I need to know."

"If you think so." She looked doubtful. "He's a jerk, you know."

"I'll run up a flag if I need help."

She gave me a hug and took me out to the balcony that overlooked the river. A heavy smell rolled in off the water, as if rain were on the way.

Jonathan Longnecker was nuzzling the neck of a college boy. He looked up, annoyed at our interruption, then realized who we were and straightened in a flash.

"Jonathan," said Lexie, "Nora is my friend. Play nice or I'll cut you off at the knees. Come with me," she said, crooking her forefinger at the boy. "I'll get you another Pepsi."

With Lexie's daunting power and influence backing me up, I seemed to have gained a few respect points in Longnecker's mind. But he wasn't ready to be completely nice to me. So he sulked. "So?" he asked. "Where's your goon?"

"Truce," I said, going to the railing beside him. "If we could go to neutral corners for a minute, we might both benefit."

He raised one eyebrow and folded his arms over his chest in the pose of a suave matinee double agent. "What does that mean?"

"I need to know about Rory Pendergast's relationship with Harold and Eloise Tackett."

"The three amigos? What do I get if I tell you anything?"

"A little closer to your Chinese folio."

His gaze flicked towards the house where Lexie's voice rose in laughter at someone's joke. He said, "I'm listening."

"Rory collected the same kind of art that Harold does, right?"

"The sexy stuff? Yeah."

"And they competed for the same pieces from time to time."

"So?"

I pinned him with a look. "If you were working as an agent for both of them, I suppose you might have offered the same pieces to both Harold and Rory."

"It wasn't unethical," Longnecker said quickly. "The pieces always went to the highest bidder."

With quite a bit of encouragement from Longnecker, I supposed, who stood to make his commission on the sale no matter what. The higher the price, of course, the higher the commission.

"And the folio?" I asked. "Did you offer it to both of them? I can ask Harold for the truth, you know."

"Then why don't you?"

I took a deep breath. "Because I'd rather hear it from you and keep the matter between us."

His gaze sharpened on me as he realized I was offering to keep my mouth closed about his business practices. "Okay," he said slowly. "Maybe I mentioned the folio to Harold. But it turned out to be useless. Pendergast fell hard and wanted to keep it. Once the folio was off the market, there was no sense teasing Tackett. Actually, I felt sorry for the old guy."

"You're all heart. Harold wanted the folio badly?"

"He practically drooled. It would have been a nice cornerstone for his collection. And I told him so. The folio would have elevated his stuff into a collection that would interest a museum. That got to him." Longnecker dimpled at the memory. "He started talking about leaving his collection to an institution someday. Even his wife got into the act."

"What do you mean?"

Longnecker looked at his manicure. "She called me herself asking if I could try again with Rory. She upped their offer by another million. But I said it was a lost cause."

I saw something smug in his expression. "Do you think she really gave up?"

"I know she didn't."

"How?"

Pausing for dramatic effect, Longnecker finally said, "I saw her the night Pendergast died. She went in to talk to him."

I caught my breath. "You saw her? Upstairs?"

Longnecker considered me. "Are you really going to keep your trap shut? I'm on the brink of my dream job right now. I don't want to screw that up."

"Give me more incentive. I gather you didn't tell the police that Eloise was in the upstairs corridor?"

"I may have forgotten to mention it."

"Did you tell the police anything about the folio? Do they know it exists?"

"They didn't hear about it from me. Look, Pendergast was supposed to give the folio to the Reese-Goldman, but he wouldn't let it go. When I figured out he'd given it to your sister for repair, I had hopes she and I could come to terms about my taking it without getting Rory involved. I mean, I have the letter he wrote promising to give it to us. I need the folio now for an exhibit. It'll make my career. It's only fair."

"Sounds like you had motive to kill him yourself."

"Oh, please." He shivered. "Who would want to touch that old guy?"

"So you thought you could convince Libby to hand it over. Just like that?"

"It was worth a shot. As soon as the Pendergast sisters know about the folio, they're going to lock it up tight. It'll take years of litigation to wrestle it out of their claws."

I wasn't so sure. The Pendergast sisters might be very happy to get rid of an item they considered offensive. The faster, the better.

I said, "Did anyone besides you see Eloise Tackett on the staircase?"

"She didn't come up the staircase. Colonel Mustard must have a secret passageway through the conservatory or something because I know she didn't use the stairs."

The elevator. Or the kitchen staircase. Chances were good Eloise had known Rory's house almost as well as her own. She'd been in his social circle for years, and as his mistress she wouldn't have needed a Clue game board to know about secret avenues in the Pendergast mansion.

I asked, "When she talked to him that night, did you hear them together?"

"I'm no eavesdropper," Longnecker said virtuously. "I just know she went in to dicker with Pendergast. She'd given up on money. She was going to offer him a trade."

"A trade?"

"She handed me drivel about having something Pendergast would want more than anything, even the folio."

Sex, I wondered? If she'd been his mistress, why would he want to trade the folio for something he'd been enjoying all along? Why buy the cow, as my grandmother used to preach, when he could have the milk for free?

Or was it the Viagra? Had Eloise planned to trade her husband's prescription for the priceless Zhejiang Folio?

All the details of various geriatric sexual relationships began to swim in my brain. I leaned against the balcony railing.

"You okay?" Longnecker asked.

"Yes."

"I know what you're thinking," Longnecker said. "Maybe I should have told the police about old lady Tackett being up there. But I have a clear conscience. I wasn't the only one who saw her."

I must have jumped. "Who else did?"

He smiled, pleased to have startled me. "Lots of people. Mrs. Treese, for one. A waitress, too, but maybe that was earlier. Oh, and that crazy woman from the newspaper, what's her name? She was up there for a few minutes, but she blasted off like a rocket after yelling at Pendergast for a while. And there was your sister, of course."

I felt my head go light, and I clutched the balcony railing.

"That's when I first asked her for the folio," Longnecker went on. "In the corridor outside Pendergast's room while he talked to Eloise Tackett."

"What was Libby doing up there?"

He shrugged dismissively. "Who knows?"

"Did you tell the police she was there?"

"Hell, no. I'm still hoping to get the folio from her."

"Did she — Why was she there?"

"I told you, I dunno. We talked about the folio, and she acted surprised that it was worth as much as it was. And when I offered her the finder's fee —"

"The what?"

"You heard me. I figured the best way to get the folio was to offer a bounty. A finder's fee. You know, to get the folio back to its rightful home."

"How much?" I asked, hardly able to summon my voice.

"I offered her a hundred thousand dollars."

I swallowed hard. "Did she take it?"

"Not yet," said Longnecker. "But she can have it the minute I get my hands on the folio."

A sudden wind blew it off the dark river, and the rain started to come down hard.

Chapter 18

At Blackbird Farm, Reed Shakespeare had insisted on escorting me inside the house. Boss's orders, he'd told me. He stood looking at the remaining mess that I hadn't managed to clean up before leaving earlier in the day. I had piled the pieces of broken chairs beside the refrigerator. An open cardboard carton of books sat on the kitchen table. Two black plastic trash bags full of rubbish were still on the floor where Emma had left them. She had not hauled anything away in her truck, as she'd promised.

Reed didn't move from the spot where he'd taken a single step inside the kitchen door.

"Reed," I said, "would you wait here while I run upstairs for a minute?"

"Yeah, okay."

I took the stairs fast and went straight to my lingerie drawer. The folio was still there. With relief, I wrapped it up in my slip again and put it away.

Downstairs, Reed had not moved from the doorway. He said, "There's a note on the table."

In all the mess, I hadn't noticed a note. It was written on one of the Post-it notes I kept for making grocery lists. Emma had stuck the paper square on a book as if she had pulled the book from the carton on the table and used it for support as she wrote.

She said, "Had to go. Call you sometime. Em."

The book was *The Killer Angels*, the one she'd been looking through over lunch. I considered hurling it against the wall. Of all the times for Emma to choose to run off with one of her boyfriends . . .

Reed stayed in the doorway, but his nonplussed gaze swept around the kitchen and over to the swinging door that led to the dining room. "You don't mind my saying, this place doesn't look like I imagined from the outside."

"Believe me, living here isn't what I imagined either." I leaned against the table. I'd thought a leaky roof was bad enough when I moved in, but I hadn't counted on vandalism to lower my property values, too. "Someone broke in here yesterday."

"Really busted it up," Reed commented. Starting to show signs of concern, he asked, "You live here alone?"

"My sister sometimes stays."

"She here now?"

I waved the note. "No."

"You got anybody else to come tonight?"

I'd been filing through my mental Rolodex to come up with someone I could ask to stay in the house with me. I didn't want to be a wimp, but I wasn't quite ready to face any returning vandals on my own. "I'm thinking."

Reed appeared to be struggling with an inward argument. Although he tried to be an adult all the time, he occasionally looked very young indeed. Slowly, he said, "I'd stay myself, but I got a test in the morning."

"This isn't your problem, Reed."

"You got a dog?"

"No."

He frowned. "Dog would be good right now. Big Rottweiler, maybe."

"I'll be fine."

I must not have been terribly convincing because after a couple of heartbeats, he said, "I'm not supposed to leave you anywhere that doesn't look safe. I think I better call the *jefe*."

"This is my house, Reed. It's perfectly safe. I only — Now, hold it!"

He must have come from a family where it was necessary to ignore the womenfolk now and then. He crossed the kitchen in three long-legged strides, picked up the phone without asking and dialed.

I knew who he was calling. "Reed, for Pete's sake, you can't just take matters into your own hands like this. I can call a number of people —"

He talked to Abruzzo anyway, referring to me only as "she." I steamed while they discussed my situation. Reed even walked to the refrigerator and opened it. He leaned in and reported, "Nothing but diet soda, peanut butter and a bag of something green."

"Reed —" I began.

"Yeah, okay," he said and hung up.

I glowered at him. "This is not the best way to endear yourself."

He glowered back. "That's not in my job description."

We continued to glare at each other while I tried to decide how best to yell at this young man who didn't want a boss or a friend or anyone else who required him to open up, admit a mistake or give an opinion. He didn't want to trust me, and until now he didn't want me trusting him, either. I hadn't been able to think of a way to get through to him, and here he was suddenly taking charge of my life.

Which was progress.

So I asked, "What about driving lessons?"

"Say, what?"

"I need someone to teach me to drive a car," I said. "My sisters are both maniacs behind the wheel, and we have trouble obeying each other anyway."

"So you want me to — ?"

"Teach me to drive."

Looking at me sideways, he asked, "Whyn't you just call one of those driving schools or something?"

"Because I think you drive very sensibly. And you seem to be a patient sort of person."

He shook his head. "I don't know."

"Think it over," I suggested.

I offered him a Diet Coke, which he accepted, although reluctantly. It seemed we had reached a new level of understanding in our relationship, if a man under the age of thirty was willing to drink a nonsugared soft drink to mark the occasion. He even straddled a chair at my kitchen table while I picked up the telephone again.

Sometimes in the face of a crisis, a girl needs to talk to her mother.

I got out my address book and placed an overseas call.

"Mama?" I said when the connection finally went through. "Mama, it's Nora."

288

"Nora! Hey, Butternut, it's Nora on the phone! Oh, he's asleep again, poor darling. I must have tired him out on the tennis court today. Sweetheart, how nice to hear your voice!"

"It's nice to hear your voice, too," I said, and it was. My mother sounded happy and carefree. Of course, in the midst of a fatal tax audit, my mother had been cracking wise and offering fashion tips to anyone who would listen. She called my father Butternut, and he called her Gingersnap, and they were happier than any two people had a right to be.

Sometimes I wished I could be like my parents. Disasters could befall them, and they managed to spring up out of the hot lava smiling. Their skewed view of the world enraged me sometimes. At other times, it sounded heavenly.

"What's going on?" she asked brightly, and I could almost see her settling back against lacy bed pillows for a nice chat, fluffing up the satin sleeves of her nightgown and fixing her hair with one hand. "Have you been to any fun parties lately? Libby tells me you have a new job!"

"*Libby* told you? Mama, have you seen Libby? Is she there with you?"

"For heaven's sake, why would she be

here? No, we talked on the phone a month ago. Was it a month? No, not that long. Maybe just last week. Well, anyway, she said you're going to fabulous parties and having a fabulous time!"

"Well, it's not quite that fabulous, Mama."

"Oh, you take things too seriously, Nora. Why don't you just cut loose and enjoy yourself? Be a little more like Libby. You deserve it, sweetheart."

"I'll try to do better," I promised and felt a smile growing on my face despite my mood. Libby and my mother shared a philosophy of life, and it was hard not to appreciate their naïve high spirits.

"Are you seeing any men?" she pressed. "I know you have a hard time letting anyone into your life, but it's high time you found a nice young man who will give me a grandchild."

"You have grandchildren, Mama."

"I will never have too many! Of course, looking at their pictures is so much easier than dealing with them in person. Until they're twenty-one, of course, and can have a cocktail with me when I start actually *looking* like a grandma. So? Are you going on any dates? Seeing anyone I know? A big strong man to snuggle up with?"

I felt my face turn pink as I realized Reed was listening to every word I said. I prayed he couldn't hear my mother. His face was impassive, so I hoped for the best. "No, no dates, Mama. I'm just working. And keeping tabs on my sisters."

"Why would you do that?" my mother asked, laughing. "They're perfectly capable of managing their own lives, you know."

"I think you're wrong about that," I muttered.

"What? What, dear?"

"Nothing, Mama. I just wanted to see if Libby was — if she had contacted you lately."

"Well, naturally we stay in touch, but it's just not the same. A mother hen needs to see her chicks once in a while." Her laughter trilled. "Can you get away this summer, do you think? Would you join us for a few weeks, perhaps?"

I doubted I could afford cab fare to the airport, let alone a ticket to their sumptuous new digs. But I said, "I'll try, Mama. Listen, I need some help. Do you remember any of Libby's college friends? Any school friends? Anyone named Sylvia, maybe?"

"Why would you — ? Oh, there was a Sandy, I think. That girl from Boca. No, Cyndi Lauper, right? Oh, no, that's a singer!" My mother laughed. "Sylvia, you say?"

"Yes, a school friend of Libby's."

"No, I don't think so. But I was never very good at remembering any of the friends you girls brought home. I just — Wait, there was a Sylvia, I think. Sylvia Whiteman. Or Blackman? It was a color. Her name was a color."

"From New York?"

"Heavens, dear, I can't remember her name, let alone her address! Let me think. It *was* Sylvia, but I can't quite recall her last name. Besides, wouldn't she be married by now?"

"Do you think Sylvia was at Smith with Libby? Or at Miss Porter's?" I could try tracking Sylvia through the school alumni records.

"Well, it seems a very long time ago, so it must have been Miss Porter's. But why on earth do you want to know?"

"Oh, I'm just tracking her down," I said vaguely. "For the wedding, you know."

"Which wedding? Are you invited, dear?"

"Of course, Mama. Ralph's son is the groom."

"Ralph?" she asked.

"Libby's husband."

"Oh, of course. I have a mental block

when it comes to your husbands. You girls are Blackbirds through and through, and you'll never have happy marriages. How many men have your aunts been through? Dozens, I swear. I'm so glad I'm just a Blackbird by marriage." She sailed into one of her patented parental lectures. "You should forget about husbands and be independent. Make your own happiness, all of you. You can rent chairs for a party, and I don't see why you can't have a good man the same way. Just when you need him. Would you like to speak with your father, sweetheart? I can try rousing him, if you like."

"No, no, that's all right. Just give him my love."

"Of course, Emma."

"It's Nora."

"Of course, dear. Well, give hugs and kisses to your sisters, will you?" She made kissing sounds into the phone.

"I love you, Mama."

When I hung up, Reed blew a sigh and said, "My mom's a pain in the ass, too."

Half an hour later, Abruzzo arrived in a wet yellow rain slicker that made me think of elementary school crossing guards. He carried a bag of groceries in one arm and tracked rainwater into the house. Then he tossed his car keys onto the kitchen counter like a man who intended to stay a while. I could see the handle of a toothbrush poking up from his shirt pocket.

I said, "I do not need a keeper."

We faced each other across the width of the kitchen table. We must have both had thunder on our faces because Reed mumbled something and left in a hurry.

"What happened?" Abruzzo demanded, when we were alone.

"Nothing happened," I snapped. "We got home and Emma wasn't here, so Reed took it upon himself to call the cavalry."

"You're pissed," he said, eyeing me as if I were going to explode. "Because we won't let you do something foolish?"

"Because you think I can't take care of myself. Maybe I was raised like some kind of hothouse flower, but I'm on my own now, and I'm doing just fine."

Which was a lie. My head hurt. My heart felt as if it would never beat normally again. And I had hot tears burning in the back of my throat that I was damned if I was going to release. So I asked, "Do you have any brothers or sisters who act like — like knuckleheads?"

The question didn't dumbfound him, but it took some of the heat out of his expression. "Sure. One sister and three brothers. Well, two brothers."

"What happened to the third one?"

He looked away and shook his head. "Nora —"

"What happened?"

"Really, you don't want to know." He peeled off the yellow slicker and slung it over the back of a kitchen chair.

My knees gave out and I sat down in the other chair. I put my elbows on the table and put my face into my hands. "My family is making me crazy."

"Yeah, I noticed." He began to unpack the groceries. He'd brought a bag of bagels, along with a box of pasta, some veggies and assorted other staples.

"I can't find Libby. I really can't. And I'm afraid she's gotten herself into something so huge that I — that nobody can get her out of it." I looked up again. "On top of that, tonight of all nights, Emma has obviously decided to run off with one of her ten thousand boyfriends, leaving me holding the bag!"

He came around behind me and used both hands to smooth my hair away from my face, then draw it into a ponytail at the back of my head. He leveraged my head gently backwards so I had to look up at him. He said, "I brought dinner."

"Is that your answer to everything? Food?"

"Call it a cultural stereotype. You can't help anybody if you're weak from hunger."

"I'm not weak. I'm just stark raving."

"Same thing. Go change into whatever you wear when you're not dressed up in a ball gown and I'll cook. You'll feel better. You'll be able to think straight."

I looked up at him and felt my heartbeat start to steady. I hadn't realized how hard it had been pounding. "If I promise to eat, will you tell me what happened to your brother?"

He released my hair. "This is the wrong time for that discussion."

"He's in jail?"

Abruzzo walked over to the stove and examined the selection of pots I kept hanging there. "No, my other brother is in jail. And the youngest one is working in Vegas under a name he won't even tell his mother. But Little Frankie is probably dead, so my family is hardly the yardstick for you to measure against."

"He's probably dead?"

"Probably," said Abruzzo.

So I burst into tears, naturally, and felt like an idiot all over again.

Abruzzo came over again and gathered

me up in a hug. "I'm sorry. I didn't mean Libby's dead."

"I know."

I slid my hands up his back and proceeded to make a big wet spot on his shirt. I babbled for a while, and he wisely didn't say anything until he'd handed over a clean handkerchief from his pocket and I stopped hiccoughing.

He told me to go upstairs and change in a tone that allowed me no wiggle room, so I went up to my bedroom and stripped off my grandmother's clothes and hung them on the padded hangers in my closet. Then I sat on my bed and composed my emotions. I congratulated myself on not fainting and began to feel a little better.

At last I dug out a pair of cashmere lounging pajamas Todd had given me one Christmas. I put them on and looked at myself in the mirror. They were loose and unrevealing, but comfortable and, okay, I knew the pale blue color made my skin look fabulous.

Meekly, I returned to the kitchen where pasta boiled on the stove and my guest flipped something aromatic in a sauté pan. He did not look like a blacksmith except maybe for the shoulders. And the glance he gave me when I entered in my pajamas made me feel as if the time I'd taken to comb my hair and reapply my lipstick had been well spent.

The kitchen was warm and smelled spicy. The salad from my refrigerator had been revived and sat on the table in a yellow bowl, the greens supplemented with strips of red pepper and tomato slices. A bottle of wine with a label in Italian stood breathing beside it. Two glasses gleamed in the glow of the old chandelier. The sound of steady rain beat on the roof, reducing the kitchen to a cozy port in the storm.

"Sit," he said. "And tell me what's happened."

"Tell me first what went on between you and Detective Bloom. You saw him today?"

"We didn't go over anything we haven't covered many times before. That, and he wanted to know what I discussed with Rory on the phone."

"Did you tell him?"

"Of course. I am a law-abiding citizen." He turned and offered me a taste from the wooden spoon.

I met his gaze over the steaming spoon and let his words hang in the air.

A heartbeat later, I asked, "Are you really law-abiding?"

His expression held steady — mild and a

little amused. But I thought I caught a flicker of uncertainty in his eyes, something I'd never seen before. He said, "What happens if my answer scares you?"

I took a deep breath. "I'm not afraid of you, Michael."

"Damn," he said softly. "I was hoping to intimidate you into bed pretty soon."

"Sorry," I replied. "You're out of luck."

We smiled at each other.

I noticed he didn't answer my question. Instead, he said, "Try the sauce."

I tasted the sauce on the spoon and nodded my approval.

The moment was over.

He turned back to the stove, saying, "Anyway, I gave Bloom the highlights of what I said to Rory, and he kindly spared me the handcuff routine. Your turn."

I sat on the chair and curled my feet up under me. I was surprised to realize how much I had learned since I'd seen him last, which hadn't been so long ago.

"In a nutshell," I said, "it was Grand Central Station upstairs in Rory's house the night he was murdered. Libby was there, and so was Jonathan Longnecker, who offered her a hundred thousand dollars to give the folio to him and not to Rory."

"But she didn't do it. The folio is here."

"Why?" I asked. "Why give it to me?"

Abruzzo continued to attend to the stove. "Maybe she doesn't need the money."

"As a matter of fact, her husband is paying for part of a very expensive wedding this weekend and could probably use every penny he can find."

He put down the sauté pan and came over to pour us each a glass of wine. "So how come she gave it to you?"

I sighed. "I don't know. Now that Longnecker has dangled such a huge finder's fee, I'm scared. It's upped the ante."

"Longnecker is the asshole at the restaurant?"

"Uhm, yes." I accepted the glass he handed me.

Abruzzo took a drink of the wine and held it on his tongue for a moment while he considered things. It occurred to me again that he might have a better insight into the criminal mind than I had, and I watched him think. Mostly, though, he seemed to be contemplating whether the wine was good or just passable.

Then he swallowed and said devastatingly, "What if Libby killed Rory and ditched the folio because it links her to the murder?"

I took a deep breath. "Oh, God."

"It's possible."

"She hasn't a violent bone in her body."

"Maybe she was angry. Maybe she attacked him and didn't realize he was dead."

"But why would Libby kill him?"

"To get the folio free and clear? If Longnecker was willing to pay a hundred grand for it, maybe somebody else would pay more."

"Harold Tackett," I said unsteadily. Or Eloise.

"Who?"

"A collector I know. He wanted the folio and was willing to pay Rory a lot for it. You don't suppose Libby tried to sell it to Harold? No, I can't accept that. She's not the sharpest knife in the drawer, but she's not that stupid. Or that desperate."

Abruzzo went back to the stove. "Okay, maybe she gave it to you so she wouldn't be tempted to sell it."

"How like Libby to ask me to enforce her moral code." I drank some wine. It went down like warm embers and cleared my head. "What if the folio isn't connected to the murder at all? What if I'm just making an assumption?"

"What do the police think?"

"Last I knew, they were still focused on Peach Treese."

Abruzzo looked over his shoulder at me.

"And you still think that's impossible?"

"I don't know anymore," I admitted. "Peach's granddaughter said Peach was furious to find Rory with Eloise Tackett. And I can vouch that she was really provoked about something when she came downstairs."

"Man, musical beds for Rory. Who'da guessed?"

"It gets worse," I said, steeling myself to tell him the rest. "Eloise took a bottle of Viagra to Rory. Either she intended to use it with him, or she hoped it would help convince him to sell the folio to her husband."

Abruzzo looked amused. "Which was it?"

"I don't know. I'm afraid to ask Eloise."

He nodded. "Being Emily Post has its drawbacks."

I bristled. "Some questions you just don't ask point-blank."

"In my family we ask and hope the other guy's right hook is slow."

I smiled at the joke. "It's not in my nature to be rude, even when murder is involved."

He tested the pasta, drained the pot with a practiced technique and tossed it with a dash of olive oil. He served portions onto two of Todd's grandmother's Limoges and then finished by neatly sliding the contents of the sauté pan over the gently steaming pasta. He slipped a plate in front of me and put one for himself on the opposite side of the table.

I inhaled the fragrance of sweet sausage, tomato, vegetables and basil. I said, "You cope well with hysterical women. And you can cook."

"I'm good-looking, too," he added, sitting down and reaching for the wine bottle. "And I don't need Viagra. At least, not yet."

On the other hand, he could blithely prepare a delicious meal while discussing cold-blooded murder.

He was correct about some things, though. Todd had been a little boy. And Mama was probably right, too. I had to make my own happiness, and that didn't have to include another husband. Maybe I should consider the possibilities.

I said, "Did you bring dessert?"

On Thursday morning, I tried phoning Emma at her apartment while Abruzzo showered upstairs after carrying his pillow and blanket up from the sofa where he'd spent the night. Emma did not answer. I turned on the *Today* show until Katie and Matt went outside to talk to the weatherman. I always turn off the sound when the people in Rockefeller Plaza start screaming. For a while it frightened me. Now it's just annoying.

Abruzzo came down with his hair still wet from the shower and took over making breakfast. I got out my address book and looked up a friend from Miss Porter's. Not a friend, exactly, since during her school years Rose Stine had stuck to her books and her one extracurricular club, a particularly hostile feminist group. She had gone back to the school after four years at a repressed southern college and now had a part-time job in the administrative offices. She had no sense of humor and a heightened loyalty to school procedures.

I asked her if she knew anyone named Sylvia Whiteman or Sylvia Blackman.

"Nora, I shouldn't give out that information." Her voice was as cold as if I'd asked to sell naked pictures of her classmates on the Internet.

"Rose, it's not an emergency, but it's getting there." I told her about Libby taking a powder and hiding out in New York. I might have fabricated a bit by suggesting Libby could have run away from an abusive husband.

Immediately, Rose promised to e-mail me a list of women in Libby's graduating class. I promised not to sell the list to any sexual terrorists.

While eating scrambled eggs and bagels, I decided to try reaching Emma at Paddy Horgan's place. Abruzzo poured coffee while I looked in the phone book. Paddy had two phone numbers, one in the house and one in the barn. I phoned the house first, but nobody answered. Paddy answered the barn phone himself, gruff and annoyed.

"Emma was supposed to be here last night," he said. "And again this morning."

"You mean she didn't arrive?"

I heard him spit tobacco before he said, "She didn't show."

"Why — ? I mean, do you — ?"

"I know she's working hurt," Paddy snapped. "Maybe she's not physically ready yet."

"I'm sure she's the best judge of that," I said hastily. "She didn't call to cancel?"

"No, she just didn't show. I can't have people like that in my barn," said Paddy. "I need responsible help."

I could barely shut off the phone because my hands shook so much.

"What?" said Abruzzo. He'd been looking through the books on the table while he ate his breakfast, but my conversation with

305

Paddy had drawn his attention. "Where's Emma?"

"I don't know," I said, suddenly sick. "She didn't go to work yesterday afternoon or this morning."

"She's with a boyfriend, did you say?"

"I assumed so, but this doesn't feel right. Oh, my God. She'd never miss work."

Don't panic, I told myself. *Think.*

I turned on my computer and went on-line. The e-mail from Rose Stine had come in already. She must have gone immediately to the database and sent me the names of Libby's classmates along with phone numbers, addresses and — heaven be praised — maiden names, too. I skimmed down the list. No Whiteman or Blackman.

Abruzzo had tipped the screen so he could read along with me. He pointed. "What about Redmond? Sophia Redmond. It's a New York address."

I grabbed the phone and tried to read the number and punch the right keys on the handset. I fumbled and tried a second time.

Abruzzo took the phone from me. "Let me try. Drink your coffee."

I let him dial and prayed Sophia Redmond stayed at home in New York.

"Hello," said Abruzzo into the phone, making eye contact with me across the table. "Sophia Redmond? No? Is she at home? Uh, *¿Está en casa, Senora Redmond?*"

He listened to the Spanish on the line for a moment and asked, "*¿No? Uh, ¿La conta usted con ella hoy? ¿Se quenda en la casa Senora Kintswell? ¿He llamado Kintswell?*"He waited while more Spanish flowed back at him. "*¿No? Gracias, gracias.*"

He disconnected the line and said, "Nobody's home and the maid has never heard of Mrs. Kintswell. Libby's not there. I can understand more than I can speak, but from the sound of things, she never was."

I got to my feet. "Maybe it's the wrong person. Maybe my mother got the name wrong. Maybe I should call Ralph to double-check."

Abruzzo and I looked at each other, and he did not hand over the phone.

I said, "You think Ralph is doing something wrong."

"I think he knows more than he's telling you. Either that, or he's not thinking many moves ahead."

Ralph wasn't stupid. But he was gentle and perhaps he was keeping the truth to himself to protect me from something. It was the kind of thing he might do, I thought. Wasn't it? I said, "Why would he keep Libby's whereabouts a secret?"

"Money. A business deal gone bad." He didn't finish his list.

I clutched my head. "I don't understand what's happening."

"You want some advice? I think it's time to call your buddy Gloom."

I sat down at the table again. "But if Libby's in legal trouble . . ." I began.

"Nora," he said, "it's past that."

Chapter 19

Detective Bloom told me he didn't handle missing persons and I should contact my local police. He was so busy — or so uninterested — that he didn't let me finish my sentences. It wasn't until I mentioned Libby's name on the phone that he said, "Your sister is Libby Kintswell?"

And I realized how long it was going to take the police to get up to speed. My own investigation was light-years ahead of where the police were, and by the time I could prove everything I felt sure I knew, God only knew where Libby would be.

"I'm scared," I told Abruzzo when I'd disconnected his cell phone.

We were in his Volvo and already halfway to Libby's house.

"Breathe," he advised and turned on the windshield wipers.

I obeyed. "He said to call the local police, but he wants me to come to him to talk, too."

"Not a good idea," advised Abruzzo, driving through puddles of rain. "He'll hold you for days."

While the trails for my sisters got colder and colder.

I dialed 911 and was transferred to a New Hope policeman who took my information and invited me in for further conversation at my earliest convenience. I said I'd come as soon as I could, but I had things to do first. By then, we'd arrived in Libby's driveway and had climbed out of the car. I said I'd call back and hung up.

"What now?" Abruzzo asked when Arlo came over to say hello. He patted the damp dog, and Arlo wagged his tail. "Looks like nobody's home."

"The kids are probably at school. And Ralph's gone to work already."

"Listen," he said, "I'll stay out here by the door unless you call me. You can go in, but I'll be breaking and entering."

He was a useful person to know.

I went into Libby's house, calling her name. The place was still an appalling mess, perhaps more so. It had begun to smell even worse than before. A stack of pizza boxes had grown to an alarming height in the kitchen. Upstairs, the bedrooms looked like a train wreck.

Libby's matching set of tapestry-sided suitcases were still in her closet.

I went back outside and reported.

Abruzzo, with Arlo sitting at his feet,

stood looking across the driveway. "What's in the barn?"

We went over to the barn, and he put his shoulder to the heavy door. It slid open.

Inside, Libby's minivan.

With my hands almost too weak to function, I opened the passenger side door. On the floor between the seats sat Libby's Coach handbag. Hyperventilating, I pulled it out of the van, opened the zipper and found her wallet.

The next thing I knew, I was sitting in the Volvo with Abruzzo hunkered down on the driveway beside the open door, patting my hands.

He said conversationally, "I can see why you don't drive. You black out like somebody's thrown a light switch."

"I'm going to stop fainting," I said.

He nodded. "Okay."

"No, really. I'm going to learn not to do this."

"I'm thinking of learning to ski."

"If Libby's purse is here," I said, "she isn't shopping in New York."

"I know." He pushed my hair away from my face and studied me for signs of panic. Finding only a manageable quantity, he said, "Let's go find a pay phone."

"Why?"

311

"Because I need to make a couple of calls from a phone that's not necessarily wire-tapped."

"Do I want to know who you're calling?"

"No," he said and fastened my seatbelt.

He got in beside me and drove to a car wash that had a public telephone mounted near the change machines. While he spoke to someone who I hoped looked like Mike Tyson and had the counterintelligence smarts of James Bond, I used his cell phone to try Emma's number again.

He got back into the car two minutes later, his shoulders wet with rain. "Okay, somebody's going to keep an eye on the farm today. Now what?"

"Emma still doesn't answer her phone. Let's go to her place."

I gave directions, and we arrived in less than ten minutes. Emma lived in an apartment over an antiques shop in New Hope. The shop didn't open until eleven, so the parking lot in the back was empty. Not even Emma's truck was there. I ran up the rain-slick wooden steps to the second floor rear balcony. Emma's door was locked. I knocked and peered through the glass, but her lace curtains obstructed my view.

I leaned over the balcony railing. "It's locked. Should I break a window?"

Abruzzo came up the stairs. "No key under the mat? Over the door? In a flowerpot?"

We searched, but Emma hadn't left a spare key.

"Let me break the window," he said. "I can do it without making too much mess."

And he did. Rather than smashing the whole window, he flattened a credit card against the glass and used his pocket knife to tap the first crack. The crack grew as he rapped until it made a slightly irregular six-inch line, creating a triangle in the corner of the window. He slid the knife back into his pocket, the credit card into his wallet. Then with a sharp whack of his elbow, he broke in the triangle and slipped one hand carefully inside to unlock the door. The neat job took a quiet two minutes.

I looked up at him. "Sometimes you make me nervous."

"It's mutual," he replied. The door swung wide.

I stepped over the glass and went inside alone.

If Libby's house had been a veritable demolition site, Emma's apartment was the picture of spare living. She had little furniture, although all good stuff that had probably been begged from various relatives — a

John Widdicombe gateleg table with two chairs, a comfortable-looking slipcovered sofa, some reading lamps on mismatched tables, a pair of mahogany bookshelves packed tight with books, a Tabriz rug on the floor. Her queen-sized bed had been neatly made with an Amish quilt, and her closets were tidy except for the jumble of boots and shoes on the floor. She had a sweater drying on a rack in the bathroom. I laid my palm flat on the sweater. It was still slightly damp.

In contrast with the simple furnishings, all the walls of her apartment were covered with horse paintings. She hadn't hung them with much precision, but there they were in plain view, not safely stowed in some storage facility. I found a stack of other pieces from the family art collection leaning against the bedroom wall, each frame tidily wrapped with padded paper.

From the doorway, Abruzzo called, "Anything?"

I went back out to him. "No. I think we'd better go to the local police."

I found some duct tape in a kitchen drawer, and we taped a hunk of cardboard over the hole in the door window. It didn't seem wise to leave the paintings so vulnerable, but I decided even the most imaginative cat burglar wouldn't peg that modest second floor apartment for the home of a multimillion-dollar art collection.

But I planned to discuss home security with Emma as soon as possible.

As soon as we found her, that is.

Abruzzo drove me to the police station but declined to come inside with me. "I'll just complicate things," he said.

He gave me his cell phone and a number to call when I was ready to leave. Then he disappeared.

The New Hope police kept me for the entire afternoon with questions, questions and more questions. I felt as if I had gone to Mars and nobody understood my language. The state troopers were called, and I gave the same information to them. Three times. I was nearly screaming with frustration at their lack of action until a woman poked her head into the room where I'd been quarantined and announced that a patrol car had found Emma's truck. The cops nearly knocked each other over trying to get out of the room to learn the details.

The woman raised her eyebrows at me. "You want a Coke or something?"

I thanked her and she brought me a soft drink.

She sat down in the chair beside me as I popped the top and drank the caffeinated sugar. "I'm Judy Tandy. I'm the rape coun-selor, but I figure you could use a friendly face. I just want to tell you not to worry. These jerks won't tell you anything, but the cops out in the cars are doing everything they can."

"Where was Emma's truck?"

"At an expired meter on Main Street."

"Was she — ?"

Judy shook her head. "The keys were gone, the doors were locked. Nothing unusual. They're looking in nearby shops now."

I thanked her. The chances of finding Emma shopping were slim to none, I knew.

The rape counselor sat with me until the cops came back, then she patted me on the shoulder and left.

I thought they'd never let me go. I finally asked, "Am I under arrest?"

Hastily, they said I could leave, so I phoned the number Abruzzo gave me. I told the gruff male voice on the other end where I was, and he told me to sit tight. Fifteen minutes later, Abruzzo arrived in a vintage Lincoln Continental.

"Where's the Volvo?"

He shrugged. "Better to keep everybody guessing today. If people think I'm involved, it's going to get unnecessarily complicated."

He took me back to the farm where two

men were changing a tire on a black SUV near my mailbox. In the house, I checked my answering machine and found two messages from Detective Bloom among assorted unimportant calls. I telephoned Bloom only to get his voice mail. I told him I'd try again later. I phoned Lexie next and packed an overnight bag.

Abruzzo carried my suitcase out to the car. When we left the farm, I noticed the two men were still changing their tire. Abruzzo lifted one hand at them, and they jutted their chins back at him in recognition.

He took me to Lexie Paine's boathouse in Philadelphia. Two more men were changing a tire on her street.

Lexie came outside in the dark and hugged me hard. "Oh, darling, I'm so glad you called. So glad!"

"You don't mind a slightly bedraggled houseguest?"

"Of course not. And this must be your . . . friend."

I introduced them, and for the first time in my life witnessed Lexie Paine completely speechless as she shook Michael Abruzzo's hand.

He said, "Nora needs some food and some rest."

Lexie could only nod.

Hiding a grin, Abruzzo said to me, "I'll come back in the morning."

"Thank you," I said, smiling too.

He kissed the top of my head and departed without further ceremony.

Lexie closed the door behind him and leaned against it, her dark eyes wide. "My God, Nora."

"I know. He looks like a felon. But he's been very kind."

"Are you sure? Does he carry a gun?"

"Of course not. He likes fly-fishing."

Lexie gathered her breath and took my arm. "Well, you know what you're doing. I hope! Come in and have a glass of wine. I'll order some food. I want to hear the whole story about Libby and Emma, and then you can tell me what I can do to help."

"Did you have time to learn anything about Rory's van Gogh?"

"I had time to make a few calls after you phoned me earlier. It was legitimately purchased at auction about fifteen years ago. Rory has always said he's going to leave it to a museum. Heywood Kidd tells me Peach and Rory have argued about it for years. Something about the frame being wrong. Now it's your turn."

One glass of wine couldn't subdue the nervous adrenaline in my system as I filled

Lexie in on what was happening. The second glass of wine blunted my nerves, and the spring rolls helped restore me, too, while we hashed out a plan. But the third glass of wine at midnight knocked me for a loop. I fell into Lexie's guest bed around one and slept for several hours.

I wasn't the first one awake. I slipped into Lexie's kitchen at seven in the morning, and there she was spreading cream cheese on a bagel, dressed in a razor-sharp Prada business suit, stiletto heels and marquis diamond earrings the size of small caliber bullets. Across the kitchen counter from her, Abruzzo sat on a stool reading the paper and drinking coffee from a Starbucks cup. He looked even more dangerous than she did.

Lexie saw me and made an instant diagnosis. "You need aspirin."

"Oh, yes," I gasped.

"I got her drunk," Lexie explained. "It was the only way she could sleep."

"You did what you had to do," said Abruzzo. To me, he said, "Good morning."

I kissed him on the mouth. It felt like the natural thing. He tugged my ponytail.

Lexie turned away and got very busy with orange juice and the aspirin bottle. I could see her smiling.

Abruzzo said, "What's the plan?"

"I hate to say it," I told them, "but I need to go to a party tonight. The rehearsal dinner for the Treese-Kintswell wedding."

Lexie came back with pills and juice. "The whole cast of suspects will be there."

"And Ralph will have to explain one way or another where Libby is."

Abruzzo said, "The New Hope cops kept him half the night. He still claims Libby is visiting a friend in New York. They're looking into it."

I didn't ask how he came by his information. "With the wedding tomorrow, Libby has to show up. Or Ralph's story will have to change."

"And Emma?" Lexie asked.

The question hung in the air. I popped the aspirin and washed them down with juice.

Abruzzo said, "I think we should go talk to the people Emma works with. The cops did that yesterday, but maybe you know better questions to ask."

"And," I said, "Lexie, you'll go see Jonathan Longnecker?"

She nodded. "I'm gonna twist his balls until he screams."

"Yeow," said Abruzzo with a grin.

"If he has anything more to tell," she promised, "I'll get it."

Outside, we got into our respective vehicles — today a snub-nosed white Corvette for Abruzzo and me, another new BMW for Lexie. The two guys still changing tires watched Lexie slide into her car. When she drove past them, she tilted down her sunglasses and took a long look, too.

I said to Abruzzo, "You have resources I never imagined."

He smiled. "People come in handy."

"Do all these men work for you or something?" I asked without thinking.

"Or something," he admitted.

We drove out to Paddy Horgan's barn, just a few miles north of Blackbird Farm. The morning sun shone on his house, three pristine stable buildings, a large indoor ring and an outside exercise yard. White-painted fences surrounded pasture that rolled away from the buildings in undulating hillocks. From a paddock below the stables, a trio of fat mares swished their tails and watched our arrival. When we stopped, a Jack Russell terrier burst out from under a parked horse trailer and attacked the tires of the Corvette.

We got out of the car and could hear voices inside the indoor ring. I made a dash in that direction while Abruzzo sacrificed himself as a decoy for the dog.

Paddy Horgan stood in the center of the

ring, breathing dust while riders cantered two enormous chestnut horses around an obstacle course of elaborate hurdles. The riders took turns leaping their lathered mounts over the impossibly tall jumps. The horses snorted with each stride and kicked up clouds of sawdust. The sharp noise of hooves rapping on the rails occasionally rang out. Leaning on a cane, Paddy bellowed instructions. The riders grimly obeyed.

Paddy, a burly man with little patience and a lot of arrogance, came over and told me exactly what he'd said the day before about Emma. She hadn't come to work, she hadn't called. Then he waved his cane and chewed me out for making the police come to cross-examine him yesterday when he had work to do.

I snapped that maybe he could be a little helpful considering all the work Emma had done for him over the years, which sent him into a tirade.

Then Abruzzo loomed in the doorway, cradling the tamed terrier in one arm and rubbing her tummy. Paddy quit shouting and went back to work.

Abruzzo said, "Horgan has a lot of charm."

"That doesn't mean you can steal his dog."

He sighed and put the Jack Russell on the

ground. It raced us back to the car, where a motley crew of even more dogs had gathered, all with tongues lolling. A woolly black Newfoundland lay panting in a puddle, her swollen belly evidence that she had a litter of nursing puppies somewhere nearby. Two miscellaneous hounds and a Dalmatian joined the terrier in joyously chasing us down the driveway to the highway.

"Learn anything new?"

"Just that you like dogs."

"Don't you?"

"I love dogs. I just don't want to own one."

We didn't get three miles down the road before a police car drew up behind us and flipped on its lights and siren.

Abruzzo glanced into the rearview mirror and cursed.

"What?" I asked, craning around. "Were you speeding?"

"Listen, this happens all the time. Just keep your hands out where they can see, and don't get upset."

"But —"

"Here's my phone. If they take me for questions, call Reed. He'll drive you where you need to go today." He pulled over and shut off the car.

"Why would they arrest you?"

"They're not arresting me. You've heard of the usual suspects? Well, I'm number one on their hit parade. The good news is this means they're looking for Emma and Libby."

"But you have nothing to do with that. This isn't fair. Do you have a lawyer?"

He laughed at me, rolled down the window and placed his hands on the steering wheel.

The cop asked for his license, and Abruzzo said it was in his hip pocket before he moved to reach it. Another patrol car pulled in behind the first, and while the first cop spoke with Abruzzo, the second came to my side of the car and asked me to step out of the car. I did, and he asked if I was okay.

"Of course I'm okay. What's going on here?"

A third patrol car pulled in front of the Corvette and suddenly the incident began to look like a capture on *America's Most Wanted*. Red lights flashed. Police radios squawked.

"This is ridiculous," I said. "You can't do this!"

"Just step over here, Miss."

Despite my protests, they put him into a patrol car and took him away.

I phoned Tom Nelson, the lawyer in Philadelphia. He said he'd look into it, but he imagined Abruzzo had lawyers up the wazoo and didn't need any further assistance. Besides, unless somebody filed charges, he'd be out by tomorrow.

To me, tomorrow sounded far away.

I made phone calls all afternoon. Lexie reported in, saying she was in touch with the Reese-Goldman museum. The local police wouldn't discuss Abruzzo, but they finally reported the discovery of Emma's truck and were officially declaring her missing. At last I got through to Detective Bloom, who said he wanted to see me.

"Why? Am I being arrested?"

"No," he said patiently, having already endured my diatribe about false arrest, unlawful imprisonment, slipshod police work and the general state of law enforcement. "We just need more information from you. Are you coming into the city today?"

I told him about the rehearsal dinner for the Treese-Kintswell wedding. He said he'd meet me there before the dinner.

I dressed in another of Grandmama's Saint Laurent masterpieces, an austere ice-blue sateen that balanced on my collarbones. My hands trembled as I fastened the small hooks. My missing sisters had never felt so far away.

Before Reed arrived to drive me, I sat in the quiet kitchen, closed my eyes and tried to arrange all the information that seemed to float inside my head like a hundred goldfish swimming in a too-small bowl. All the thoughts seemed random. I couldn't make them organize. I could make them slow down if I concentrated. But I couldn't quite manage to bring all the clues into a pattern.

I just needed a little more information for it all to make sense.

Reed picked me up and drove me to Shively House in Philadelphia.

The Shivelys had been a family who imported munitions during the Civil War, and their restored home was open for daylight tours and nighttime special events. A favorite place for Ralph Kintswell, who served on the board of the foundation, it was just the right size for a small dinner. He had rented the whole house and gardens to celebrate his son's upcoming wedding, and Main Events was catering.

I arrived early, as agreed with Detective Bloom. He was waiting for me on the steps of the house, eating a hot dog like a kid at a baseball game. He wolfed the last bite and came down to the car, wiping his hand on a paper napkin. His black raincoat blew open in the light breeze.

"Hey," he said, slamming the car door behind me as I stepped out. He ignored Reed. "I'm glad you could come early." He took my elbow and hustled me onto the sidewalk.

I glanced back at Reed and waved before asking Bloom, "Do you have some news about Libby?"

"I'm sorry, no. We talked to Ralph Kintswell, but he still claims his wife is in New York and will come tonight."

"I hope so," I said.

"Me, too. Let's go into the park to talk, okay?"

Other cars were soon to arrive, so he ushered me around the side of Shively House along a brick sidewalk that was shielded from the street by a tightly grown privet hedge, about knee high. Alongside the house, a precise, geometric knot garden had been planted with herbs, pansies and tiny white alyssum. We entered the space through a break in the hedge. I could see the trucks from Main Events parked behind the garden, and waiters moved between the trucks and the back door of Shively House.

Bloom headed for a stone bench in the center of the formal garden.

I said, "Have you learned anything at all?"

He shoved the crumpled paper napkin into the pocket of his raincoat and sat down. I realized how exhausted he looked. Like a boy who'd stayed up too late, he had blue circles under his eyes. I'd been angry with him for not finding Libby for me, but now I could see he'd been plenty busy looking for Rory's killer.

My heart softened. But I did not sit on the stone bench. I might have been upset, but I wasn't crazy enough to sit on outdoor furniture in my grandmother's Saint Laurent. "You've been working hard."

He nodded. "Maybe so, but not hard enough. Listen, the investigation's gone in a direction I don't like. But my own leads haven't panned out. There's a lot of pressure from upstairs for an arrest."

"You think the wrong person will be arrested?"

He looked up at me. "It's very possible."

"Who?"

"Mrs. Treese."

"But that's ridiculous!"

"Maybe to you, but she's the best we've got. At least we're holding off until this wedding is over tomorrow." He ran one hand through his hair. "If we're wrong and arrest the woman on the day of her granddaughter's wedding, the department will never live it down."

I saw his point. No amount of spin could undo the damage of a weeping grandmother hauled off to jail on the evening news.

"There's just not enough physical evidence," he went on, "tying her to the murder. We know she spent time in Pendergast's study, but there's no sign of her in the bedroom."

"No DNA?"

Bloom shook his head. "Nothing. Which is weird in itself."

"What do you mean?"

"Pendergast is covered in stuff because he shook hands with nearly a hundred people that night. But the pillow is clean. Nothing but his own and the housekeeper's. She made the bed."

"What do you want from me?"

"I'm sorry," he said. "I shouldn't be asking you. My ass is in a sling already, but I need somebody's slant on this. Somebody who knows these people better than I do."

We heard a shout from the back door of the house — a waiter calling to someone in one of the Main Events trucks.

I said, "What do you need to know?"

"If she and Pendergast were lovers, how

come we can't find even so much as a hair of hers in that bedroom?"

"They were together," I said, "but that doesn't necessarily mean they were physically intimate."

"Get this," he said. "We found out that the prescription for Viagra was Harold Tackett's. Does that make sense to you?"

"It does. The thing is —"

Another shout from the caterers. This time we both looked up.

One of the waiters ran from the house to the truck. A chef came hastily out of the kitchen next, and two more young women followed him at a trot. I saw Jill Mascione come outside, too.

I called to her and waved.

She saw me and headed into the garden, jumping over the pansies instead of taking the brick pathway. She shouted, "We're evacuating! Everybody's supposed to get out of the building."

"What's wrong?" Bloom was on his feet.

Jill shook her head and looked back at the house. "I don't know. Somebody said it was a bomb threat."

"A bomb!" Involuntarily, I caught Jill's arm. "Good Lord, here? At Shively House?"

"I know," she said. "But it sounds serious."

Bloom took off at a run.

"I can't believe it," said Jill. "This has never happened to us before. What bastard would do this? It's so sick! For a wedding rehearsal, for godsake!"

She didn't look frightened. Angry was more like it. She said, "If Ralph thinks he's going to get out of paying this tab, he'd better think again. We bought all this food!"

I looked toward the street, hoping Reed had stayed behind.

At that moment, I saw Libby's minivan pull up to the curb.

"Libby!"

I forgot about Jill and ran across the brick sidewalk and through the privet hedge. By the time I reached the street, the minivan doors were open and the kids spilled out into the evening sunlight. I caught Lucy's hand.

"Aunt Nora!"

"Lucy, is your mom here?" I peered into the van.

But it was Libby's son Rawlins behind the wheel.

"No," said Lucy. "But she's coming back soon."

"How do you know, sweetheart? Did you talk to her?" I knelt down to be closer to Lucy. "Did she telephone?"

"Nope," said Lucy. The child's hair was wild, barely combed, but her face was clean and her smile bright. "But Uncle Ralph said she'd come soon. Do you like my dress? It's very itchy."

"I'm sorry it's itchy, Luce, but it's very pretty. Don't go inside just yet, okay? Rawlins, don't park the van yet. Just wait."

The Philadelphia police arrived, and quickly cordoned off the block. I crossed the street and stayed with the children. After fifteen minutes, a police officer came out and told us the dinner would have to be postponed.

As we watched, another car drew up and parked behind the police. A white Mercedes. I saw the license plate. MEOW.

What the hell was Kitty doing here? She got out of the car with a notebook in hand, an incongruous figure among the swarming police. Her suit was fuchsia, her high heels electric blue. I saw her sweep her lacquered hair back from her determined face.

Lucy pointed. "Who's that, Aunt Nora?"

"A lady I know, sweetheart. She's a reporter."

"She has a lot of colors."

Kitty saw me, but immediately pretended she hadn't. She set off walking unsteadily towards the police line.

With Lucy's hand grasped firmly in my own, I headed straight after her. We caught up with Kitty within twenty yards.

I said, "You're too late for the party, Kitty. Or too early for the bomb."

Kitty spun around and wobbled on her too-high shoes. "What are you talking about?"

I held my ground. "I thought you weren't invited to the party."

"I wasn't," she snapped. "But we heard something on the police scanner. I just happened to be available to cover whatever's going on here."

"This is hardly your beat."

"I'm a journalist," she said harshly. "I can cover any story if I have to."

She swept off, looking more ridiculous when her heel caught on the pavement and sent her stumbling. But she pulled herself together and kept going. I watched, wondering if she was determined or desperate. For one crazy moment I wondered if Kitty had phoned in a bomb threat just to get a story. Was she planning a new era in her newspaper career?

Lucy tugged my hand. "Is that lady your friend, Aunt Nora?"

"No, Lucy. She's not my friend."

When a K-9 car arrived with the bomb-sniffing dog, Detective Bloom came out and told me to take the kids away.

"They have to shut this place down for the night," he said. "The party's cancelled."

I treated the kids to McDonald's and tried not to think about my sisters.

Chapter 20

The bomb-sniffing dogs were the first thing I saw again when I arrived at Peach Treese's Main Line home on Saturday morning for the wedding.

"They've thoroughly searched the house," Peach told me herself, amazingly composed, but distracted as she greeted guests in the gazebo at the top of her garden. "And they looked all over the tent and the garden. The police assure me there are no bombs. Can you believe what happened last night? What times we live in!"

"It still seems unreal," I said. "Is Pamela upset?"

"No, actually. She says she didn't feel like eating, so maybe things worked out for the best."

We were standing at the corner of her house, looking down on the peach orchard. An enormous white tent had been erected for the day in front of the rose arbor. The tent seemed unnecessary, however, because the sunshine was brilliant and the cloudless sky was perfect. Other guests had begun to arrive, and they filtered down across the lawn in beautifully dressed groups of two and three.

Ushers in dove-gray tails passed a silver flask. A slight breeze wafted through the flowers. I could hear the string quartet tuning up among the roses. The violinist played a few droll bars of "Jailhouse Rock."

I said, "It's an ideal day for a wedding. Let's enjoy it."

"Nora, you're such a tower of strength." Peach hugged me again. "I do appreciate the note you sent about Rory. And with your own troubles. Everyone is whispering. Has Libby truly run away from Ralph?"

"We're still trying to sort that out. I hope she'll come today and put our minds at ease."

"Oh, yes, I hope so, too. But men can be such animals, can't they? Even dear Rory. I suppose underneath it all, Ralph could be a rat, too."

"Peach," I said, "about Rory."

She looked at me from beneath the brim of her hat. Like me, she had chosen to wear black despite the early hour of the wedding, to recognize Rory's passing. I had revived my grandmother's favorite Mainboucher for the wedding. Peach had brightened her trim suit with a spray of peach-colored roses and the matching picture hat, along with pearls, white gloves and a brave smile. "Yes?"

I took a breath. "I know about the Viagra."

She colored at once and raised her finger-tips to her mouth. "Oh, dear."

I decided to put away Emily Post and try the Abruzzo-approved technique of asking the tough questions. "I can't imagine Rory intended to use the Viagra with Eloise Tackett. It doesn't make sense, Peach. She's over the moon for her husband, and Rory was obviously devoted you. They never had a real affair, did they? She only wanted pieces of his art collection for Harold and was willing to try anything to tip the scales for Harold. But I need to know. Did Rory ever — did the two of you — ?"

Peach's expression crumpled and she groped in her pocket for a handkerchief. "I was afraid of this. Oh, Nora."

"Peach, this is important." I slipped my arm around her to guide her behind a Japa-nese maple tree for some privacy. "I know it's very personal, but believe it or not, it may answer a great many questions. Did you and Rory use Viagra?"

"Of course not!" she burst out, then quickly lowered her voice. "Rory couldn't."

"He couldn't take the drug?"

"No, he'd never been able to" — her color turned even brighter — "to perform."

"Never?"

"He was more interested in the pictures than the actual activity."

"The two of you never . . . ?"

She shook her head. "Oh, heavens, no. When Viagra first came on the market, he said he might try it, but then his heart attack came along and the doctor said he shouldn't."

"But —"

"And what did it matter? I certainly didn't care!" Peach cried into her handkerchief, managing to add, "Sex was never what our friendship was about."

"I'm sorry you're so distressed, but —"

"I don't know why the old fool thought he should try it now, after all these years. What was he thinking?" She noticed her makeup had smudged on her white gloves and began to tear them off her hands.

"He probably wanted to make you happy."

"Oh, hogwash!" she cried, ripping one glove as she yanked. "Men are all the same! He was just trying to be a randy goat! I am so furious with him!"

"That will pass," I murmured. "It's a stage, Peach. Soon you'll —"

She threw her torn glove to the ground. "Bullshit."

And she stalked towards the house to freshen up before the wedding began.

I looked after her. Automatically, I bent and picked up her glove. Then I stared at it.

And the goldfish in my head suddenly made a perfectly clear pattern.

Main Events had parked their trucks behind Peach's house, strategically near the tent. I found Jill Mascione behind one of the trucks, chilling bottles of champagne in ice-filled barrels. She was elbow deep in ice water, but her face was hot.

Ralph Kintswell, dressed in his Civil War uniform, stood arguing with her on the opposite side of the barrels. His scabbard gleamed in the sunlight. In his right hand, he held his uniform gloves, jerking them with annoyance. "I don't see why," he was saying. "The party was canceled."

"Don't be a moron, Ralph. You owe us for the food that went to waste. We can use the wine, and we won't have to pay the employees for all the hours we scheduled, but you're definitely going to owe us some bucks. You didn't buy the insurance, remember?"

"How am I supposed to remember a tiny insurance clause? I didn't see it on the contract!"

"You scratched it out!" Jill snapped. "Of course you saw it! Oh, why I am bothering? You don't pay us, you'll hear from our lawyers!"

And she walked away.

Ralph turned and saw me. His hands went still. "Nora."

"Ralph," I said, "let's talk."

He backed up a step. "The wedding is starting in a few minutes. They'll need me."

"This won't take long. I want to know what you've done with Libby."

"Done with her?" He manufactured a laugh. "She's the one who left."

"Stop it, Ralph." I put Peach's white glove down on the caterer's table. "You saw the folio when Libby worked on it. And when Jonathan Longnecker offered the finder's fee, you thought it was easy money."

Ralph's face had turned magenta. His voice went hoarse. "How do you know?"

"Trouble was, Libby wanted to return the folio to Rory," I went on. "Didn't she? And you overheard Eloise Tackett trying to convince Rory to sell the folio to her husband, and you thought your chance was slipping away. So you put on your gloves and you smothered Rory with the pillow while the folio was still in Libby's possession. It had to be you. Nobody would wear gloves to a

340

cocktail party except you. You thought it would be easy to sell the folio to the highest bidder once he was dead. Only Libby wouldn't give it to you."

For an instant I thought Ralph might have a stroke. He grabbed the hilt of his sword as if it could sustain his balance.

I said, "Libby wouldn't tell you where the folio was, so you took her away or hid her somewhere until she told you where it was. And you broke into my house to look for it. Tell me she's alive, Ralph. Is she all right?"

I felt the black wave of faintness start to undulate around my knees, but I fought it down. Surely Libby wasn't murdered. Ralph had smothered Rory, but he couldn't have killed his own wife.

Ralph pulled out his sword. Sounding resigned, he said, "You Blackbird sisters are gonna kill me yet."

He lunged and grabbed my arm. The sword blade flashed up against my face. I was so startled by mild-mannered Ralph's sudden metamorphosis that I floundered to stay on my feet.

"Ralph!"

The only thing I could seize upon was a bottle of champagne. It came out of the ice water with a whoosh, and Ralph staggered back to avoid the splash. In another moment, he was dragging me away from the tent, away from the wedding guests.

"Ralph, stop," I choked. "You've done too much already."

"First Libby, then that bitch Emma," he gasped, hauling me into the peach orchard where we'd be hidden from view. "She was strong! I had to break Emma's arm. Now you, and today of all days!"

"Ralph, think!"

He was very heavy and surprisingly strong. He wrestled me the length of the orchard with my arm twisted up behind me and the sword pressed to my throat. I prayed the weapon was only for show and dull, but a glimpse of my arm showed spatters of blood. I didn't feel a thing, but the sight of blood on the Mainboucher gave me a spurt of adrenaline. My heels sank into the turf, but I flailed out with the bottle and hit him across one kneecap. He yelped and punched me in the head with the hilt of the sword. I saw stars, and my head rang.

But he wasn't going to get away with hurting my sisters. I swung the bottle again and it connected with a crack. He hit me harder, and a pain like fireworks went off in my head. I twisted and kicked with everything I had.

At last we reached the end of the orchard.

Panting like a steam engine, Ralph shoved me through the hedge. I staggered ahead of him and found myself in Rory Pendergast's garden near the polo field.

"Why, Ralph?" I whirled around to face him, furious. "Dammit, why did you do it all? Was it money? Just money?"

"Just money!" he laughed, half weeping. "That's the way you Blackbirds think of it, don't you? Only money, nothing important. I've given to wonderful causes all my life, but finally I have a chance to do something really important — something of historical value."

"The Shively House?" I guessed.

"Of course not! Only a family like yours would care about a crumbling old pile of bricks! But the hallowed ground of the battlefields! We should long remember the ground where sacred blood was spilled. Where great men, living and dead, consecrated the — the —" He wailed, "I pledged half a million dollars to save a cornfield near Gettysburg so it wouldn't be turned into a motel!"

"But, Ralph —"

"They were going to give me a commemorative plaque! But with the stock market the way it is, I didn't have the cash anymore." He began to cry, his chubby face twisted and blotchy. His whole body drooped, and the sword trailed on the grass.

"But Libby could have helped, surely?"

"Libby!" he cried. "She inherited all that ugly furniture and do you think she would part with one measly stick of it? She had it hauled away to some storage barn and wouldn't even tell me where it was! I've shared my life with her! I've been good to those monster children!"

"Ralph, tell me where she is. Is she alive? And Emma?"

He didn't hear me and sobbed like a baby. "When Libby said Longnecker would give her a hundred grand for those sex pictures, I figured it was our chance. I thought we could bargain with him, get the price up. But, Libby — Oh, it would have been easy!" he bawled.

"Ralph," I began, taking a step toward him.

"No," he said, lifting the sword. "There's still hope. If I can just shut you up, too, it could still happen."

I had my chance. And I only had one weapon — the bottle of champagne. I braced my thumbs against the cork and took aim just as Ralph lunged with the sword.

I popped the cork.

It exploded off the bottle and hit Ralph

square in the eye. Then the champagne came frothing out, and I sloshed it in his face.

My Israeli commando training came back in the next instant. I kicked the sword.

Not hard enough. Ralph staggered down on one knee, clutching his eye with one hand. With the other, he fumbled for the sword in the grass.

I kicked it aside again. "Ralph, stop! It's over!"

He didn't listen. He abandoned the sword, clambered to his feet and set off running blindly down the polo field.

"Ralph!" I shouted.

He did not escape. A second pop exploded nearby. Only it wasn't a champagne cork. Ralph jerked in midstride, missed a step, stumbled and crashed to the grass, spread-eagled flat on his face.

"Oh, my God." I sank down on my knees and the horizon swam. I struggled up again.

Then Eloise Tackett was there, holding me back. "You're okay," she said several times. "You're going to be fine, Nora."

"Eloise —"

"It's all right," she said. "I got him. Damn! My aim isn't what it used to be. I only meant to wing him. I think he's a goner."

"But Libby. And Emma." I tore free of her grasp. "He can tell us where they are. If they're alive."

"Oh, they're alive, all right," Eloise said. "They've been screaming out the windows of my gatehouse since yesterday."

"Eloise?" I stared at her.

"I know, dear. I should have told you. But they seemed just fine, and Ralph kept saying I could have the folio any minute and then they could go free. It all turned out rather badly, though, didn't it?"

Chapter 21

Four weeks later, my sisters and I formally got together again. Except we didn't go out for spinach salad and white wine at a genteel sort of restaurant where ladies lunch.

"I call to order this meeting of the Blackbird Widows," Libby said as she cut the take-out pizza.

Because Emma's arm was still in a cast, I opened the beer. Summer sunshine splashed the porch of Blackbird Farm, casting leafy shadows over our wicker chairs. The fragrance of pepperoni wafted around us.

"At least I managed to keep most of this out of the newspaper." I passed around the bottles. "The newsroom was very kind because of my help with the mayor's story."

"What do you mean, they were kind?" Libby demanded. "They called me his hysterical wife!"

"You *were* hysterical," Emma said. "You were bonkers, nuts, totally bananas. Let me tell you what a delightful roommate you were for two days in that damn gatehouse.

347

the screaming."

"Let's not argue," I said, although I found myself smiling. It felt ridiculously good to be squabbling with my sisters again.

"It's Eloise who went bananas," Libby said, aiming the knife at Emma. "Can you believe they let her out of jail already? Those lawyers Mr. Abruzzo found must be worth their weight in gold. I mean, she killed my husband in broad daylight. And she walked!"

"Libby," I warned, "everyone decided it was an accident. Anyway, Ralph was probably going back to the gatehouse to kill you and Emma."

"Eloise helped him keep us there!"

Emma lifted her bottle in a call for peace. "Only because he told her some cock-and-bull story and promised her the folio. And she redeemed herself, didn't she? By explaining Ralph's plan to sell the folio to her to pay for his battlefield?"

Libby sighed. "Dear Ralph. He really meant well."

Emma rolled her eyes. "By hitting me over the head and breaking my arm? Not to mention kidnapping me? He held a paring knife to my throat while I wrote that note — and left it on that Civil War book, which was supposed to be your big tip-off, Nora."

"Sorry. I didn't make the connection at the time."

Emma's tirade continued. "Sure, Libby, Ralph slipped you nice, gentle sedatives. You even slept through Nora visiting your house on Sunday morning and him dragging you into the gatehouse. But Ralph had to beat me unconscious!"

"Which surprises me. I thought you could have fought him off."

"He hit me with a chair, Lib. So I wasn't exactly at the top of my game, but thanks for your concern. I think, by the way," she said to me, "Ralph would never have surprised me in the first place if you had a dog."

Libby said, "You're getting a dog?"

I sighed.

Libby shrugged and rearranged the pepperoni on her slice of pizza. "Well, Ralph will be happy, I'm sure, that we buried him in his uniform. The poor dear. I sometimes feel a terrible tug on my heartstrings for him. But — Never look back, right? Things happen for a reason."

Libby put on a brave front, but I felt sure she wasn't so philosophical when she was alone.

She went on blithely. "The bullet hole in his jacket is an extra bonus as far as he's concerned, don't you think? He'll fit right in with all those dead soldiers he knew so much about. And it was kind of Peach Treese to give us that Civil War flag from her family, too. Ralph must be swooning in heaven."

I refrained from pointing out that Ralph might not be enjoying the pleasures of heaven at the moment. "Peach was relieved that it was all over. She paid Ralph's bill with Main Events just for some closure. I mean, Rory was killed. Her granddaughter's wedding was ruined —"

"Not just ruined," Emma said. "It never happened."

"Well, the elopement happened without any problems," I said. "Peach just wanted it all over with. She couldn't face another disaster."

"I don't know," said Libby. "A van Gogh might ease a lot of disasters."

Emma lit up a cigarette one-handed. "She bought a van Gogh?"

"No, Rory gave it to her," I said. "Apparently, they always argued about whether is was hanging straight, so he left it to her in his will. The Poison Gas Sisters didn't get that, at least. Kitty Keough interviewed them for *The Back Page* and got the whole ugly story. The editors say it received more reader response than anything Kitty's written in years. She's more popular than ever."

Emma snorted. "The Pendergast sisters sure unloaded the porn fast, didn't they? Harold Tackett must feel like a kid on Christmas since he got to buy most of it."

"It isn't porn," I corrected. "It's art."

"Hmm." Libby slid her eyes sideways at me. "I guess you'd know. You had it long enough. Did you practice the positions?"

Unruffled, I said, "I needed time to decide what to do with it. You were busy with Ralph's funeral and the children. And Emma wasn't much help, being in the hospital."

"Sending the folio to the museum was the right choice," Emma said. "Even if that Longnecker guy lost his job for his unethical business practices."

"Well, Rory's sisters certainly didn't want it. And I figured Harold has enough pieces from the auction of Rory's collection. So the Reese-Goldman has the folio now, and they even sent me an invitation to the opening of the exhibit."

Emma grinned. "You're not going, are you? To an exhibit of sexy pictures? You?"

"I just might," I said. "If I have enough frequent flyer miles."

"That's the only way you'll be able to afford the airfare," Emma cracked. "With the roof practically caving in on this house —"

Libby clanged the knife on her beer bottle. "Oh, let's not talk financial matters. That's so boring. Here we are, dear sisters! The Blackbird Widows again. I don't know about you two, but I'm not planning on any more marriages."

"I give you six months," I said with a grin.

"I'll be busy in six months." Libby put her hand on her belly, which had already begun to show. "I'll have Ralph's child to look after. Do you know, I've been wondering if maybe Ralph went a little off the deep end when I told him we were going to have a baby."

Emma and I chose not to express opinions on that subject.

I said, "Okay, then, I give you a little more time. But you'll have another husband. Mark my words."

"Nope. I'm finished. We're cursed."

Emma drank some beer direct from the bottle and said, "Personally, I don't think I'm cut out for monogamy."

"What about you, Nora?" Libby asked. "Think you'll get married again?"

"I don't know. Right now," I said, "I just want to practice my fly-fishing."

Michael had been dozing in a wicker chair beside me with his feet up on the footstool and a bottle of beer balanced on his chest. I nudged his boot, and he became aware that the three of us were looking at him. He'd spent quite a bit of time at the farm lately and was beginning to look very comfortable there even when my sisters came around. He opened his eyes and looked at me. "You're cursed?"

"It's a thing," I said. "A Blackbird thing. Our husbands die."

"Okay." He closed his eyes again and relaxed. "Remind me not to marry you."

About the Author

Like her heroines, the Blackbird sisters, Nancy Martin comes from a distinguished Pennsylvania family whose ancestors include Betsy Ross and a signer of the Declaration of Independence. She has written numerous romance novels, directed a few Shakespeare plays and raised two delightful daughters. She lives in Pennsylvania.